Karson Pleiades
and the Treasure of
Nova Scarm

by Bill Muir

Karson Pleiades and the Treasure of Nova Scarm

Bill Muir

Methinx Publishing

Methinx Publishing
methinxentertainment.com

Printed in the United States of America
First paper edition by Methinx Publishing
ISBN: 978-1-7347696-4-7

Art & Design:
Contributing Editor: Kathryn Tedrick
Cover Art: Digital Coast Media, LLC

Chapter 1

Karson Pleiades

In the year 2847, the outer-core planet Nergal was a revolving door of shipping and commerce in the Outer Core of planets under the Galactic Federation. Besides its native Nergals, a completely hairless race of tall, thin humanoids with violet eyes, the world hosted a diverse population made up of species from numerous planets and star systems.

Karson Pleiades, an eighteen-year-old human boy with light green eyes, jet black hair, strong muscles, and a handsome face, worked the space docks along with his best friend, Hague C'avt. Hague belonged to the species Rungho, a blue-skinned humanoid with bulbous, glittering, eyes, short blond hair, and suction cups instead of fingertips. They spent their days transferring heavily loaded metal containers on anti-grav lifts from freighters to shuttlecraft to warehouses planetside. It was tedious work needing little intelligence other than for the dock worker to check the labels and make sure the shipment was delivered to the correct warehouse or shuttle.

Karson had bigger dreams for his life, but his family was poor and needed his income to survive. Most kids his age were either attending college, trade school or had entered the academy for military training and planetary defense. Karson thought about signing up with the Galactic Academy, but he wasn't sure. He needed to save up more credits to even get an application. Still, everything he worked for usually went back to keeping him and his mother alive on Nergal. The Galactic Academy was a way to get started to work for the Galactic Federation. If one got good scores, they could become a solo fighter pilot. Or perhaps get more lucrative deals by being a captain on a larger vessel.

That afternoon, Karson and Hague worked planetside, unloading shuttles and taking the cargo to their designated space within the warehouse. A warm breeze blew through Karson's dark, shoulder-length hair as he and Hague guided an anti-grave skid loaded with several containers of varying sizes toward the warehouse. Nergal was a hot tropical planet. When Karson stopped to wipe the sweat from his brow, his buddy came to a rest behind him. As they rested, Karson spotted a pair of small personal fighter ships break the atmosphere of Nergal. They were Osprey fighter ships, usually reserved for pilots of the Galactic Federation.

"One day, I will leave on a ship like that," Karson declared. He loved working on the various alien cargo ships, seeing the different types of military ships, and meeting people of different races with all their diversity.

"Yeah, and how are you going to do that?" Hague responded with skepticism. He ran his blue fingers through his blond hair. His light locks a stark contrast to his deep blue skin. Although he knew if anyone was smart enough and determined enough to find a way to buy a ship, it was his friend.

"Maybe I'll join up with the Federation."

"You think you will have freedom with the Feds?" Hague said with a shocked expression on his bulbous eyes. "You could get stationed on some backstar planet with virtually no resources as part of a Terraforming attempt. You know how well those work out."

That was a reality Karson had neglected to think about. After the twelve central planets formed the Galactic Federation in 2200, there were various Terraforming attempts. The Feds sent teams to foreign planets to create them sustainable for various life forms. This was initially put in place for the members of an ancient planet in the Milky Way that had used up their planet's natural resources and needed to evacuate the world. Earth, more commonly referred to as Terra Firma to its descendants, was that planet. While several of these Terraforming missions were successful in the early years of space exploration. In the last few decades, more and more worlds were deemed too hostile to support "sensitive" life. Karson had ancestors who were on the original escape flights of Terra Firma before they settled on their home planet Tecmula.

"Well, maybe I'll just find a treasure on some uninhabited planet," Karson declared.

"And how are you going to *get* to an uninhabited planet?" Hague asked with a grin.

"I'm still working on that," Karson replied with a laugh.

The two boys were best friends. Anyone in the spaceport city could tell you that if you saw one, the other would be nearby.

"You are a pretty good pilot, even for mainly using anti-grav, one-man shuttles. Given enough years, you could buy a shuttlecraft with the credits you make gambling," Hague suggested.

"Yeah, some broken-down heap with enough room for a pilot and little else." He pressed a button on the skid, and they continued through the warehouse door.

"Then you have plenty of training here," Hague chuckled as they entered the warehouse.

Just ahead, two Nergal males struggled with an oversized anti-grav skid overloaded with two massive containers too heavy for a single skid. Especially one that was old, uninspected, and in need of replacement. No one cared to check that it was overdue for maintenance. If anyone had taken the time to look, it would have been evident that the equipment should have been replaced or refurbished years before. Until it broke, however, no one cared.

As Karson and Hague walked through the open doorway, a scanner passed over the cargo, recording its origins, destination, and contents.

"Please take this cargo to Section 22 Delta," a computer with a female voice told them.

"Confirmed," Hague replied as they guided their cargo down the central aisle.

Like most people on this multi-race planet, the boys wore a medallion-sized translator on a chain around their necks. Few people bothered to learn a foreign language in this day and age. Why bother when the translator device was programmed to understand every known language in the universe?

The boys were so deep in conversation; they did not notice the defective skid loaded with duranium was headed for a significant shipbuilder on Nergal. Duranium was a powerful metallic substance used in building the hulls of starships and space stations. As the boys waited for the cargo to pass, the computer in charge of warehouse operations contacted them.

"Workers Pleiades and C'avt, please move to the side of the aisle to avoid colliding with the shipment heading your way."

"Affirmative," Karson replied. He checked his timepiece. "Anything to get us out of here on time," he told Hague.

"You going out for cards tonight?"

"Maybe," Karson said with a shy smile.

"Why maybe?"

"I first need to learn how to handle the crewmen from Ashnar. They're oversized brutes twice the size of a human, and they get outraged when they lose their credits to me."

"There's a new ship in port from Dulthar filled with a crew itching to spend their earnings," Hague challenged his friend. "Dulthar is an Inner Core planet too, so they should have quite a bit of credit. You can make their pockets a little lighter tonight."

"Maybe."

The skid ahead began wobbling dangerously. A handful of handlers, Nergals, humans, and other species alike, jumped in and helped steady the cargo tilting wildly in the air. They tried to lower it to the floor, but the controls froze. They knew the shipment had to be removed from the warehouse and loaded aboard the shuttle before anyone could go home. They tried to steady the load. Nothing worked.

"Let's try forcing it down," one Nergal suggested.

The two work boys standing nearby were so engaged in their conversation; they took no notice of what was happening overhead.

"Back home on Rhungiah, it never gets this hot" Hague complained

7

"Isn't it pretty cold?" Karson asked.

"Oh, yes. Practically an ice planet during our fall and winter months."

"Does it warm up in the spring and summer?"

Hague grinned. "Highest weather record for my planet was 70 degrees Fahrenheit at one point."

Karson chuckled, "Well then yeah, Nergal is a pretty different planet then. Though I thought you would be used to it by now, C'avt."

"I don't think I will ever get over these summers, Pleiades."

They usually referred to each other's last names in a tongue-in-cheek fashion when they were picking on each other.

The dockhands continued pulling downward on the skid until the controls exploded, making it rock so violently that the cargo tipped over and fell straight down toward the boys. The noise made Karson lookup. All he could see was the bottom of a large cargo container falling straight down toward them. He shoved Hague out of the way before jumping aside. The warehouse shook from the impact, knocking everyone to the floor and toppling smaller nearby containers. The boys slowly stood up and studied the damage. The explosion had strewn the cargo across a large area. They looked at each other and grinned.

"Thanks, Karson," Hague said as he helped his friend up and gave him a hug. "You saved my life."

"No, I didn't. I just pushed you," Karson replied with a smile.

The funny thing about Karson was that he was cool under pressure, but he didn't like the attention or admiration. There was a shy side to him.

The Nergal supervisor hurried over. "Everyone okay?"

"Yes," they replied.

"Day's over, you two," the supervisor told Karson and Hague. "Store away your cargo and go home. We need to repackage this material in new containers before anything else happens. We'll start back up tomorrow morning when the second sun rises."

The boys were routed around the mess and put their load away and returning the skid to storage. They left with the other tired dockhands not needed in the cleanup. The two companions hopped on their anti-grav scooters and broke away from the rest of the spacedock workers.

****

The boys drove all the way to the cliff that overlooked the spaceport. Parking their scooters, they dropped to a sitting position on the ground to calm their excitement. As their breathing slowed, they listened to the native Nergal birds call out to each other. The two friends watched the graceful birds dive along the surface of the choppy water, returning to the air with wiggling fish clamped in their beaks. The sound of giant spaceship caught their attention, and they watched it descend from above. These docks were specially made for space ships more massive than a shuttle, but small enough to land rather than dock in the *Atlas*. The *Atlas* was a Galactic Federation space station that was stationed above the planet. The space station was used for more military or even more extensive craft than typical commercial ships to dock.

The blue and white gleaming ship was a breathtaking sight. The main body was shaped like an eggshell with two powerful engines located on each side of the narrow end. A dozen gun turrets were mounted above and below the ship, hidden behind seamless doors that opened instantly upon the correct spoken command to the ship's computer. A row of windows covered both sides, allowing the crew and others, who might be on board, a view of the wonders of space. Manufactured on the planet Lodi, they were in high demand by merchant carriers across the galaxy.

"Someday, I will own a ship like that," Karson said, his voice dreamy.

"Yeah, right, and someday I'll be the Supreme Potentate of the Federation," Hague replied.

When the land shuttles started down the dock toward the parked ship named *Stardust*, Karson jumped to his feet.

"It's getting late, I'm heading down to the Planetary Rings Tavern."

"Oh, you are?" Hague asked.

"Yeah, I'm feeling lucky," Karson replied as they raced down the cliff toward their scooters. The first sun on the planet Nergal was just starting to set.

Chapter 2

Captain Grimlocke

One of the Capitol Planets, Cesaroma, had numerous shipbuilders located in orbit above the planet and circling the moon. Built as a large scale cargo ship for interstellar travel, the *Antares* was seized by pirates on her maiden voyage in deep space. The ship was then taken to their base on the planet Oblistidon. Where it was outfitted with a more powerful star drive, new phaser banks on the top and bottom of the ship, and photon torpedo launchers placed all about the ship's outer hull. Making the *Antares* a formidable enemy. Pirates not only roamed the oceans of water worlds. They plagued the shipping lanes in space, especially those routes that were not as heavily patrolled.

Traveling from the Tiger Star System, the ship had a cargo hold more than half full of stolen artifacts that would fetch a princely sum from the right buyer. The giant pirate ship was captained by the notorious pirate Captain Flint Grimlocke, who was wanted in at least twelve planets within the Federation systems. Standing 6'5'' tall, he towered over every man on the ship. His black eyes matched his tight black beard. A long scar zigzagged from his left ear to his pointed chin, giving him a look so fierce that even the bravest to face him grew afraid.

Captain Grimlocke pulled on his size, thirteen boots, and smiled. The shoes were absolutely the most comfortable things he'd ever had on his feet. Stolen from the body of a wealthy merchant, they fit perfectly and made the captain's day just a little more bearable. He squinted at the small window in his cabin and smelled the air. A portion of the filtration system that kept the air running through the life support, fresh and clean, was on the fritz, leaving a stale smell throughout the ship. Grimlocke scowled. *Haven't they got that repaired yet?*

Throwing a mug half full of lukewarm coffee across the room, Captain Grimlocke stared out the little window in his cabin. Cargo ships weren't built for luxury. Most areas had no windows at all. And the ones that did had viewing ports no larger than two feet by two feet. Fortunately, the bridge had a much broader view screen, so the captain spent most of his time there.

Blimey, what we need is another plasma storm, he thought. Plasma storms were dangerous, and most ships avoided them, preferring to wait them out along the outskirts. This made them easy targets. Leaving his cabin, he walked down the corridor to the turbolift, got on, and rode it to the bridge.

"Captain on the bridge," yelled Sharky, his lieutenant, as Grimlocke stepped out of the lift and headed for his chair, which was centered twenty feet back from the front of the view screen.

"Do ya see anything, Fingers? That ship out of Nergal should be passin' today."

Fingers, aptly nicknamed after his long, twelve fingers that his species possessed, had been at the helm all night. "Nothin' yet, Cap'n."

It had been 35 days since their last capture of a vessel. The captain knew the men were growing anxious over the lack of contact with any merchant ships. *Let's hope we spot her first. She's a fast ship and might outrun us if she realizes who we are.* He needed strong coffee and a bit of luck. They were low on rations, and his crew needed a good battle to get their spirits up.

Checking the time on the lower right-hand corner of the viewscreen, he stepped down from his chair and rode the turbolift to the engineering section. Entering the room, he walked toward his men, who were gathered in one of the open areas for a judgment. The crew wore a variety of clothing, depending on their planet of origin, and what they stole off their victims. A few were dressed very colorfully, but most at first glance looked no different than any other space traveler. Swift, agile, and hard-hitting, the ruthless pirates were the scourge of deep space.

They parted, forming an aisle as Grimlocke walked to the center of the men. Thirty-five pirates stood huddled in the room as an old pirate human named Henry, was dragged before the captain. Henry was unfortunate enough to have been caught stealing food, not much, but that didn't matter to these hungry crewmen.

"Shoot him," screamed one pirate.

"Feed him to the trash disintegrator," yelled another.

Captain Grimlocke stood over the unfortunate Henry who shook with fear.

"I'm sorry, Captain, but my stomach got the best of me," Henry explained.

"Since we are a democracy, my old friend, we will take a vote regarding your punishment," declared the captain. "How many of you want this man to be whipped?"

A loud yell went up.

"How many want our brother here to be shot?"

A louder yell went up.

"And, how many of you want him to be fed to the trash disintegrator?"

The yell now was louder than the whipping, but lower than the shooting.

The captain quickly pulled a phaser from his belt and shot the man dead before he could beg or protest. The corpse collapsed to the deck.

"Let that be a lesson to everyone. Stealing from one man on this ship is stealing from all of us. Now we have another agenda for our meeting today. As you know, Andrew is new to our ship, and today, he is being promoted to a navigation officer. As is our custom, he will be blindfolded and made to cross the walkway to the plasma cooling tanks."

Andrew's eyes grew wide as two engineers swiftly blindfolded and forced him up a ladder to the third level.

"Andrew, you are to cross the walkway to the coolant tanks," the captain shouted up to him. "The safety shields have been removed. If you don't fall off the walkway, you will be our new dayshift, navigation officer."

"But I don't want to die," Andrew pleaded.

The men laughed.

Grimlocke climbed to level three and pushed Andrew forward with the point of his phaser to the edge of the walkway. The young man slid his feet one in front of the other. Without the safety fields, which prevented the maintenance crew from accidentally falling to their death, the blindfolded Andrew could quickly lose his balance or misstep right off the walkway.

"Please, don't do this to me. I want to see my mother again before my life is over!"

The men laugh even louder as the captain poked his phaser harder into Andrew's back.

"Now, walk!"

The young man eased forward, but quickly lost his balance and fell three stories, screaming his head off. But instead of hitting the deck, he landed in a safety net. The safety feature had been set up after he was blindfolded. The men burst into laughter and applause. Andrew didn't suffer so much as a bruise. Hurrying back to the first level, the captain pulled off the blindfold and helped the boy out of the net. It was all a joke.

"I hope you're a better navigator than a fighter, or we're all in trouble," yelled a pirate named Lonnie.

The men quickly crowded around the young man and patted him on the back for his promotion. These men, who would kill everyone on a ship they attacked, thought of each other as brothers. It was them against the universe.

The crew drifted back to work. The best part of the day, this entertainment was over. Most of the team on the ship were there out of necessity. They were either unemployed living on some low level, backward planet, captured from a cargo ship, or greedy for quick loot. Being a pirate gave them an opportunity for the wealth they would never find working planetside, and it sent them into space with the promise of a better life.

Life aboard a pirate ship was hard. The ships were often not designed for the number of spacers they carried. The crew of a pirate ship always had to outnumber the fighters of the ship they were attacking. Unfortunately, this meant they often ran out of food and supplies before they found another spacecraft to plunder.

Any starship had much to do. Keeping the warp drive running at peak performance, and the various systems that ran throughout the ship in good repair was a never-ending job. Other men handled the day-to-day operations of the ship, keeping her space worthy. Handling repairs caused by plasma storms and other anomalies or their latest battle with another vessel. Today the men were repairing a leak in the coolant system that had been damaged by phaser fire.

Meals were nothing to write home about. The longer the ship was in deep space, the worse the meals became. They went from eating the meat brought onboard and kept in refrigeration to hard biscuits morning, noon, and night. The cook was a position customarily given to the man who couldn't do anything else, and the *Antares'* cook, Chef, was that man. Though he was not a man at all, he was an android. Old and beaten, he did his best to perform his duties lest he end up melted down for scrap metal.

The captain returned to his cabin, sat at his desk, and studied a map of the star system. He scoured for a planet capable of supporting life, with few inhabitants that were centuries away from any sort of modern civilization. Terraformed planets were easy enough targets. Usually, just given the basic needs to start a world, they rarely had weapons enough to stop a pirate attack. When his cabin boy informed him of a commotion in the mess hall, he shut down his computer and joined them. He was a strategic leader, even though he was a pirate, and he knew that by observing his men in play, he could judge them for battle.

Chapter 3

Luck

Across the street from the space dock, happy crew members, returning from deep space with money to spend, filled the crowded taverns and shops. As usual, the streets were crowded with pedestrians, shopping, working, or just going about the usual routine of their day.

The Planetary Rings Tavern, a white, three-story wooden structure that was a favorite of the space ship crews. A large sign showed the planet with its rings done in brilliant colors. In front of the planet was the upper torso of a Nergal drinking a glass of spirits. Since cargo ships came from planets across the galaxy, the owners wanted to make their taverns and shops easily recognizable. The second and third floors had rooms rented out by the day of the week.

Aside from being a hotel, the tavern has a small stage that featured nightly entertainment. Singers, small musical groups, comedians, and others would take the stage. Happy customers meant more liquor sales. Even Karson would benefit during very entertaining nights. The card games didn't pay out a whole lot, and sometimes Karson lost more than he won. But he made sure he did not spend too much, and any extra money went right into helping out his mother.

Although the bar did a brisk business, often taking most or all of a crew member's hard-earned wages, the tavern looked worn and well used. A long wooden bar, scarred from fights as well as general use, was the centerpiece of the room. Booths lined two walls, and round wooden tables with plain wooden chairs filled most of the space. When the pub was crowded, which it usually was, there was barely enough room for the barmaids to get through.

The servers used small, hand-held computers to keep track of what each customer was drinking and eating. Locals and crew personnel that visited the planet often had a little wrist computer that was used for such functions. When anyone one any of the gambling games, they would receive a code that was required to claim it. Then once that code was redeemed, the credits were transferred instantaneously.

Since they often led a lonely, hard life with trips to their home planet few and far between, many crew members on the freighters drank too much. Which usually led to bar fights. The damage was often extensive. Although the combatants paid for the damages, the owner couldn't see the point of buying anything expensive. Chances were the new stuff would soon be broken anyway.

Karson sat at a table, playing a game of cards. It was a gambling game, and Karson was fortunate. Two strong, ugly Ashnar crew members, one male, one female had decided to take a chance. The male sat in front of Karson, the female a few places away on his right, the other three players had left the game soon after they lost. This was probably due to the Ashnar's threatening appearance. Besides their considerable height, the hair on their heads was massive, long, and auburn. To keep it out of their way, the Ashnar people tied it behind their back in a braid as thick as a man's bicep. Ashnars also sported jagged, sharp teeth. They were the last contestants and the only ones from the same crew. Karson quickly checked the screen in front of him. 2,000 credits were in the pot, if he won this, he could not only help his mom but start real savings for the academy.

The male clicked his screen and spoke, "Raise 500."

The screens in front of the players, as well as the central screen keeping track of the event for the onlookers, all showed the screen change from 2,000 to 2,500 credits.

Hague stood a safe distance behind Karson. Hague was an excellent pickpocket with his suction-cup-ended fingers and usually would wander around the bars on occasion to loot. He would typically do that when Karson attracted a decent crowd with his gambling. But this was the biggest pot the tavern had seen in a long time.

"I bet the male Ashnar wins," a patron spoke to his friend.

"No, the little human has got it," his friend protested.

He can't keep on betting like this Hague thought to himself. *He is gonna run out of credits at this rate.*

The ugly Ashnar male looked confident. However, perspiration slowly ran down his face from his temples. He glanced at his cards, gave the female a brief look, and studied young Karson's face.

The female Ashnar, catching the look from her companion she played her next move. She spoke as she typed on her screen, "Fold."

The screens all removed her from the game with the word *Fold* scrolling horizontally across the screen. It was just Karson and the male.

Hague leaned forward and whispered. "You don't have enough money to cover that bet."

Karson looked nervous as he typed his response into his screen, "Call."

The male Ashnar laughed as he revealed his hand, "Three Black Comets."

The cards appeared on the screens.

Hague sweated, *Great Griplar! Karson, I hope you can beat that.*

Karson smiled as he revealed his hand, speaking the same time the images appeared on the screen. "Pair of White Dwarves."

The table and screens began to make various noises as the words *Player 2 is the Winner* scrolled across the screens. Karson had the winning hand!

The claim code for 2,500 credits pinged on Karson's screen. He quickly typed it on his wrist-computer when he heard a mighty roar. The male's hand slammed down on the table, splitting it in two and sounding of various alarms and signals to alert the owner of the destruction.

"You cheated me, human!" His companion also roared and began to advance on Karson and Hogue.

The crowd scrambled to get out of the way of the raging Ashnar as quickly as possible. Karson and Hague knew the routine. They would split up and head to the back alley. They also would only wait twenty minutes for the other, then they could go back or get going. It was a plan both had relied on growing up on Nergal, though the second portion had never come up before.

Hague got to the alley first and sat down. He panted and whipped his brow, the humid evening taking a toll on the already thirsty Rungho. Thankfully he did not have to wait long as Karson showed up from the opposite side of the alley.

"Didja keep it, Pleiades?" Hague asked.

"Kept it and claimed it, C'avt," Karson replied.

"All of it?" Hague jumped to his feet.

"Oh yeah," Karson beamed as he patted his wrist computer.

"That is some luck you got there," Hague said as the boys began to make it out of the alley.

" 'Born under a lucky star' that is the Pleiades motto," Karson chuckled. "That is what my mom tells me anyway. Guess sometimes it's actually true."

They were distracted by Karson's good fortune that they did not pay attention as they bumped into an elderly human male. He had long white hair, a pointed beard, and was dressed in a bright-colored space station uniform.

Karson looked up into the man's face. "Uncle Jasper!"

"My my, Karson Pleiades and Hague C'avt. Now, where might you boys be headed at this time of night?" The elderly man chuckled.

"I was just heading home myself, sir," Hague spoke up as he shuffled away. "See ya tomorrow at work, Karson." He whispered as he raced back to his home.

"Now, what about you, son?" Jasper asked.

"I...I... was just going to the... store! To buy food for the evening meal," Karson nervously replied.

Jasper looked around, the night was dark, and the stars were shining. "Bit late if you were supposed to bring home preparations for dinner? The second sunset hours ago."

"Uh, well…" Karson looked down dejectedly.

"Why don't we sit down somewhere and talk? Unless you'd like me to tell your mother about me finding you so late after work?" Jasper kindly threatened.

Karson had no choice. If his mother found out he was making extra money by playing cards, she would be distraught with him. She didn't like the idea that he had to

21

work on the dangerous spacedocks. Still, she would definitely not like him gambling, especially anywhere near a tavern.

Chapter 4

Family Time

They sat at a small cafe near Karson's home, the Blue Star. Karson offered to pay for Jasper's meal as an attempt to show good faith. Jasper readily accepted the offer.

Jasper Tinsmith was a mechanic for the reactor coolers on the space station *Atlas*. While he was older than most of the other mechanics, Jasper was the most knowledgeable. He stayed near where Karson and his mother lived, he had been a family friend for years. He had worked alongside Karson's father before his death and had done what he could to help his widow and son. While he was not a blood member, Karson called him Uncle Jasper, since he was the only family he had.

Once he got his drink, Jasper asked. "What do you want to do in life more than anything else, Karson?"

Karson looked out the cafe's window and imagined the *Stardust*. His voice filled with wonder as he daydreamed about an exciting life in space and all the different planets he would visit. "I would love to join the crew of the *Stardust*. Or at least see what she looks like on the inside. I've seen plenty of ships, their cargo bays at least, but the *Stardust* is different. Father showed me around the transport ship when we left Tecmula, but I was too little to remember much of what he showed me. All I know is that ever since then, I knew I wanted to captain, or pilot, a spaceship someday."

"Have you thought about joining the academy?" Jasper asked.

"If I could save up enough credits. I even have to have money to apply. That's part of the reason I play cards. Extra money for mom and me."

Jasper thanked the waiter as his meal was served to him. "I understand, Karson. I just don't want you to get into trouble. I know you think that because this is a busy port that you can turn a lot of tricks but still. Workers like myself and others don't often leave. Plus, I wouldn't want your mother to get upset."

Karson starred as his water as he spoke, "I know. I know. Tryouts for the academy are eight months away from now. If I could get in, that could take care of mom and me more than working these docks."

"How much did you make tonight? If I may ask."

"2,500 credits."

"That's a pretty penny," Jasper commented on.

"It is a start. Applications are 50 credits, the enrollment fee is 3,000 credits. Granted, it pays for your whole training and equipment, and even the slowest recruit gets out in three years, but it's a lot. Plus, how would I take care of mom during training?"

"How much would you need to be comfortable with before you signed up?

"I don't know, 6,000 credits or something would be nice," he chuckled as he and Jasper laughed at the notion.

"Might as well get the lost treasure of Captain Nova Scarm too, lad," Jasper laughed.

Karson laughed at the old story that he remembered Jasper telling him the ancient legends so many years ago. When he was younger, he loved the tales of the dreaded pirate captain and how much loot he stole. Though much had changed during his time on Nergal, Karson still longed for the old legends to be true.

****

Bacon snapped and crackled as it fried in a pan on the stove in the kitchen. Gloria Pleiades, Karson's attractive but tired-looking mother, mixed the dough for biscuits. She had been working late at one of the planetside military stations. She was a dishwasher, and the station never seemed to run out of dishes for her to load into the machines and load back into the dish serving units. She heard the door click open.

"Why are you home late tonight, son?"

"Bumped into him and got a quick drink, Gloria," Jasper replied.

"Oh hello, Jasper. But out this late?"

"A couple of anti-grav lifts broke again, had to wait till a mechanic could repair them."

"Alright, son."

Because they were poor, their apartment was small with a combined kitchen and living room, a bath, and two bedrooms. A bed and a wardrobe for Karson took up most of the space in one room. Gloria slept in the other bedroom. Aside from the table and stove, the room contained a refrigeration unit and a small pantry. Two clean but beat-up upholstered chairs sat in front of one wall with a small table between, holding little more than a lighting fixture with a crack in the base. A sagging couch sat next to the opposite wall with an old metal crate at each end to serve as end tables. Each held a mismatched lamp, and a few trinkets Gloria had brought with her from her home on Tecmula.

"I just don't know," she said to Jasper as Karson cleaned up in the next room. "I know the academy is a dream, but I can't afford it. Even pulling a double shift, we'd never make enough money in time."

"I know, Gloria," Jasper assured her. "But, Wally would've wanted him to go."

Wallace Pleiades was Karson's father. He was a spacer for the merchant starship *Magellan* stationed on the planet of their origin: Tecmula. They all had lived there until Wallace was offered a position on a ship stationed on the Central Core planet of Fenrir. They sold everything they could and chartered a voyage from their outer-core planet when their ship was waylaid by a cosmic flare. The flare was so bright that it blinded those who saw it and scrambled the systems of their vessel. Jasper and Gloria, along with a much younger Karson, were able to board an escape pod. Wallace, however, did not. The pod drifted for days until it landed on Nergal.

"I know, Wally and I always spoke about him joining the academy, but that was all before…"

"I could try to get him a job at the *Atlas*?" Jasper offered. "The boy is supposed to be a pilot, but he might make a good mechanic."

"No, but thank you, Jasper. The more he could stay planetside, the better. Thank you, old friend." She wiped her eyes and returned to the kitchen to finish the late meal.

"Night to ya, Gloria." Jasper Tinsmith said as he excused himself from the humble abode of the Pleiades family.

****

When the meal was ready, the mother and son ate and talked.

"I hate that you have to work at the space docks, but without your earnings, I don't know what we would do, " Gloria said.

"Well, if I went to the academy, we could make more earnings," Karson attempted.

"That is true," Gloria admitted defeatedly, "But we just don't have time. Time to earn the wages in time for you to register and time to cover for wages gone while you train."

Karson put his hand on his mother's hand, "I won't leave until its the right time."

She smiled at her son.

"Or unless I get lucky, you know the Pleiades family motto," Karson winked.

Gloria laughed. "You remind me so much of your father."

"Do you still miss him?" Karson replied.

"With all my heart."

Chapter 5

Cloudracer

Thousands of light-years from Nergal, a privately owned luxury cruiser, named the *Cirrus* sped through the Inner Core system. Non-military spaceships, they were favored by wealthy members of the galaxy. Though, those with connections to the Galactic Federation usually got the best in non-military cruisers. Pirates craved them, too, and were delighted whenever they could get their hands on one. The ships didn't hold as much cargo. Still, their speed and maneuverability were perfect for escaping galactic and planetary law enforcement.

But the owner of this ship wasn't a pirate, just a wealthy technology developer, and his family on their way to their winter vacation on a tropical planet with six moons called Weth. The planet was so popular with otherworldly visitors that over 460 years ago, the Wethian people turned their entire world into a vacation hot spot. For those who could afford it, it was *the* place to go.

The owner and captain of the *Cirrus*, Viscount William Cloudracer, had been a starship captain in Galactic Federation's space fleet for twenty years. Before retiring to take over the commercial spacecraft design business, his great grandfather had started 150 years ago. His family consisted of his wife Margaret and their beautiful eighteen-year-old daughter Serena.

His daughter was his pride and joy with cornflower blue eyes, a slender nose that turned up slightly at the tip, and full lips that caught everyone's attention. As a member of the Federation, their life was one of privilege. Besides the cruiser, the family-owned a vast mansion on the core planet Cesaroma. Unlike Karson, Serena had android servants to grant her every whim that, like her parents, spoiled her. Whatever she wanted, her father made sure she received it. Her mother supplied her with the most beautiful clothes, jewels, and accessories money could buy. A highly intelligent girl, Serena attended a prestigious academy. Being from a wealthier core planet, her father wanted her to become whatever she desired; and he showered her with all the latest technology. She loved math, science, and medicine. During school breaks, she would often go to work with her father, spending hours in one of the many labs developing some new technological medical breakthroughs or working on improvements for the latest model android.

Her dream was to be a doctor on a starship. That would be the best of both worlds, but she knew she would have to work very hard to obtain such a position. Still, that didn't stop her from dreaming. She loved flying through space. She and her father spent hours together on the bridge of his ship. He taught her everything he knew. Every day, her mother invited her to their quarters for afternoon tea, but Serena would stay on the bridge. When not at the helm, she worked with the navigator, tactical officer, communications officer, or the science officer. She especially loved working with the onboard physician, an android simply named Doc.

Her mother knew she had lost her daughter to space when the girl was only seven. The family has gone to the spaceport to see off some friends who were boarding a ship owned by Centennial Cruise Lines. A centuries-old, well-renowned company that offered cruises of space. Just before they were about to leave, Serena went missing in the crowd. Hours later, after frantically searching the port stores, they found her. She was being escorted off the ship by a captain who told her parents she was hiding behind a container in the ship's storeroom. She'd declared herself to be a stowaway to the captain, who'd only laughed at a beautiful little girl with long blonde curls, dressed in the latest fashion.

Serena, however, was a bit of a tomboy, which bothered her mother. Once, she cut her hair short, which had angered her mother for weeks. She loved sneaking around her father's ship dressed in the crew's uniform, which she had secretly purchased before they set sail. The outfit consisted of a white waistcoat with gold trim on the lapels. Beneath the jacket, she wore a grey, long-sleeved padded shirt that zipped up in front and had a V-shaped collar. Black trousers tucked into a pair of black dress boots completed the uniform.

When she became bored with typical ship's operations, she would climb into access ways, tall enough to stand up in, that ran throughout the ship. Maintenance crews used these corridors to access various parts of the ship where repairs were needed. These access ways sometimes became dangerous with power surges, caused by damaged power couplings or computer panel access points. There was the off chance of being hit by space debris or laser fire. Those dangers could blow a hole in the hull, sucking anyone inside the tube into space and immediate death. Whenever her mother found out about one of these excursions, she always panicked, and her father always laughed. Aside from the crew and her android servants, the only thing Serena didn't have was friends. She was too engrossed in her studies, the technological advances in her father's company, and her family's travel, be it across the planet or in outer space.

Today, her father let her be at the helm. Instead of observing her from the captain's chair, he was in his private office just off the bridge. Reading a book in his favorite chair near the window, which gave him a fabulous view of space as they passed through it. Serena gave orders confidently to the men and women crew members, calling out course adjustments and listening to the various science and communication reports. When her father returned to the bridge, she would accurately relay those reports to him along with any other pertinent information. The crew would smile whenever she increased the speed past what her father would take the ship.

As they were enjoying their fun, a meteor collided with a nearby planet, causing a powerful shockwave that sent waves of electric discharge towards the ship. They violently shook the *Cirrus* and tossed the crew members about like rag dolls. Several people were injured. On the bridge, most were minor injuries, although one woman received knocked unconscious and had a concussion. But the worst one hurt was the science officer, Jeffrey Holbrook, who had just returned to the bridge and was still standing. He was tossed so violently against one of the chairs that it broke his arm. Serena clung to her seat at the helm and with the help of the navigator, steered the ship away from the planet's shockwave. The collision was unforeseeable and not her fault, but she felt terrible. Everyone on that ship was dear to her.

Serena turned the helm over to the navigator and ran to the man's side. His arm was bleeding from a compound fracture. She calmly helped the man hold his arm against his body and escorted him into the turbolift and down to sickbay. Doc had his hands full, helping several injured members of the crew from other sections of the ship. So she led the science officer over to an empty biobed where he sat down.

"I can fix this for you, but if you'd prefer to wait for Doc…," she said tenderly.

"I trust you," Jeffery said.

Serena nodded. Pulling over a tray on wheels that contained the instruments she would need, she gave him an injection for pain from a needless syringe, which painlessly administered drugs through the skin.

His relief was instantaneous, and he smiled. "Thanks, Serena."

Before she could take the next step, her mother entered sickbay and rushed over to her.

"There you are. Are you all alright? When they told me you went to sickbay... I was worried, sick."

"I'm fine, Mom. I just brought Jeff down to take care of his broken arm."

"Maybe he should wait for Doc."

"Doc is so busy; it'll take forever before he has a chance to work on Jeff."

"It's okay, ma'am. I trust Serena." Jeff said.

Margaret was about to say more, but she took one look at the compound fracture and promptly fainted.

Serena shook her head and told Jeff to lie down on the biobed, which instantly scanned his entire body and high-lighted the injury. Using the scan as a guide, she carefully straightened the arm, pulling the bone back inside the skin. Then she aligned it until the broken ends of the bone were set correctly.

Her father walked in just as she was reaching for the bone knitter. He had come to check on the well-being of his crew. After speaking with each injured member, he quietly walked over to his daughter. He watched as she passed a handheld instrument over the broken bone. The bone knitter emitted a thin stream of light that literally replaced the missing fragments of bone and sealed the ends together. Changing the setting to heal the broken skin, she glanced up and saw her father smiling at her.

"Keep going, sweetheart," her father said encouragingly. "I'll carry your mother back to her room.

Serena carefully repaired the science officer's skin as though she had done it a thousand times. Still, other than her practice on virtual patients, this was her first time with a living patient.

"There you go. All healed," she said. "Just take it easy with that arm for a couple days. You wouldn't want to damage the new skin and bone.

"Thank you, Doctor Serena," Jeff said with a smile.

Checking with Doc, Serena helped a few people with minor injuries. When she finished, she went back to the helm and assumed her duties without losing a beat.

Chapter 6

Opportunity

The next day was an off day for Karson and Hague, the Ashnar from the day before stood outside the tavern, talking and laughing with a couple friends. When he spotted Hague, he roughly grabbed him by the arm and shook him.

"Hey, you're the partner to the human who swindled me out of my money."

"I have no idea what you're talking about," Hague said, lying through his teeth.

The Ashnar's female friend piped in. "Yes, you are. I remember you being with him during the game. Too close, in my opinion. You and he must've cheated Grut and me!"

"You have me mistaken for another Rungho."

"It's not good to lie," Grut said as he slugged Hague in the stomach.

Hague bent over gasping for air.

At that moment, Karson turned the corner and saw what was going on. It was tempting to run in the opposite direction, but his loyalty to Hague wouldn't let him.

"Hey, let go of him!" He yelled.

The Ashnars turned their attention to Karson as Hague ran in the opposite direction. He assumed that once he was free, Karson would also take off running and communicate with him later.

Karson didn't run, and the aliens quickly surrounded him.

"Hey, it's gambling boy," Grut sneered. "He's probably planning on cheating another crew member out of his hard-earned wages, eh, Connie?"

"Yeah," the female Ashnar, Connie, said, giving Karson a shove. "Awfully bold of ya to mess with an Ashnar, to say the least," she snickered.

The others laughed.

It was about then that Karson realized he should have been smarter and run off when he had the chance.

"Maybe we ought to break his arm," one overly broad Ashnar suggested.

"He only needs one arm for cards," another one agreed.

"You're right," Connie agreed.

Karson suddenly realized that he was being braver than smart and wished he would have been quicker than heroic. He looked for an opening, but there weren't any, just angry Ashnar crew members standing shoulder to shoulder and shoving against him.

"What? You gonna fight me? You think you're man enough, puny human?"

The Ashnars snickered.

Karson threw himself at the Ashnar and tacked him. But the alien quickly got the upper hand and lifted his right fist to teach the boy a lesson.

A crowd formed on the street as the fight began. Karson held his arms in front of his face. After a flurry of punches to his body, he dropped and rolled onto his stomach. He tried to squirm away from the Ashnar, who simply grabbed his belt and pulled him to his feet. The two locked together as they rolled around until a ship's captain, hearing the commotion, pushed through the crowd and broke up the fight.

"Stop this fighting, or I'll have the lot of you thrown in the brig," he said, pulling them apart.

Grut didn't want this fight to end; he was having too much fun.

Grabbing hold of the ugly Ashnar, the captain, who was tall and muscular, punched him in the jaw and shoved him into the arms of the male's friends. "You! Get him out of here, and don't let me see the lot of you hanging around here again. Aren't you all that lot from Captain Howing's ship? I know the Ashnar personally. Stay shipside from now on, or I'll have to have a talk with your captain. A month in the brig ought to settle you down."

The captain knew that Ashnars hated imprisonment. They were so large; they were claustrophobic. Locking them up in the brig was nothing less than sheer torture for one of their kind. Grut righted himself and jerked away from Connie, who had a hold of him. He turned to Karson. "Stay away from us. Or next time, there won't be anyone around to save you."

As the men walked away, grumbling, the captain turned his attention to Karson and Hague. "Haven't I seen you boys working on the docks?"

"Yes, sir," said Karson.

"Affirmative," Hague said

"What the devil was you, boys, doing picking a fight with a bunch like that? Those hired hands are here because of brute strength, you know. You could have ended up with your skull popped."

"Just my luck is all, sir," Karson retorted. His left eye was closed and turning black and blue. He went inside the tavern and contacted Hague, telling him it was safe to come back.

****

The inside of the bar was full and noisy when an alien sharply dressed in an officer's uniform walked up to a crowded table of dockhands.

"The *Stardust* is offering a bonus and advancement of payment in Federation credits if anyone interested signs up today," the first mate, a reptilian-like male belonging to the species Venomae said.

One or two males took him up on his offer but most ignored him. He was about to leave when Karson, stood up, "The *Stardust*?"

"Karson, what are you doing?" Hague asked his friend.

"Hang here, I'm going to talk to his guy." He made his way to where the Venomae was standing.

"Hello, um I'm Karson Pleiades, and I am interested in signing up."

"Tuscon Scalemander," the officer extended his hand and shook Karson's. "You ever sailed on a merchant starcruiser before, lad?"

"No, but I work at the docks not too far from here."

"So, you have some experience with labor and machinery?"

"Indeed. Where is this ship heading to?"

"The first voyage is to the Terraformed colony on New Kansas. An Outer Core planet. The other two voyages are confidential until you become a member of the crew. Any other questions?"

"Just one more: what would be this bonus and advancement of pay add up to?"

Tuscon smiled and replied, "Well, the bonus is 2,000 credits. Given your limited experience and the roles that would be assigned…" He began to mentally calculate.

Karson waited, the sound of his own heartbeat echoing in his head.

"Six thousand credits," the Venomae first mate finally stated

Karson's hopes rose. Here was the answer to everything. "I'll take it!"

Tucson smiled and handed Karson a small device that would allow him on board the ship. "Hand this to the security officer before boarding. We leave at first daybreak tomorrow."

"Yes, sir," Karson replied.

****

"You did what?"

"I took the opportunity."

"Karson, your mom is going to kill you!" Hague said as he walked his friend back to his home.

"Well, hopefully, Uncle Jasper can hold her off before that happens," Karson replied.

"Well, make it back alive, alright? We can still hang out before you go to the academy."

"I will, my friend, I will," Karson replied.

They both hugged each other for a moment before Karson went inside.

****

Karson sat with his mother and Jasper in their makeshift living room. He had just finished explaining what he did earlier today, and the place was dead quiet.

"I'll send communication as soon as we make port," Karson said.

Jasper smiled and turned, "Gloria?"

38

Gloria looked up and at her son and only her friend. "I can't stop you. I know your father would've wanted this."

They all stood up and hugged. Gloria cried, holding on tight to her son. Proud of him for thinking of the family. Afraid for him for what he would endure out in deep space.

Chapter 7

All Aboard!

Karson stood in front of the *Stardust*. He was alone, save for a pack slung over his shoulder. His mother was at work, and Jasper did not start his shift for several hours, so he was asleep, Karson deduced. He began to make his way to the portal of the ship when he heard a call.

"Pleiades! You better not get on that ship without me!"

He turned around to see Hague C'avt and Jasper Tinsmith walking down the lane to meet him.

"Hague? Uncle Jasper?"

"Didn't think I'd let ya go alone on this one, didja?" Hague winked one of his bulbous eyes.

"You signed on?"

"Yes sir, brought my device and everything." Hague showed him the exact same device Karon had received from the first mate.

"I found him this morning," Jasper said. "As luck would have it."

"Guess I was born under a lucky star," Karson chuckled.

"Well, we better get going," Hague urged Karson. "The ship is leaving today, and we better get on before they're ready to blast off." The two friends then headed over to the portal.

"Good luck, lad," Jasper said, a small tear forming in his eye.

When they reached the ship's portal, they handed their devices to the man standing guard, who nodded. They scanned their wrist computers, letting the internal network on the Stardust know who they were and their levels of clearance. As they walked up the plank, Karson became very excited, touching, and drinking in everything he saw. Stepping inside to the outer corridor, they were met by an attractive human female, who would be their guide.

"Good morning, gentlemen," she said with a smile. "I am Lieutenant Adira Shawnees. I'll be showing you around before we take off." She checked her tablet and looked up at them.

Anxious to begin the tour, Karson asked, "Do we get to see the engine room?"

Adira smiled. "They always want to see the engine room first. We'll pass a few other points of interest on the way, but I promise you'll see the engine room soon."

As they walked down the gleaming corridor, Adira talked about the ship. "Since the *Stardust* is based on the Capital Planet Yusie, most of the crew is human. However, we also have plenty of crew members from different planets."

"Are any of them from Ashnar?" Hague asked nervously.

"I'm afraid not," she replied as she stopped in front of a door that slid open automatically. "Their size would make it difficult to accommodate them. Plus, their disposition would not fit in with our personnel." Leading them inside, she continued. "Now, this is one of ten cargo bays. As you can see, it is equipped with the latest technology, making the job easier and safer."

They returned to the corridor and continued through the ship. "I'm sure you've noticed the panels along the walls in the corridors." She stopped in front of one. "Using one of these, a crew member can find his or her way to anyplace on the ship. It is also useful for contacting the captain or other officers if something an emergency comes up."

"How does it show me where to go?" Karson asked.

The guide touched the panel. It became brighter, and a computer voice spoke from it.

"How may I help you?"

"Computer, I need to find the engine room. Can you show the way?"

"Of course." Suddenly, a line of panels lit up with arrows displaying the proper direction. "Please follow the green arrows to your destination."

"Thank you, computer."

Excited, Karson took the lead as the others followed. Sure enough, he soon found himself standing inside the engine room. "Wow!"

"It is an impressive sight," Hague agreed.

The room was massive, with work stations lining all but one wall with several others stationed throughout. Even Hague was impressed. He followed Karson to the massive engines and cooling tanks that stretched four stories upward. From there, Karson explored the work stations, fascinated with the different operations taking place to keep a starship this large in peak operating condition.

"I never realized what it took to run a vessel like this," Hague said in awe.

When Adira was finally able to pull the friends away from the engine room. She led them through sections of the remaining four floors, showing them the sickbay, mess hall, kitchen, and other areas.

"Would it be possible to see the captain's quarters?" Karson asked.

"Another frequently asked question," the lieutenant said with a smile. "No, I'm afraid not, but I can show you the crew quarters."

Karson looked disappointed at first. "I guess that would be okay."

Adira took them down another corridor, passing several doors before stopping before one. These doors did not open automatically in their presence.

"Adira Shawnee requests permission to enter this room."

"Access granted," the computer replied.

They stepped inside of an attractive, but plain room that served as both living room and bedroom. It also had two other doors. One led to a bathroom and the other to a closet/storage area.

"They look much nicer once the occupant adds their own personal touches like pictures, colorful pillows, and other décor," Aida said.

"Wow, even without, this is better than my bedroom at the apartment. I think it would be great to serve on this ship," Karson said in awe.

"I'm glad to hear that," Aida said with a smile. "Your quarters will be similar for the duration of your contract with us. Although built to accommodate two."

"We get to board up together?" Karson asked excitedly.

"How long exactly is this duration," Hague asked skeptically.

Karson blanched. In all the excitement, he realized he didn't even know how long this trip would be. Based on the number of credits, it might be longer than he anticipated.

"Could be a few months," Aida said. "All depends on travel and speed."

She showed them to their rooms. They went down a long hall of other rooms, bunks shared by crewmembers on this section of the ship, until they reached the one that would house Karson and Hague.

"Room 186. I suggest getting some rest. Your immediate supervisor will be here after we takeoff to inform you of your duties." She nodded and excused herself back to perform her duties.

The room was similar to the one they saw before. But it was designed to have a slightly larger living area with two bunks on opposite walls. However, there was still only one closet and bathroom. It also looked a lot dingier and beat up than the first room. But still, the boys were happy.

"I'll take the left one," Karson called.

"Fine by me," Hague said.

****

The *Stardust* had been speeding through space for several hours when Paulie, a large bear-like Zanoform, unlocked their door.

"Get up!" Paulie shouted as he banged on the wall and doors.

Hague woke up in a daze and fell off his bunk. His fall awoke Karson, who had nodded off by accident.

"Lights 70%," Paulie ordered the computer.

Karson attempted to get up as a thought occurred to him. He stood very still, trying to decide if he felt any motion beneath his feet. Nothing? Did that mean they hadn't left the planet Nergal yet?

"Are you, our supervisor?" Karson asked. "Have we taken off yet?"

Hague sat on the chair placed under his bunk, nursing his head. He had never seen a Zanoform before, and neither had Karson. But clearly, his friend was too excited to see if they had embarked to question anything else.

"Have we?" Paulie snorted. "We left hours ago. We're light-years from Nergal."

"But I don't feel the ship moving," Hague asked. "Have we stopped somewhere else to make a delivery?"

"You'd better not feel this baby moving. Aldar Dietrich, our engineer, takes great pride in how smooth he keeps his engines running. Look out your window, if you don't believe me."

Karson turned and walked over to the only window in his quarters. In the distance, a giant gaseous planet was just coming into view. His heart rose.

"Well Karson Pleiades at your service," Karson replied

"Hague C'avt," Hague introduced himself.

"How can we support you, sir?" Karson beamed. "Need us to transport dangerous cargo from the end of the ship to the other? Have some pirates intercepted us, and you need us for combat? Or are we training today?"

Paulie laughed and handed him a mop. "Here's how you can support me, start cleaning."

Karson looks dejected as he stared at the metallic mop.

"You both signed up to be cabin boys, according to First Mate Scalemander," Paulie spoke. "You'll start mopping this area, Pleiades. Now C'avt, come with me to the stalls."

"Stalls?" Hague asked as he rushed after their now leaving supervisor.

45

Karson picked up the mop and programmed the computer to track where the mop was moving. He walked out to the hallway, sighed, and began to mop.

****

The livestock aboard the ship was being delivered to a deep space Terraforming colony called New Kansas. Even though the ship had food packaged and stored for use in their processors, the cook would use the fresh milk and eggs as primary means of sustenance. Only if the trek went longer than planned would they break into the packaged food.

"It stinks in here," Hague complained, pinching his nose.

"It'll get better once it's cleaned up," Paulie responded. "The infiltration system will be able to keep up with it then, as long as you keep the place clean. In the meantime, smell or not, get to work and clean up this mess."

Hague looked around the large room. Stalls held cows and bulls. A penned area contained dozens of pigs, and several rows of nests were stacked two shelves high for the chickens and two roosters. These animals were all descendants from the original animals on Terra Firma, and due to their ability to reproduce relatively quickly, they became a primary commercial food source. It would take more than a mop to clean up this mess.

"Once you muck out this room, you can feed the animals."

Hague got to work. *Well, at least an anti-grav lift won't fall on me.*

The smell was actually getting better. The more he dumped down the waste disposal, the better the air filters freshened the air. It was a dirty job that took two hours to complete.

****

During those two hours, Karson continued to mop. While he cleaned, he racked his brain for a way to get out of this placement. *Cabin boy. So that's what Scalemander was offering Hague and me. Well, it is my own fault, I should've asked. But I am so much more than this!*

The longer Karson cleaned, the worse he felt. *The captain, whoever he is, will never release me from duty unless I can prove myself more than a cabin boy.* Karson frowned. After emptying the bucket, he stood unmoving, deep in thought. *Somehow, I have to learn how to fly a shuttle. It's my only chance to escape out of this job.*

Paulie yelled at him. "Next time I catch you doing anything other than your job, you'll be disciplined and tossed in the brig. And believe me, boy. You won't like being disciplined."

****

On the bridge, the helmsmen punched in a new set of coordinates. Captain Abernethy stood behind him. Captain John Abernethy was an Osira, a species of aliens from the planet Rasiris, located in the Inner Core. Osira had the heads of many different animals but had the bodies of humans. Abernathy's head was that of an eagle. His white plumage standing stark contrast to his golden beak. He stood on the bridge, taking in all that he was observing. This mission was of the utmost importance, and his own pride would not allow him to fail it.

"Our speed?" Abernethy asked.

"Warp three, sir."

"Captain, we're coming up on another vessel. Its transponder is putting out mixed signals," the helmsman said.

"Shall I open a hailing frequency?" Lieutenant Adira Shawnees, the communications officer, asked.

"Delay that. Are you getting any kind of distress signal?"

"No, sir," Shawnee replied. "If I may, sir, I think we should steer clear of it. It may be a pirate vessel."

"Gut instinct, Shawnee?"

"Woman's intuition."

The captain smiled. "If there's one thing I've learned over the years, lieutenant, it's to always trust your instinct. You've never steered me wrong." He turned to the navigation officer. "Mr. Tavish, change our heading to four, five, zero, mark thee."

"Four, five, zero, mark three, aye, sir."

Captain Abernethy turned back to the helmsman. "Increase our speed to warp five. Since we've spotted them, there's no doubt they also have us on their scanners."

"Increasing speed to warp five."

The captain smiled. "That's better. Let's not waste time losing them. It'll take us a bit out of our way. Still, I'd rather avoid any unnecessary skirmishes, a battle, and subsequent repairs would delay us even further. I'd like to get those animals in our cargo hold delivered sooner rather than later."

Chapter 8

Working on the Ship

When Karson finished his job, Paulie took him to a storeroom near the galley where the provisions were kept and had him help out Hague. Besides the grain and food used for the animals, the cargo bay contained large walk-in units with shelves of pre-packaged processor-ready food, sugar, flour, spices, coffee, tea, and other liquid beverages. Oranges, grapefruit, lemons, and limes were also preserved in containers.

"Just be careful and don't spill any of it," Paulie warned. "If we lose too much food, we'll all starve. We're traveling through a section of space with few populated planets, and most of those have only minimal technology or worse. Plus, we don't want to attract rats or other vermin when we dock to resupply."

"Other vermin?" Hague asked.

"Aye, I've seen plenty of strange beasts try to sneak aboard a ship for a quick bite. We don't know what kind of fauna we will encounter when we land. So you two better keep it clean back here."

When Karson and Hague finished feeding the animals, the crewman escorted him to their next duties.

"C'avt, you are to report to the galley and help the cook with the cleaning. Ask the central computer where to go if you get lost. Pleiades, you got laundry duty, I'll take you there myself."

Hague made to the galley, with minimal help from the computer, and found an enormous mound of plates, cups, silverware, pots, and pans. More would come later, as a crew of eighty-five finished eating. Nearly every surface was stacked with additional tableware. The dish sanitizer was also filled with dirty dishes that Boris, the cook, had not bothered to run yet. *How lazy can you get?* Hague programmed a short sequence code, and the sanitizer turned on. Using chemically created steam to clean, and a blast of hot air to dry. The entire process took ten minutes. Even so, with the number of dishes to be cleaned, this was going to take quite a while.

Once the first part of the task was finished. The first wave of dishes put away in cupboards with doors that sealed shut to prevent breakage during the occasional rough turbulence, Hague reflected. *Well, at least there are no Ashnars.*

****

Karson walked into the laundry room through a jungle of bins on wheels containing the crew's dirty clothing. Fortunately, someone had already sorted the darks from the lights and whites. Grabbing one of the containers, he rolled it to a large machine and loaded it up. Like the dish sanitizer, the dirty laundry was also cleaned using chemical steam. The room contained six washers and six dryers. After loading all six machines, he looked for a chair to sit and wait. He noticed the long tables along one wall filled with clean clothing, ready to be folded or hung up and delivered to the various crew members.

He was halfway through the mountain of clothing when all six washers buzzed. Sighing, Karson emptied the machines and loaded the dryers. Then after turning them on, he reloaded the appliances with more dirty clothes and went back to sorting, hanging, and folding. He placed the folded laundry into containers, both marked with room numbers and loaded them into a chute, which scanned the number and sent the containers to the corresponding rooms. The others were hung, again according to room numbers on long racks where the crew could pick them up, all except for the officers' clothing.

Karson had to hand-deliver those to their quarters. After working through the second round of laundry, and making sure the officers' clothing was finished, he started his deliveries. *I'm sure glad their quarters are all in the same corridor,* he thought. As he approached the captain's quarters and said, "Karson Pleiades delivering Captain Abernethy's laundry. Permission to enter."

"Permission granted," the computer replied, and the door to the captain's stateroom swished open. A human steward in his mid-thirties was inside. For some reason, he gave Karson a dirty look as he marched over and snatched the clothing before the newest crew member could step foot into the room. When the servant turned and walked toward the captain's bedroom, the door swished closed right in Karson's face.

****

Nighttime finally descended, and the ship quieted down as the shifts changed and tired crew members headed for their quarters to snatch a few hours sleep or to the mess to get a bite to eat. When Paulie finally said the cabin boys were done for the day.

They stood in line and eventually received a plate of food. Looking around for two empty places on one of the benches, Karson finally sat at a table with several muscular crew members.

Hague brought over two plates of ill-colored food. Looking down at the slop on his plate, Karson made a face. It didn't smell that great either.

51

"How does someone mess up a meal using a processor?" Karson grumbled.

"Doesn't the cook have any decent recipes to program?" Hague said bitterly. "I was there earlier, cleaning the dishes. Didn't know the meal processor needed rebooting too."

"Guess we will have more work cut out for us tomorrow," Karson said as they continued to finish their lackluster meal.

****

"Lights on 10%," Karson said in a quiet voice as he woke up. He needed to see but kept the light at a minimum so as not to disturb his sleeping roommate. Sighing, he searched for the ladder on his bed to climb down. He was so tired, and his muscles ached. Frustrated, he decided to take a walk around the ship.

He began to walk down the hallway. The light was low, but the ship was still active. Various members of the night crew were out and about performing checks on the systems. A member of the team saw Karson wandering. Karson did not know the crewmember. Feeling sorry for the newest crew member, he touched Karson's shoulder.

"My name's Sam. First time on a deep-space vessel?"

Karson shook his head. "Yes, sir."

"Ah, makes sense. It took me a while to get used to sleeping in space too."

Although Karson's eyes were getting used to the low light, it was apparent that this man could see a lot better. Karson wondered if eventually he, too, would be able to see as well in the dark. His crewmate seemed thirty years older than he thought the man to be. Life was hard on anyone who labored on a cargo vessel, thanks in part to the pirates. Although the officers had it pretty cushy, the rest of the crew labored hard, especially when delivering goods to backstar planets with limited technology. Much of the work had to be done the hard way.

Most freighters were captained by harsh men, and the luxuries built into military and private ships were considered a waste of money. Their owners figuring the men didn't need the perks, which would cut too heavily into their profits. The *Stardust* was a modified exception. Captain Abernethy, the owner of this vessel and had allowed a few exceptions since his ship was also his home.

"How long did it take for you to get used to spacetravel?"

"Mark my words, in a couple weeks, you'll get used to the way things operate out here in the black recesses of space. I have to go run some checks, nice meeting you."

Karson nodded as his new friend walked away.

Well, we are stuck here. But I refuse to be a cabin boy any longer. Maybe I should head to the hangar bays and check out the ships.

Chapter 9

Fly by Night

With only a skeleton crew on duty, the corridor lights were dimmed, and everything was quiet. Although deep in his mind, he knew it was impossible, Karson was determined to locate the shuttle bay and learn how to fly one. He walked toward the turbolift, thinking, *All I have to do is tell the computer where I want to go, and the lift will take me to the right floor. But once I'm on the correct floor, how will I find the right door?* Then he remembered the panels on the corridor walls and smiled. All he had to do was ask for directions, and the computer would light the way.

Ten feet from the lift, he heard it come to a stop. Someone was coming! Glancing around, he remembered passing a corridor behind him on the left. He took off at a run and flew around the corner just as the lift's door swished open. Footsteps came toward him, and Karson crouched down, plastering his body against the wall. The sound continued toward him, and he wracked his brain. *If he sees me, he'll want to know what I'm doing here. Maybe I should stand up. I could tell whoever it is that I just got off shift and was trying to find my quarters.*

The man was almost there.

But if I remain crouched, he might not see me in this dim light.

Karson was about to stand up, when the man came into view, turned and headed down the hallway right past him. As soon as the crewman was far enough away, he slipped around the corner, stood up, and headed straight for the turbolift, which immediately opened at his approach.

When the doors closed, Karson said, "Shuttle bay."

"Which one?" The computer asked.

"There's more than one?"

"Affirmative, the *Stardust* has two shuttle bays. Which one do you want?"

Karson thought a moment before answering. "Is there any activity going on in either one?"

"Shuttle Bay 1 currently has two crew members doing repairs," the computer informed him.

"What about Shuttle Bay 2? Is anyone on duty there?"

"Crewman Washburn is due to arrive at 0800 hours."

"What time is it now?"

"It is currently 0150 hours."

"Then take me to Shuttle Bay 2."

The lift smoothly took off sideways before heading upward. *Can I learn how to fly a shuttle that quick? If I can't, I can come back again tomorrow night to practice. Either way, I'd better be out of this bay before 0730 hours.*

When he arrived at Shuttle Bay 2, the doors automatically opened, and Karson was grateful he didn't need to ask permission to go inside. He entered and stepped to the side, allowing the door to close. When it did, the room was pitched into darkness once more. Aside from a few small green lights on a control panel that operated the space doors and, in case of fire, vented the atmosphere to kill the flames.

"Lights 50%," Karson ordered. With the bay illuminated, he walked around in amazement. "Wow, I never knew they carried so many shuttles on one ship. I wonder if the other bay has this many, too."

"Affirmative. Both bays contain the same number of shuttles."

Karson jumped and spun around, facing the door to the corridor. His heart hammered in his chest. Then he realized that the computer had thought he was talking to her and answered his question.

Heaving a sigh, he walked along the rows of small, one-man spacecraft, caressing their metal exteriors. He finally stopped at the one nearest the outside bay doors. Laying his hand on a small touch plate next to the spacecraft door, it opened upward with a hiss of air. Karson walked inside and examined everything. It was one of the smaller crafts used for personal transport rather than to haul cargo. He sat down in the pilot's seat and touched the panel in front of him. It came to life, and Karson felt the magic of space fill his soul. *This is why men go to space.* He imagined himself flying this shuttle to freedom and smiled for the first time since waking up to this nightmare.

"So, this is a personal spacecraft?" The question wasn't aimed at anyone, but once more, the computer answered all the same.

"Hello."

"Oh, hello, are you the autopilot?" Karson asked, this time specifically.

"I am the Central Intelligence Program designed to aid and assist all pilots who operate the T3-M1 personal fighter craft. I am also capable of operating the autopilot."

His hopes rose. "How do I open the space doors?"

"I am capable of opening the doors. However, unless you seal the door to this shuttle, you will die when the oxygen is sucked out through the bay doors."

Karson's face lit up. "Great! Open the bay doors once you tell me how to turn this ship on."

"Are you an authorized pilot?"

Karson's face fell. "Ahhh, I guess not. Can you show me how to pilot this?"

"Permission denied."

"Permiss... What?"

"Permission denied. You are not authorized to take a craft out. I have notified Security."

"No! No, wait. Please don't notify security. I...I was just kidding. I'll go back to my quarters now."

"I am afraid that it will not be possible."

"Computer...computer...do you have a name?"

"I do not," the female voice replied. She sounded testy.

"We should definitely give you a name. I can think of one if you like." When the computer did not respond, he said, "Look, I'm new here. I don't know all the rules. Can't we just forget this even happened?"

The sound of the door opening brought him to his feet as a security officer walked in, his phaser drawn. "Stealing a shuttle is a capital office, son."

"I wasn't stealing it. I just wanted to take it for a test-drive. Honest! Tell him, computer."

"He did not say that theft was his intention," the computer confirmed.

"Doesn't matter. You are not an authorized pilot. You could cause massive damage to this vessel, if not the whole *Stardust*. Even worse, you could kill yourself or others by accident. No, this was a horrible idea on your part." Grabbing Karson's arm in a firm grip, the officer marched him below deck and threw him in the brig.

The light in the security office was just bright enough to see by, but the light in the cells was off. Each jail was significantly sufficient for three prisoners. They contained three shelves large enough to sleep on, one on each of the three inner walls. No blanket or pillows were provided. The fourth wall opened onto the security office. After pushing Karson inside, the officer keyed in a code, raising the force field.

Karson jumped to his feet and ran at the opening, hoping to get through, but the force field was quicker. It was like running into a brick wall. He slammed into it and was pitched backward against the back wall sleeping shelf.

"Let me out of here!"

"Quiet down," the officer shouted. "I scanned your wrist computer. Your supervisor will be here tomorrow to see how to deal with you."

As soon as the officer left, Karson's frustration overwhelmed him. He wanted out, had to get out. He approached the shield once more and cautiously extended his index finger.

"Ouch!" He jerked it back and sucked on the injured digit.

It was useless. He stood there, wondering what to do next when the hair on the back of his neck stood up. He wasn't alone. Turning, he stared into the dark recesses of the cell, trying to see by the dim light in the security office. As he strained to see, he could just make out a dark figure squatting on the floor in the corner. As his eyes adjusted, he got a better look. What he saw made his blood run cold. It was a man's face; long stringy hair framed his head in wild abandon. His maniacal expression sent chills up and down the young man's spine. The prisoner's eyes had a cunning look. Then he gave Karson a wide, gap-toothed grin and began to cackle, making the frightened boy want to crash through the force field and escape, but he couldn't.

He was trapped.

Chapter 10

Celestial Paintings

Captain William Cloudracer stood on the bridge, enjoying the sight of a beautiful nebula in oranges, blues, greens, and browns. This one was named the Horsehead Nebula, and that's precisely what it looked like. The upper body and head of a horse rearing up at some unseen danger. Nebulas are created by gaseous pockets expelled by a dying star, each one different in shape, size, and color. Cloudracer's hobby was to see and record as many nebulas as he could find. He was in his element, enjoying the fruit of his hard work and wealth as captain and owner of his beautiful ship. His family slept in, which was their regular routine while in space. Still, William enjoyed the quiet comfort of working a few hours with the night crew, until shift change at 8:00 a.m.

Below, Serena woke up with a smile like she did every morning in her private quarters with her android servant, Sarah, who had brought her breakfast. Fresh fruit, two over-easy eggs, and a thick slice of ham were placed on a bed tray over her lap. Sarah reached behind Serena to fluff her pillows so she could sit up in bed. She turned to leave, but her mistress called her back.

"Stay," Serena told her.

"Is there something else you need me to do?"

"No, please sit here on my bed. Have a piece of toast."

Serena treated Sarah like a best friend, although Sarah's mother always reminded her that she needed to keep an emotional distance from their android servants.

"I don't eat. You know that, and I have other chores I must…" but before she finished her sentence, Serena giggled.

"I know you don't eat, silly. But could you?"

Sarah cocked her head, her positronic brain searched for an answer. "I don't believe that is possible."

"If you weren't a servant, what would you like to do?"

"That question is illogical. I was programmed to be a lady's maid."

"You can be reprogrammed. Isn't there anything you'd rather do than this? Can you dream?"

"I am incapable of dreaming, but…."

"But what? You're sentient. I know your mind is always working. Have you ever seen or hear about something and thought it might be nice to try it?"

Sarah's features lit up. "Yes. I like to look at paintings. It would be…nice to create such beauty. Is that dreaming?"

"Yes. It's called daydreaming. So let's dream together," Serena urged her. "If you could do something else, what would it be?"

Serena sat silently with a soft, inviting smile, while Sarah visualized all the paintings she had ever seen.

"I would like to be a famous painter," she finally replied.

With those words, Serena jumped from her bed, grabbed Sarah's hands, and pulled her to a wooden easel in the corner of the room. On it sat a blank canvas, and the table next to it contained brushes, a pallet, and numerous jars of paint in beautiful colors.

"My Mother wants me to paint, but I hate it. From now on every morning you are going to paint in here. I will tell Mother that I've given you some chores, and while I do something I really enjoy, you can paint."

"Miss Serena, I have never painted. It is not in my programming."

"Look, you are more than the sum of your programming. You can learn new things. I know you can. I've seen you."

"Yes, that is true, but…"

"But nothing. Find some books on painting on the computer and read them. I'll bet you'll be painting in no time. I order you to do it," Serena said with a smile.

"I cannot refuse if you order me." Sarah went to the computer and sat down. "Computer, I want to see a book on painting pictures."

"I have 227 books on painting pictures. Please be more specific."

"I wish to see them all. Start with the easiest and continue on from there."

The first book, *How to Paint*, came up on the screen. Sarah began reading. "Faster."

The computer sped up the rate in which it flashed the pages.

"Faster…faster…faster."

Serena walked over to stand next to Sarah, and her mouth dropped. The pages were flashing by so quickly, the words were nothing more than a blur to her. Even at this rate, it would still take a while to absorb all 227 books.

Two hours later, the computer said, "You have finished the last book."

"Thank you, computer," Sarah said. Standing, she walked over to the easel, hesitantly picked up a paintbrush, and studied the white canvass. Her eyes rapidly flitted from left to right as she mentally ran through all the pictures she has seen in the books. Free to think and free to paint. She couldn't hide her smile. She looked at Serena and back at the canvas.

"Is there anything special you would like me to paint?"

Serena thought a moment, and then looked out the window and grinned. "How about that nebula? Could you paint that?"

I will do so. Sarah began painting, while Serena made the bed and picked up her clothing. She kept stealing glances at Sarah's canvas and thinking how amazing she was. It took three hours to finish it, and when it was done, Serena propped it on a chair in her parents' bedroom. That night when she joined them in their cabin for dinner, she found them both beaming with admiration.

"This is magnificent!" Her father exclaimed. "Even better than the images I recorded."

"You seem to have quite a talent for painting. Now, aren't you glad I made you do it?" Her mother asked.

"Yes, I was pretty surprised myself." Her response was accurate. She was surprised at how quickly Sarah had been able to create something so beautiful on canvas, but she felt a bit guilty for lying to her parents.

"Tomorrow, I'd like you to paint something else."

"Anything, in particular, Mom?"

"Your choice."

Serena left the room and returned to her bedroom, where she found Sarah cleaning the brushes and pallet. A new canvas was already sitting on the easel for Tomorrow.

"My parents love the painting. They can't wait to see the next one, and frankly, neither can I." She gave Sarah a hug. "But you should probably be a little less perfect for a while. I don't want them to get suspicious.

"Very well, I find painting very satisfactory," Sarah agreed. "Thank you for showing me how to expand my programming."

With those words, she left the room with a little paint on her hand and a smile on her face.

Chapter 11

Night Lessons

The *Stardust* continued her journey through deep space without incident. Karson could hear his heart pounding in his chest as he saw the crazy eyes of his neighboring cellmate.

"What are you in for?" A voice with a slight mechanical accent asked.

Karson spun around, thinking someone outside the cell had spoken.

"I asked you a question, spacer."

Karson turned back around in confusion. The voice did not match the man's appearance. "Trying to fly a fighter ship while being unauthorized."

"That's bad," the man replied. "You'll be taken to a prison planet and left to rot for the rest of your life."

Fear filled Karson's eyes. "Really?"

"No," his cellmate replied, "but the whippin' will hurt."

"Nobody does that anymore. It's an ancient punishment."

"Ever work aboard a freighter before?"

"Only to load or unload them."

"Then you don't know what happens on these ships. The officers can get real mean."

Karson remained silent. He didn't know whether to believe the man or not.

"My name's Dawson. What's yours?"

"Karson." The young man sighed and plopped down on the shelf against the right wall. He looked at the man. Dawson looked like any human from any planet from his left side. But once his face turned, Karson could make out the mechanical skin grafts, wires poking out of the skin, and a few mechanical digits. He looked up and realized why Dawson's eyes had scared him, one of them looked like human eyes, the other was animatronic.

A cyborg! Karson thought. Cyborgs were few are far between on Nergal. They usually were spacers who were injured during their flight and needed extensive medical treatment. Though sometimes cyborgs were the result of personal means. Pirates would sometimes trade their limbs for extra mechanical assistance. He did not know why Dawson had these, though.

"Don't let these gears and wires fool ya," Dawson chuckled. "Lost the side of me head and various digits during a charter around Ashnar."

"Did the Ashnars do that?"

Dawson laughed harder, "No boy. It was an explosion. Leaky canister of fluid. I was lucky, let's just say that. At least my hair grew back." He ran his fingers through his thin, dark brown hair. It had grown back, but it was more patchy and stringy on this right side.

Daniel smiled, feeling he could trust this cyborg. "What are you in for, Dawson?"

Dawson smiled, feeling the same mutual trust forming. "I discovered a mystery on this ship. One they don't want anyone to know about."

The man's words pricked Karson's curiosity. "What is it?"

"Don't know. That's why I called it a mystery, but I do know where they've stashed it."

"Tell me more," Karson said.

Dawson sat upon his sleeping shelf and rested his back against the smooth metal wall. By the expression on his face, it was apparent he was delighted to talk about this so-called mystery.

"I figure it has to be something of the confidential"

"That makes sense," Karson agreed. "Have you touched it?"

"Never got the chance before getting locked up in here."

"It's probably just a bunch of important papers," Karson said, losing interest and slumping against the wall.

"Maybe so, but if that's the case, they must hold great value. Enough value to put a specialized lock on the door."

Karson sighed, his mind returning to the fix he was in.

"Look, if that doesn't interest you, I know something that will," Dawson said. "This ship isn't just going to some planet to deliver and pick up goods. Once we deliver the cargo to the New Kansas Colony, we're headed off on a private mission."

This statement piqued Karson's curiosity. "It's not? What's the special mission?"

"Before you came on board, Captain Abernathy announced that we're going after treasure; ever hear of the Lost Treasure of the Planet Tarkees?"

"No."

Dawson smiled. He knew he had Karson's interest now. "It's massive and filled with a fortune in gold and jewels."

Karson sat up straight. "Is it still on Tarkees? Who did it belong to?"

"It belonged to a famous pirate: Captain Nova Scarm."

"Captain Nova Scarm! The pirate who looted hundreds of ships and planets? The same pirate who was eventually captured by Captain G'oge?"

"You're a smart kid."

"Nah, I just grew up with these tales from my uncle."

"They also captured the other vessels in his fleet, which contained an enormous amount of stolen treasure and rare, valuable items," Dawson said. "Nevertheless, Captain G'oge didn't find everything. Before Scarm's men were tried and sent to a penal colony, some of the guards overheard them talking about a massive chest and the vast fortune it held. Some of the guards tortured them for its whereabouts, but no one talked. The only thing they learned was that it was no longer on Tarkees. As for the actual whereabouts, the pirates took the knowledge of its location to the grave. People have been hunting for it ever since."

"Didn't that happen back in 2385?" Karson asked.

"Yes."

"If no one has found it in over 400 years, why is this ship looking for it now?"

"New information has surfaced along with part of a treasure map the captain suspects will lead us to its hiding place," Dawson said.

"Part of the map?" Karson asked. "Are there other parts?"

Dawson shook his head, "that part I do not know. I just know that if we find it, he's offered to share it with us."

"This is a pretty large crew," Karson said thoughtfully. "How much would each of us receive? Especially if there is only one chest left."

"I haven't the faintest idea, but according to the rumors, it would be more than enough to give every man onboard a large stake in his future."

Karson's mind churned with ideas about what he would do if he could get his hands on that much treasure. He and his mother would never be poor again. It might even be enough to buy a starship and take her back to Teculma. He allowed his imagination to run wild until he heard footsteps approach. Paulie approached the cell and turned off the force field. Lights on.

"Let's go, boy."

"Where are you taking me? To the captain?"

"Nah, worse."

"Are you going to strand me on some underdeveloped planet or moon?"

"You haven't worked off the credits yet."

"Then what?"

"You're going to work for the cook."

From the shadows of the cell, Karson heard Dawson mumble, "That's not good."

Hague worked with him yesterday, Karson thought, *he did not mention anything too bad. Guess we will see when we get there.*

Paulie entered the cell, grabbed Karson's arm, and after re-engaging the force field, dragged him to the transport, which took them to the mess. When they arrived, they found a fat human with a large, round nose standing over the dishes, his head bent low.

"Here's your help," Paulie told Boris.

69

The cook looked up. Seeing Karson, he said, "You're kidding, right?" Boris lowered his head and fell back to sleep. When he awoke, he saw Karson sitting alone across from him at the table. "Get to work! Start with the dishes and then fix breakfast."

Karson went to the galley. Although he knew that Hague had cleaned up the dirty dishes from last night's meal, he discovered still more dirty dishes crammed in an adjoining storeroom. Food and grease caked the inside. Getting them clean would take time. Karson sighed and got busy.

He put the first load into the sanitizer. The job seemed to take forever, and when he was finally finished, he went to the storage room to see what he could find for breakfast. *I have no idea how mom did it as a job as well.*

Remembering all the animals he saw yesterday, he thought about making eggs. When he entered the storeroom, however, he discovered Hague milking the cows.

"Where have you been? I didn't see you this morning when I woke up." Hague questioned his friend as he entered.

"Went exploring. I tried to do a little night flying and got nabbed. Spent the night in the brig as they call it. And now I'm helping the cook with dishes and breakfast," Karson told him.

"You got to fly?"

"Never even got it to hover," Karson laughed a bit at the situation.

"Well, let me finish with these cows, and I'll help you with the galley. I worked with him yesterday, and...you could use all the help you can get."

"I don't suppose you have any ideas or suggestions on what to make for breakfast, do you?"

"Actually, I do."

****

Returning to the galley, Karson programmed the processor to make coffee and two huge pots of oatmeal. Hague showed up later with eggs and started cooking. He also programmed the rehydrator machine and placed it in the dehydrated bread meal.

When breakfast was ready, two men helped carry the containers into the mess, placing them on the serving table, next to the coffee, fresh milk, and sugar. The crew filed in.

Chapter 12

The Conspiracy is Formed

Having served the men, the boys ate. Karson pulled out a deck of cards and shuffled them. This caught the attention of a few spacers in the room.

In the galley, several crew members sat around drinking coffee as Karson and Hague played a card game at the other end of a large silver metallic table.

"Hey, any chance you a gambling man, son?" One crewman shouted, gaining the attention of the others.

Karson grinned. "I am as a matter of fact."

"Let's play a quick round then," another human male said.

Very quickly, Karson and Hague found themselves in the company of two human males and a female Krillien, a crustacean species from the planet Krell. This time it was a friendly game with no real betting going on. Karson figured this would help create a friendship with the crew.

"I fold," Cecelia, the female Krillien said.

"Same," one of the male humans said.

"I'm out," Hague said.

"Call," said Karson.

The other male, Alexander, revealed his hand, "Three White Dwarves."

"Three Red Giants," Karson smiled as he showed his cards.

However, instead of violence like at the tavern, everyone at the table laughed. Alexander shook Karson's hand as he and his partner went back to their security division.

"Can we play another round at dinner?" Cecelia asked as she cleaned up her area.

"Only if we can actually bet this time," Karson winked with good humor.

His response brought cheers and good wishes. Life aboard a freighter could be monotonous and boring. Karson's entertainment brought a bit of laughter and happiness to the crew they usually wouldn't have.

The rest of the day passed with Karson and Hague helping the cook make the evening meal. The pile of dirty dishes and pots seemed endless. While Karson finished the last of them, Hague swept and cleaned both the galley and the mess. For the first time that day, the cook had a smile of anticipation on his face. After a final round of cards and a swift nightly clean-up, he sent the cabin boys to bed and headed off to pass the night away in his own comforts.

In their quarters, Karson stripped his bed and made it up with fresh linens, tossing the dirty ones down the laundry tube. He had meant to do this last night, but he was too tired. Hague appeared out of the restroom already changed into his night outfit. Karson figured it would be the best time to tell his friend.

"There's a cyborg on the ship. He told me something about a mystery or a secret that is on this ship."

"Really?" Hague asked. "What do you think it is?"

"Not sure, especially when the truth of this mission seems far more like a secret."

"I thought we were just delivering supplies to New Kansas?" Hague ran his suction-cup fingers through his blonde hair.

"That's what First Mate Scalemander told me when I signed on too," Karson interjected. "Though, according to the cyborg, after that, we are searching for the Lost Treasure of Captain Nova Scarm."

"That old spacer tale? I thought we signed on for a simple delivery, not chasing Rhungo geese."

"Well, we can figure out the truth of his claims once we land in New Kansas," Karson reassured his friend. "Though still, if we got that treasure, we'd be set for life."

"It is tempting. But how much could we really get if we split it among all the crew here?"

"What if we went for it ourselves?" Karson suggested.

"Well, that I don't know about. You don't think the cyborg got his wires crossed?"

"I'm not sure. But let's keep it to ourselves just in case all right?"

"You got it Pleiades," Hague responded as he wrapped himself in his blankets.

Karson smiled gratefully. Still, he was unable to doze off. Although he smiled when he played cards with the crew, it did nothing to relieve the loneliness and emptiness he felt. He missed his mother, Uncle Jasper, and recently, his old life. More than ever, however, he had a reason for a little hope, the Lost Treasure of the Captain Nova Scarm.

****

Back on Nergal, Gloria Pleiades sat in her home with Nuba C'avt, Hague's mother. Their advancement credits had been transferred to their parent's accounts. However, both mothers would have much rather had their sons home instead.

"It has only been a few days, but it feels longer," Nuba commented as she sipped a drink that Gloria had offered her. Nuba worked as a waitress for one of the local taverns on Nergal.

"It really does," Gloria commented. "Thank you again for coming over so late."

"It is no trouble at all. My shift doesn't start for another hour anyway."

The ladies had talked about work and missing their sons for the better part of the early evening. Nuba and Gloria were close, but not as close has their sons were. Then came a knocking on her door. Gloria told the visitor to come in and in stepped Jasper Tinsmith.

"I just came in to check on you, Gloria. Oh, hello there Nuba," Jasper said.

He leaned against the wall as the three adults continued to talk. Life seemed to still be going on, despite the absence of their boys.

"Another Terraforming project failed today," Jasper commented

"Not New Kansas, right?" Gloria asked worriedly.

"No, no, they wouldn't have sent supplied over to a failed project," Jasper assured her. "It was a planet out in the backstars."

"Another failed project from the Galactic Federation," Nuba blinked her bulbous eyes three times quickly, a Rhungo action similar to rolling one's eyes. "Well I better get going, I know there's a late shipment coming in tonight so the tavern should be busy. Night to you all!" Nuba excused herself out of the room. There was silence for a full fifteen minutes before Jasper spoke.

"He's doing fine, Gloria. I know it."

"We haven't been on a starship since...the accident. I'm just so scared."

75

"I know he's alive," Jasper smiled.

"How can you be so sure?" Gloria asked.

"I know he is. If he wasn't, you would know." He smiled as he took her hand in comfort. "Born under a lucky star, remember?"

Chapter 13

Dark Space

Viscount William Cloudracer had selected the *Cirrus* because of her speed. He hoped it would give him a better chance of escape, should pirates ever attack, always a concern for freighter ships. He also hired a former worker of his to be the captain during the trip.

Tonight with nothing ominous showing up on the scanners, the captain had assigned a minimum crew, allowing most of those on board to get a good night's sleep. His consideration was one of the reasons his men were loyal to him.

Later that evening, when most of the crew was asleep, a cloaked pirate ship caught up to them. Boarding four shuttlecraft, two approached each of the *Cirrus'* shuttle bays. On the bridge of the *Antares*, their chief engineer waited until the shuttles were in place. Upon receiving the signal from each of the four shuttlecraft, he punched a coded sequence into the computer.

"Open shuttle bay doors." The doors on the *Cirrus* sounded a warning alarm and began to open.

The shuttle bays were soundproof, so no one heard the alarm, which was only meant as a warning to personnel inside the bay. On the bridge, a light began to flash on the helmsman's console. Still, at the moment, he was telling the security officer a joke. By the time he looked back at his console, the pirate shuttles were onboard, and the doors closed, which turned off the warning light.

"It looks like the information you bought was correct," Captain Grimlocke said, grinning to one of his lieutenants, another human named Cosa.

The pirates, who had landed in the *Cirrus*'s shuttle bays, swarmed through the ship like an invading army of ants.

The invaders headed for their assigned posts. Three men led for engineering and quickly took control of the two-man night crew; sneaking up behind them, they knocked them out before they could sound the alarm. Others headed for the bridge. When the turbolift door swished open, the security guard turned and was immediately stunned by phaser fire. The other three crewmen jumped to their feet, drawing their weapons, and a battle ensued.

The pirates spread out, firing at the crew as each side ran for places of cover.

"Careful not to hit any of the equipment," Sharky the first mate yelled. "We want this ship left intact!"

The crew fired back, but not as carefully as the invaders. If part of the ship was damaged, the pirates would have to either tow their vessel to base or take the time to fix it here. Phaser fire flashed back and forth across the bridge, most of the time hitting nonessential equipment, walls, and chairs. Strangely, it seemed almost like a casual game of laser tag, until the security officer clutched his chest and screamed. His dead body dropped to the floor and rolled toward the captain's chair.

Suddenly, everything changed. With only two men left to defend the bridge against six pirates, the fight accelerated. When the helmsman took a hit to the right shoulder, his weapon clattered to the carpeted floor, and he raised his hands in surrender. The remaining crewman kept firing, taking out one of the pirates with a hit to the head.

But with five against one, he didn't stand a chance. He was quickly surrounded and rendered unconscious.

After gathering up the dead pirate's and the crew's weapons, the remaining crewman was stunned, and the invaders took control of the ship. In a lower deck, a handful of pirates hurried to Viscount Cloudracer's cabin. The door swished open, its sound covered by the music playing inside. Margaret's back was to them. She did not hear or see the invaders until a calloused hand clamped over her mouth. Another pirate grabbed the captain. They dragged the two struggling in protest, to the bridge, until one of the pirates placed a phaser to the captain's head.

The pirates searched the ship for treasure and other passengers. Killing who they found on sight. Aside from some jewelry belonging to Margaret, and the money they carried for their trip, the pirate's haul was disappointing. When the couple was herded onto the bridge, William and Margaret frantically searched for their daughter. When they didn't see her, hope blossomed. Maybe she had managed to hide somewhere, and the pirates hadn't found her.

"Listen up," the Captain Grimlocke shouted as he approached Cloudracer. "This is a fine vessel yer got here, Cloudracer. I think it will make a fine start of my own starfleet."

William wanted to spit back a nasty remark, but he realized that the lives of his family and crew hung on the precipice. Acting foolishly could get them all killed.

"You can say yer peace," Captain Grimlocke said with a wicked grin, "We already took out yer captain and the crew. I got me, boys, doing a final sweep, just in case."

"Coward. Not even offering a chance to surrender peacefully?" William said to the pirate captain.

"Don't take me for a fool," the pirate laughed. "I know yer connections to the Federation, *Viscount* Cloudracer. I didn't escape out of Cesaroma with the *Antares* just to slip up now."

Captain Cloudracer blanched. "The *Antares*? Then you're...you are..."

"Captain Flint Grimlocke?" The pirate captain laughed. "In the flesh and bone, sir. I should thank ye now for the lovely ship. The *Cirrus* will be the perfect first ship in my fleet."

William couldn't speak. This was one of the craziest pirates, according to the Federation. It was over for him and his wife. His thoughts were broken as he heard screaming.

"Got us a stowaway, Captain!" A pirate named Lonnie called as he dragged what appeared to be a young man out of the hallway. "Found this one hidden in one of the storage holds."

Once Margaret and her husband got a good look at the 'young man,' William's face went deadpan. His wife had to bite her lip to keep from crying out. It was their daughter, dressed as a crewman. Both Cloudracer and his wife knew that if the pirates discovered she was female, everything would go wrong. Although pirates in this century could be both male and female, there were still some captains who preferred an all-male crew and were superstitious about women being onboard a ship. They felt that women were too much of a distraction.

"We do, do we?" Grimlocke asked Lonnie. "What's his position, Cloudracer? Doesn't look like a federation uniform to me."

William thought fast, but his wife replied before he could open his mouth.

"He's our yeoman," she replied.

"Yeoman," the pirate captain repeated with a contemplative look.

Serena sweated.

"Take him to the ship," Captain Grimlocke ordered. "We could use a new cabin boy."

Serena was about to make a comment when Lonnie started dragging her away. She knew if she called out now, it was over for her too. Tears streamed from her eyes as she was dragged away.

Now with the *Cirrus*'s crew under the control of the pirates, more pirates came aboard and took up positions on the captured ship, preparing it for its new owner. While the original crew started moving the loot over to the *Antares*.

"What about us?" William Cloudracer asked.

Captain Grimlocke seemed to think it over, but it was just for show. "Well now, I suppose I could send ya out on a pod. But that would be a waste of resources I'd argue."

William remained quiet. He knew the pirate would never allow him to live.

"Let's make it quick then, out of respect for your former title," Grimlocke said, grinning at his men.

****

Serena looked out the connection tube between the ships. She has marched along in a clear tube. She began to open her mouth to scream, but she could not.

81

All she saw were her parents' faces briefly. Then a flurry of bright phaser beams in succession. She was about to turn around to see if her parents were really dead, but Lonnie shoved her harder as she entered the bay of the *Antares*. Grief encircled her heart. She straightened up and put on a brave face. It was the last time her parents saw her, and she wanted them to believe she was courageous and had a fighting chance to somehow escape her plight and live.

Chapter 14

The First Stop

Karson and Hague began to get settled into their work routine, which meant doing whatever Boris or Paulie told them. Karson figured that if they were stuck in the kitchen, they might as well try to appease the crew and, ultimately, Captain Abernathy. One night, he decided that they should make a delicious stew.

"Seems simple enough," Hague said as he cut the potatoes. "Us dock boys know how to cook a good stew that could be eaten in the morning, noon, or night."

"Maybe it will impress the pilots enough to talk to us."

"Still sticking to your plan to get us promoted?"

"At least changing stations," Karson said. "I mean, I figured we'd be doing more of what we were used to or something different."

"Cleaning laundry, swabbing floors, and cooking is technically different than the docks," Hague grinned.

Karson rolled his eyes as he gathered some packaged soup base. He would not be as good as the soup at home, but he did not have much of choice. Earlier that day, Captain Abernathy made a voice transmission throughout the *Stardust*, saying that they would be making an unexpected stop within the next few days to resupply. He ordered the cooks specifically to use as many protein packs and packaged food as possible.

"Should we be concerned about the stop we need to make?" Hague asked as he tossed the potato skins into the trash compactor shoot.

"I'd rather make an unexpected stop than be stuck out here in space."

"True enough."

****

After traveling half the distance to the planet Gestalt, their next stop, the tactical officer picked up something troubling on the scanners.

"Captain, I'm reading an anomaly ahead on the scanners."

Captain Abernethy and his science officer both checked their screens.

"It appears to be a beacon of some sort," Commander Wagoner, the science officer, said.

"Slow to impulse speed," Captain Abernethy ordered.

Once the ship drew close enough, the beacon turned on, and a humanoid male with white skin, no nose, and blue eyes, commonly known as a Tregon, appeared on the main view screen.

"Attention unidentified spacecraft, you are approaching an area of restricted space. You must go around or turn back. Any attempt to bypass this or any beacon surrounding our space will be considered an act of aggression. Trespassers will be boarded, their ship impounded, and the crew and passengers imprisoned."

"Not very friendly, are they?" The captain said to no one in particular. He looked straight at the screen. "This is Captain John Abernethy of the *Stardust*. We are a freighter en route to New Kansas to deliver…"

Before he could say another word, the beacon's message began to repeat itself.

"It would appear this is just a recording," Commander Wagoner commented dryly.

"So it seems." Captain Abernethy turned to his navigator. "Plot a course around the restricted area, Mr. Tavish."

"Going around will take us completely out of our way, Captain," Tavish said after determining the new course.

"How many days will it add to our trip?"

"At least a month," the navigator replied grimly.

Abernethy shook his head. "Thirty days? That will put a severe strain on our food and water. Are there any planets on the way where we can supplement our supplies?"

Commander studied a map of the planetary systems they would pass. "There is a class M planet marked off-limits because the indigenous people are barely past the Stone Age."

"Anything else?"

"I'm afraid not, captain," Wagoner replied.

"How long would it take us to get there?"

"Seven days at warp four."

"Then we have no choice. We can't eat the shipment of farm animals destined for the colonists. And we dare not put our crew to such temptation. Mr. Tavish, plot a course to that planet, warp four."

****

Seven days later, they arrived at their destination.

"Put us in orbit, Mr. Tavish," Captain Abernethy said. Turning in his chair to face the science officer, he continued. "Scan the planet for food and water resources. And commander, following Federation code, avoids contact with the natives."

85

The process was tedious because they had to be so careful not to allow the natives to see the shuttle. Intergalactic law was pretty harsh when it came to exposing pre-warp cultures to advanced technology. Doing so could cause the natives to think of them as gods, thereby creating a false religion. It could also change the natural development of the planet's technological evolution. Too many worlds had suffered dire consequences from gaining knowledge of advance technology before they were mentally capable of understanding it. The results had been disastrous, leading to the tough Terraforming and visitation laws now in place.

An hour later, the captain joined his science officer. "How's it look, Commander Wagoner?"

"Fortunately, the population is less than 100,000 people, and they are mostly grouped in the southern regions of the planet. I have located a continent further north that is rich in plant and animal life."

"This area," Wagoner continued by pointing to one spot in particular, "has a large freshwater lake and a high concentration of plant life. I believe the animal population is mostly herbivores, although we will need to keep watch for carnivores as well."

"Excellent. Send the teams down in groups of ten with enough containers to hold the amount of food and water we'll need to supplement our food stores. We will need enough to get us to our destination, where we can purchase more supplies. Equip the crew with hand scanners. We don't want them accidentally bringing anything poisonous or incompatible on board."

"Aye, sir."

The job took all day, but by the time they were finished, the cargo bay used for food storage was filled with fresh meat, vegetables, fruit, grain, and water. No one knew what they would taste like, but they had no choice but to eat it or starve.

The next task took even longer. The following morning, Karson, Hague, Boris, and several volunteer crew members tackled the job of processing the supplies and preserving them for storage. Aside from Boris, no one knew how to butcher meat. So the cook showed them how by making them watch and then participate in preparing the first animal. It was a gory job, and two crew members lost their breakfast while watching. They were put to work purifying the water and preparing the fruits and vegetables.

Hague's stomach was also a bit queasy. Still, with stubborn determination, he was able to help Boris and Karson and two crew members complete the task. The whole job took two days, and everyone was relieved once everything was processed and properly stored.

During their stay on the planet, Boris started showing signs of illness. Once they were back on course, cook soon allowed Karson and Hague to take over the meals again. Working only increased his aches and pains, and he refused to visit the onboard doctor.

Chapter 15

Curiosity

It had been forty-two days since the ship left the planet Nergal. Karson and Hague took over their positions as cooks for their section of the ship, at least temporarily as Boris had caught sickness before their unexpected landing. Karson had to determine the flavors of their new food stores and figure out how to cook and flavor them to taste best. It was strictly trial and error. At first, no one was happy with the meals, but they knew that once they reached their destination, the food would get better. But as the days passed, Karson learned that by mixing some of the new food with their regular supplies, he was able to come up with some reasonably good meals.

Since the processor was not programmed to handle the foreign foods, Hague had asked the science team if they could rig up a stove or two. It had taken them several hours, but by lunchtime, they had proudly delivered two stoves and six additional pots to cook with.

The two boys had continued to play cards with the crew members whenever they could. This comradery had worked to their favor as members of the bridge crew grew to like the cooks. After their shifts, they were permitted to visit the bridge. As long as an officer was there to watch them. Karson spent as much time as he could on the deck, particularly with Commander Wagoner. The crew didn't mind his visits. And when he showed so much interest in the operation of the ship, they willingly answered his questions and taught him a lot.

With his newfound freedom and friends, Karson fell in love with the bridge and all its workings. He was happiest whenever the navigator or one of the other officers let him work at their stations, under their careful guidance. Hague was learning from several of the mechanics on the ship as well. Both the boys were gaining plenty of knowledge that would never have been possible back on Nergal.

One evening while assisting the science officer, Hague made a discovery that amazed even the veteran officers. It was an ancient space probe. After bringing it onboard, he, Karson, and Commander Wagoner headed for Shuttle Bay 2 to check it out.

"I believe this probe was launched by an ancient race of people known as the Rierans."

"Is there any way to find out when it was launched?" Karson asked.

"I'm afraid I could only make an educated guess," Wagoner replied.

"Couldn't we somehow ask them?" Hague asked.

"I'm afraid not," the science officer replied. "The Rierans were in the early stages of space flight when this was launched. Sometime later, their sun went supernova. They had no way to leave their planet, which was destroyed. The only reason we know this much is because a science vessel was nearby to study the phenomenon. The ship had a crew of six and was too small to handle any kind of planetary evacuation. They met with the planet's leaders, and since the scientists could take only one extra person on board, the most knowledgeable historian on Rieran was chosen."

"I think I know why," Hague interjected.

"Yes, for the rest of his life, he made a record of the planet's history, so that his people would never be forgotten."

Karson reflected on the idea of being the only one of his kind. Would he want to have preserved the history of his planet alone? Alone.

When he went to bed that night, Karson thought about his adventures throughout their flight. Hague was asleep in his bunk, but he too was growing and changing as a spacer. *Good old Hague, not sure if I would have lasted this long without him.*

****

The next day, Karson ran into his former cellmate.

"Hey, Karson, I see things are looking up for ya."

"That they are, Dawson."

Dawson took his arm and led him into the corridor. No one else was nearby. "Given any more thought to what we talked about?"

Karson nodded. "I've got a hand in the kitchen now, so I could sneak away to find out more information."

"Here, take this." Dawson handed him a small recording device.

"What's this for?"

"It's a recording of the chief of security. Turn it on, and it will get you into any room."

****

That afternoon, after cleaning up the dirty luncheon dishes, Karson decided to tell Hague about his conversation with Dawson.

"Dawson gave me a device that can get me into any of the rooms."

"The cyborg?" Hague asked as he loaded the dishes into the dryer machine. "Think it'll work?"

90

"Only one way to find out," Karson smiled. "Can you cover me for an hour or so?"

Hague smiled, "Sure, only if you let me go treasure hunting next time."

****

Entering a part of the ship that was off-limits, he snuck down the corridors and approached the first door. He was about to play the recording when he heard someone coming. As the approaching footsteps grew closer, he dropped to the floor, slid around the corner, and hid, pressing his body as flat against the wall as possible.

A wave of fear passed over him. If anyone caught him, he might lose his bridge privileges and get thrown back in the brig. He had no plausible explanation for being in this part of the ship. He was so tense that when the crewman started to whistle, he jerked in surprise, and his left hand slid away from the wall. Just then, the man rounded the corner and missed stepping on his fingers by an eighth of an inch. Karson waited until he could no longer hear footsteps. Then rose to his feet, took a deep, shaky breath, and continued his exploration.

Heading for the nearest door, he took the recorder from his pocket, glanced both ways, and then turned it on.

"This is security chief Wiggins. Open this door."

The announcement seemed too loud, and Karson nervously glanced around once more. Seeing no one in the corridor or room, he slipped inside. Nothing. He was about to turn the corner when he spotted a man guarding the door of the next room. He grew excited. *This has to be the one.* He had to think of a way to make the guard leave his post. Karson wracked his brain. He needed to do something that would keep the man away

91

from the door long enough for him to get inside to look around and then sneak back out again.

As if the *Stardust* heard his prayers, something moved in the corner of his eye. He looked over to the hallway and saw a giant green and black rodent. It was the size of a small dog, and it was growling fiercely.

Where did that come from? Must have snuck onboard when we were planetside a few days ago. While it is big, it looks thin, must be hunting for food.

The guard also saw the giant creature and screamed. Since only the security team carried phasers unless otherwise told, he had no weapon. The terrified guard ran for the alarm stationed in the next hallway and deserted his post. He hit the alarm with a sound of sirens and lights and a computer issuing a warning.

"Foreign species detected in Sector 5. Repeat: foreign species detected in Sector 5."

As soon as he was far enough away, Karson ran to the door and used the recorder to get inside. Using a palm-sized flashlight, he looked around. Nothing. Sighing in disgust, he was about to slip out of the room when he heard Tuscon Scalemander shouting orders.

"Everyone, stay inside your rooms!" The first mate said. "The rest of us will hunt down the beastie. I don't want any more contamination on this vessel than need be."

Hearing the first mate's words, Karson panicked. Trapped with no way out. He couldn't sneak out the front door now. What was worse is that he knew that Hague couldn't cover him forever, and if he did not show up in time to start the evening meal, Paulie would send someone looking for him. Moreover, the search would grow more significant when they didn't find him. Eventually, they would check this room. With no explanation as to how or why he was there, he knew his punishment would be severe.

Chapter 16

Close Encounters

"Hold it steady spacers," Tuscon yelled, one arm raised as three members of security cornered the large green rodent.

"First Mate Scalemander," Commander Wagoner said as he walked up to the first mate.

"Ah Hector, how good to see you at this time," Tuscon spoke, his Venomae accent adding a slight level of sophistication.

"I came when I heard the alarm. We have closed off this section for now."

"Excellent commander," Scalemander responded, his eyes fixed on the beast.

"What do you think it is, Tucson?"

"Not sure. It looks like an Antilian Rous. But I have never seen one with spikes on the spine."

"How did it get in here?" Wagoner asked as he readied his phaser.

"Probably snuck on the ship when we were re-supplying on that early developed planet, Gestalt," the first mate said, eyes narrowing. He then clicked on his wrist communicator, "Captain Abernathy. This is Scalemander. We have a foreign species cornered. Capture or terminate?"

There was a faint static as Tucson waited for his next command.

****

Looking around frantically, Karson tried to find a spot where he could hide. He nearly jumped out of his skin when his wrist communicator beeped quietly. Moving into the bathroom, he leaned forward to speak.

"Yes?" He spoke as quietly as he could.

"Don't worry, Karson. It's Dawson."

"Dawson, why are you calling me?"

"I've been keeping an eye on you this afternoon since I learned you had a bit of free time on your hands. I figured you might go on the hunt again. I see you've gotten yourself in a bit of a mess."

"Are you spying on me?" Karson sounded incredulous.

"Being a cyborg has its perks kid," Dawson chuckled.

"Well, never mind. I'm glad you were. Can you help me get out of here?"

"Possibly, but it won't be easy. Commander Wagoner just showed up, and there are five other members of security there that First Mate Scalemander brought with him."

"Curse that creature, what was it anyway?" Karson asked out.

"Something snuck aboard when we landed, I'm trying to figure out a way to get you outta there."

"How about distracting the guard so I can slip out?"

"No can do," Dawson said, shaking his head, even though he knew Karson could not see him.

"Then what?"

Dawson pondered the problem for what seemed like forever.

****

On the other side of the door and in the main lobby, Tuscon Scalemander waited for his captain to reply.

"First Mate?"

"Yes, Captain."

"Stun doesn't kill. I want our science team to observe it and figure it out. Bring it to the science bay immediately."

"Roger, that."

"Commander Wagoner," Captain Abernathy called on the commander's wrist communicator.

"Here, sir."

"Do a sweep of the perimeter. Check every room close to the site where we first found the creature. Then report to the science bay."

"Will do, sir."

****

"Dawson, you still there?"

"Yes, and I think I have an idea, but it will be dangerous."

"Dangerous, how?" Karson asked.

"The only way I can think of to get you out of there without anyone knowing is by using the transporter located in the adjacent room."

"The transporter? Are you crazy? That technology is so new they only use it on inanimate objects."

"That's not completely true. They did try to transport a rat once," Dawson said thoughtfully.

"Really? What happened?"

"It made it through, but some of its parts were scrambled."

He fought against shouting at his former cellmate. "That's great. Just great! At least I won't have to explain where I was... Cause I'll be dead! If a rat didn't make it, what makes you think I will?"

"They've done a lot of work on it since that happened. Oh, and I almost forgot. Our transporter chief did some tinkering on his own. I hear he tried it on another rat before we took off, beaming it to another room, and then bringing it back."

"And?"

"It worked. The rat seemed to be just fine."

"I don't know. A rat's not a human. How do you know its brains weren't scrambled in the process?"

"No way to rightly know, I guess," Dawson admitted. "It's in a cage for more experiments, but it looks like it's acting normally. Look, what choice do you have? I'm in the transporter room right now. I can send you here once you open the side door on the west side of the room."

Karson stepped out of the bathroom and walked over to the door. "Found it. Where's the chief?"

"Gave him a bathroom break, so we don't have much time. It's now or never."

****

Tuscon held a plastic bag that contained the knocked out green rodent. "Good hunting, Hector," he said as he began to make his way to a turbolift.

A security member walked up to Wagoner, "Well sir, should we begin searching the rooms? The creature was only located on this floor and in this section. Other than the enclosed hallways, there are only a few rooms."

"Spread out. Be cautious and be ready to signal for back up." The commander replied as he began to make his way to the only room in the section that had a guard on it.

****

Karson was about to answer when he dropped his voice to a whisper. "Someone is talking outside the door. I think they're coming inside."

"Get ready; I'm getting you out of there now."

Fear ran through Karson's guts like liquid fire as he heard the door to the side room swish open. Taking a deep breath to calm down, he deliberately slowed his breathing until he felt better. He walked slowly to the next room, trying not to make too much sound. Once he cleared the door, he secured it again. In the corner of the room stood a giant cylinder. It seemed a simple design, but it was big enough for him to stand in and not feel too claustrophobic.

"Open it up, Dawson." He said on his communicator.

The door opened quietly and slowly. Karson stood inside and shut the glass door. This was dangerous, but he had no choice.

"Sending ya in 5...4...3...2..." he heard Dawson's voice say.

Suddenly, he felt a strange sensation run through his entire body. Then everything shifted, and he could no longer see anything. He was about to panic again when his vision returned, and he found himself in the transporter room.

Still a bit panicky, he nearly fell over.

"Get outta there before the transporter chief returns," Dawson told him. He reached out and helped the young man off the pad. "Can you speak?"

"Y-yes. I…think I'm okay."

"Then come on. Time to go."

Karson hurried out of the room and headed for the mess. Getting off the turbolift, he sighed with relief as it took him back to the galley.

****

Chapter 17

Old Enemies. New Friends.

Serena's nose was inches from the metallic deck, forced there by the pirate captain who ordered her to clean every single inch of the floor and walls. What was worse, he did not allow her to use the power scrubber, which you programmed and let it do all the work. He made her do it with a bucket and rag like they used to hundreds of years ago. Her smooth hands were now calloused, her nails broken and dirty, her knees now scraped and somewhat bloody from sliding up and down the deck. Life was miserable. She had lost everything she once assumed she would always have. She lost her ship, her crew, her android, and, most importantly, her parents.

Determined to remain healthy, Serena would not become a victim. She would find a way to regain control somehow, at least of her life, no matter the circumstances. After cleaning every nasty thing assigned to her on the ship, Grimlocke believed he had broken what he thought was a rebellious spirit. He informed the young lad that he would be his cabin steward. Serena accepted her new position without a word or change of expression.

She told him her name was Drake. He called her Drakey, slapped her on the back, and blew smoke in her face from his nasty cigar. Serena never flinched. She would overcome this brute, this murderer of her parents, and one day, she would control his destiny. She didn't know how yet, but she swore on the lives of her parents that she would have her revenge and destroy Captain Flint Grimlocke.

Being a cabin steward allowed Serena to overhear private conversations and become part of the rumor chain and the arrogant, boastful talk over dinner. The more the pirates drank, the less they were afraid to talk in front of the young cabin steward. She remained quiet and stealthily gathered information. The captain ignored her, except when he was ordering her around. And once she got the routine on the ship down pat, she knew where to be and when.

But at night, while the crew snored in their berths, she buried her head in the sheets and sobbed silently, her body racked with sorrow and loneliness, but not fear. Anger had replaced her fear.

The captain walked over to his desk and lifted a computer tablet that showed a map, the one he had stolen from another pirate, whom he had destroyed.

"We have one-third of the treasure map," declared Grimlocke. "On Nergal, our spies told us that the *Stardust* is carrying another third. We don't know where yet, but we will soon. The third piece is rumored to be somewhere on a lost planet in deep space."

"Where?" A pirate called out

"Of that, I have no idea."

"Legend is that it is hidden in plain sight."

"We'll be in port in two weeks, captain," one of his inner circle informed him.

"Then, eat and drink up mates." He raised a mug, slopping over with strong rum. "We are about to find the largest treasure chest in the world."

Drake, the cabin boy, sitting in the corner, quietly left the cabin. She had all the information she wanted. Being in the same room with a bunch of drunken pirates was not Serena's favorite place to be. She went up to the observation deck and found a comfortable seat near the window to lie down and stare at the stars and passing planets.

She wondered how many nights of peace remained before she experienced a battle first hand.

****

That night after the evening meal, Karson played cards with the crew as usual. It kept their spirits high throughout the day, even between games. Hague spent more time with the tech crew, continuing to learn about the technology of deep space travel.

Karson saw Dawson watching his games. When he was done for the night, Karson moved to an empty table. Hague noticed his partner's movement and followed in suit.

"What's up?" Hague asked as he sat down.

"Time I introduce you to Dawson." The young man signaled to the cyborg, indicating that he wanted to talk.

"The cyborg? Does he know that I know?"

"Nope," Karson replied. "Figured this would be a good time, to be honest."

Hague gulped, "I hope your right."

As soon as everyone's gaze was not on Karson, his former cellmate approached.

"Dawson, meet my best friend, Hague. Hague, meet my former cellmate, Dawson."

The two shook hands and smiled. Hague felt that the cyborg was friendly enough, but he still was not entirely convinced.

"I take it the Rhungo here is part of our...conspiracy?" Dawson said as he sat down.

"He is," Karson confirmed.

"You know about my people?" Hague asked in awe.

The cyborg chuckled, "I've done several tours around the galaxy lad." He winked his robotic eye.

"It wasn't there," Karson said. Sticking to the subject at hand.

"You were gone that long, and we got nothing for it?" Hague asked.

"Since there was a guard, you were in the right room," Dawson interjected.

"What if he was just guarding the transporter?" Karson asked.

"Well, the ship has security systems," Hague reasoned, "so a guard would be superfluous security honestly."

"Unless there was something important in there," Dawson smiled.

"I can try to look again tomorrow," Karson said.

"Might be dangerous," said Hague.

"It's there. I know it," Dawson replied.

"Then it is settled," Karson interjected. "Tomorrow, Hague will have to cover me at some point in the kitchen, and I can try again. Dawson, be ready in case I need to communicate to you again for the help."

"I can try, kid," Dawson said. "No promises, though."

Chapter 18

The *Pegasus*

Though he would not be able to check the next day. The area was still under surveillance due to the creature they discovered onboard the *Stardust*. The next few days were spent doing extra searches and scans to make sure that no other animals were hiding aboard. On the evening of the fourth day of the additional procedures, the conspiracy met again at dinner.

"I heard today that tomorrow the port side of the ship will be finished with the extra duties. Then our side, starboard, will be finished the day after," Dawson said as he ate.

"Finally," Hague moaned. "With the extra duties on top of pretty much feeding our entire section of the ship, I feel like I could fall over."

"Well, don't get too comfy," Karson said with a smile.

"Don't tell me..."

"The mystery?" Dawson asked hopefully.

Karson just smiled and nodded.

****

Two days later, Karson was back in the locked room, slipping in when the guard left to go to the bathroom. This time he wasn't looking for the leather box but something meaningful. He searched the area until he came upon a small chest of drawers. Finding it locked, he pulled out his computerized lock pick that he got from Dawson and got to work. Attaching the device to the locking mechanism, the red light turned on. It operated

104

quietly, with barely heard whirls and clicks. Then in no time at all, the red light went dark, and the green light flashed on. The drawers open. Among the papers inside, he found the box he'd been looking for. He had to use the lock pick once more to see what was inside. When he opened the lid, he found a set of plans.

Opening them, he studied the design. It looked like a new type of battlecruiser called the *Pegasus*. I would be the first spaceship that could fly through space and move through the ocean like a submarine. Reading the information written on the plans, he realized that the *Pegasus* was unlike any other ship he had ever heard of or seen. Its top speed was warp ten. All ships currently in use could only reach warp eight, and that put a strain on the engineers if used for too long a period.

Karson was amazed. He realized that a ship like this would help the Galactic Federation not only defend core planets and their colonies. It could be a start in ridding the galaxy of space pirates.

The ship was more extensive than any battlecruiser in service in any planetary system. Its massive size was capable of carrying a hundred spitfires, housing twenty-five ships in each of four shuttle bays. The total crew complement was 1,000 military personnel, each highly trained and battle-ready. Because of the large size of the ship, the exterior was covered with several laser turrets and photon torpedo launchers.

Although not gold, silver, or jewels, the plans for this vessel were indeed a treasure. Karson returned them to the box and placed it back into the chest of drawers. He was about to leave when he heard footsteps approached the door. He quickly hid behind some stacked crates. No sooner had he dropped to a crouch, when three members of the crew came through the door and walked to the center of the room, straight toward Karson, who tried to make himself even smaller.

"You are too suspicious, Scalemander."

Commander Wagoner!

"Hector, this is your problem, you don't worry enough."

First Mate Scalemander!

"Gentlemen, please! I invited you two here to resolve this issue, not instigate it."

Captain Abernathy!

"Now look, Tucson, I understand your fear since we encountered that creature. However, scanners have been dormant for days, the crews have successfully checked and rechecked the rooms and stations, and we have found nothing. No signs of other contamination, nothing about invasions. Hector here has even told me our science team has studied the beast, and it is just another subspecies of Rous. I think it is time we put this to rest," the Captain tried to reason with his first mate.

"You're right," Tucson Salamander said. "I think so too."

They were about to leave out of the room when Wagoner stopped.

"Someone has been in this room," he said in a quiet voice.

The three men slowly drew their phasers and spread out. The Captain made his way closer to the boxes. The first mate slowly moved towards the transporter section. Hector Wagoner then made his move towards a small device near the door.

Karson's heart was beating louder than a space cannon. While the men were not moving towards him directly, if anyone found him, it was over.

"Log says only those with clearance accessed the room," Commander Wagoner said.

"Just to be safe," Captain Abernathy replied as he retrieved the box with the plans for the *Pegasus* inside. "I'll have to keep them both in my quarters."

"Do you think anyone is actually after the plans?" Tucson asked as he returned to his companions.

"I doubt it," Abernathy replied. "But, someone might be getting hungry for the treasure map."

The three men nodded.

"We will speak of this later," Captain Abernathy said as he led the men out of the room.

When the men finally left, Karson waited until he could no longer hear their footsteps. Knowing the guard would soon return, Karson slipped from the room and hurried down the corridor to the turbolift. When he entered the galley, Hague approached him.

"Any luck?"

"No. I didn't even get a chance to look, the captain and two of his men came in. I had to hide. They took the box, though, so there was something important, I guess."

"Well, at least we found out something," Hague reasoned. "But we better get started, Paulie came by, and it seems he is getting suspicious of ya."

Karson smiled as he put on an apron and begin to help Hague with the evening meal.

He wanted to tell Hague about the plans and the map onboard, but not knowing who to trust with both, he decided to wait. *Hague would go to the ends of the galaxy to help me. But I don't know how much I can genuinely trust Dawson. I'll tell him what I just informed Hague about. However, I'll keep this information to myself until I can trust them both completely.*

****

Chapter 19

New Plans

A few days later, while Karson fixed breakfast, he overheard two men talking. The ship would be arriving at the New Kansas Colony within two days. When he completed his morning duties, he left the galley in search of Dawson. He finally found him in one of the maintenance tubes, replacing a burned-out panel.

"Got a minute?" Karson asked.

"A couple, as long as I can keep working. What's going on?"

"What's the procedure once we get to New Kansas?" Karson asked.

Dawson shook his head. "That I don't know. It depends on the mission. I've been to several different Terraformed planets. Why?"

"I was just curious. I have never been to a space colony before."

Dawson scratched his chin, "Well, I know we have those supplies and livestock to deliver. We might have some planetside leave, though how long I am not sure. Even the shortest of trips that I have experienced usually give about an hour for the crew to go planetside."

"I've also been meaning to ask Dawson, but why are we delivering so much livestock anyway? The crates I understand but animals?"

"Life in the colony is hard. They don't have all the latest and greatest technology, just enough to get them by. The same goes for animals. Some planets might have the right environment to house life, but not the right creatures needed to support it."

"I see, I think we are also dropping off some tech?"

"Wouldn't doubt it. Farming and engineering equipment. The bare basic that the illustrious Galactic Federation can give." Dawson said with bitterness edged in his voice.

"So, these supplies are of the utmost importance?"

"Aye lad. What're you planning?" The cyborg asked suspiciously.

"Not sure yet, Dawson. Not sure."

****

Karson walked back to his corridors, mentally calculating his plan. Despite his popularity on board, he was still a cabin boy, and he was not making enough of the impression needed for promotion clearly. Hague was starting to be moved to tech work now that Borris was beginning to be on the mend. Although Karson was friendly with the crew and Commander Wagoner, he still was being confined to the kitchen. *Maybe I can make a better impression of helping with this delivery*, he thought to himself. Paying little attention to where he was going, he took a turbolift to another level. He walked the corridor that ran past the officers' quarters. As he passed, he overheard the captain speaking to the first mate.

"Once we arrive at New Kansas, I have a special assignment I want you to lead," Captain Abernathey said.

"What's that?" The first mate asked as the door swished closed.

Karson wanted to stay and listen through the door, but he couldn't risk being caught snooping. He had already pushed his luck when he found the *Pegasus*, and now he needed to put it in a different direction. He headed for the galley, still thinking about a solution to his problem. He continued to ponder as he prepared lunch.

"What is on your mind, Pleiades?" Hague asked as he prepared a protein hybrid meal. Since they would soon be in port, they had been ordered to use up any perishable foods and any close to date processed meal kits. It wasn't a fantastic meal, but it would suffice.

"I need to make a better impression on the captain. Or any of the lieutenants. I'll never get to be a pilot or learn anything at this rate."

"Yeah, and with Boris back, well...ya know." Hague was referring to his continual movement to helping with the tech crews.

"Exactly. I'm not mad at you at all, Hague. But I don't want to be stuck being a cabin boy forever. There's gotta be something."

"Let's ask Dawson after we get the meal served up," Hague suggested. "He might know something.

"I already asked him, but we can try again."

****

Once they had served the crew, the boys grabbed their lunch and scanned the room for Dawson, finally spotting him at a table in the corner sitting alone.

Hague hurried over and sat across from their new conspirator. "What do you think will happen tomorrow when we make port?"

"Where do we find these new cabin boys?" Dawson said, chuckling. "Once we arrive, if they have a good landing area, we'll land planetside like we did on Nergal. If they don't, the Captain will put the ship in orbit and use the shuttles to deliver the cargo."

"Do you know if there is a decent place for landing?" Hague asked.

It was evident by Dawson's expression that he was thinking hard. "Yes, I believe there is. Based on what I was overhearing earlier. Why?" Dawson asked carefully.

"Karson wants to try to impress our superiors," Hague said. "Thinks this delivery will help him earn some fly points."

"So anything you happen to know might help me a bit," Karson asked hopefully. "We have all these supplies, I'm sure I can prove myself if I work hard with moving it. After all, Hague and I were dock boys before this."

"The livestock will be taken off by the crew, but I hear they may use that new transporter to send the crates and the tech right to the warehouse."

"The transporter? Well, there goes a bit of our thunder," Karson said.

"Do you know for sure if the transporters will be used?" Hague asked.

Dawson shook his head.

"Well, tomorrow, if you can cover me this time, Karson, I can head over to the transport chief and see if he knows anything," said Hague.

"Good idea!" Karson exclaimed. "I'll talk to Paulie then and see if we can get scheduled to help with the unloading."

****

Hague made his way to the transporter room the following morning. Maybe the transporter chief could shed some light and offer some unexpected help. The chief would soon be very busy with preparations until they reached New Kansas. Hague figured this was the best time to ask him some questions. When the door swished open, the chief expected to see the Captain or the first mate with final instructions. Looking over, he was surprised to see Hague instead.

"Hey, Hague, what brings you to my humble corner of the ship?"

"Hi, Chief Eggleton, I know you're going to get really busy in a couple hours. But, when I heard you'd be using the transporter to send the cargo to the settlers' warehouse, my curiosity got the better of me. Would you mind telling me how it works?"

The chief grinned. "Ah yes, I've heard about the night shift crew on the bridge showing you the technological ropes, so to speak. Sure thing. I'd be happy to explain it. I'd let you stay and watch, but it's going to get pretty crowded in here, and I don't think the Captain would want you in the way. But I promise. When things settle down, and we're on our way again, I'll be happy to show you what a transport looks like."

"Thanks, Chief, I really appreciate it."

Hague lost some of his fear as the chief explained how it worked. "Will the animals be transported, too?" He asked, feigning ignorance.

"Not this time. Although I believe we could, the Captain doesn't want to take any chances with the animals. They're too important to this colony to risk losing a single one. I've been spending all my spare time working on the problem and have successfully transported a rat several times. The little bugger seems just fine, but there's just no way to know if the process damaged any of its cells, brain or otherwise. We won't know that for certain until we actually transport a sentient being."

"Do you really think you could transport live cargo without hurting them?"

"That I do."

****

"They won't be using the transport for the livestock," Hague reported when he returned to the galley.

"Just the crates? That makes things a bit tricky, but it could work."

"What's your plan, then?"

"Well, I have already spoken to Paulie, to which he bit my head off."

"He doesn't want us to be there?"

"No," Karson laughed, "because he was apparently supposed to tell us that, but I beat him to it."

They both laughed as they continued to cook.

****

Chapter 20

New Kansas

When the planet's sun finally rose, the boys made their way to the room where they had tended the animals for the past two months. They watched as the crew put the chickens into crates and calmed the cattle and prepared to lead them off the ship. Gathering their courage, Karson and Hague prepared to each grab one of the boxes of chickens when the first mate saw them.

"Cabin boy C'avt, apologies, but you have been relocated to the transport room. You will stay here cabin boy Pleiades, but you'll be assisting my team with the cattle."

"Yes, sir." They both responded.

Hague returned to the transport bay while Karson stood beside the first mate.

"We will be herding the cattle a few miles away to their location," Tuscon Scalemander said as he leads Karson down to where the cattle would be unloaded. "The Galactic Federation also has men stationed to help us herd them into a giant pen. You will be asked to operate a small hovercraft to assist with keeping the cattle in line. Have you ever driven a Ferret before?"

"I have not, but I have experience with anti-grav lifts and small shuttles back on the docks on Nergal."

"Ah good, you had mentioned that. Precisely why I chose you for this mission." The first mate explained.

Karson could not help but smile with pride. *This is it! If the first mate was thinking of me for this mission, then I have no choice but to prove myself. This mission has to succeed, and I will make it happen.*

****

"Transporter room," Hague ordered the computer as soon as the doors closed.

When he arrived, the corridors proved to be as dangerous as the level where the animals were stored. Hague tried to squeeze past the loaded anti-grav lifts, but he kept getting in the way, making some of the workers angry. One crewman even yelled at him.

"C'avt! You're supposed to be at station 3!"

The only thing to do was to go with the flow, and before he knew it, he was at the proper station. He began to load the crates into the cylinder and transport them one at a time. Each time the process was simple: load the object, close the doors, check the coordinates, send, and wait for the light to glow green before doing it again.

Hague kept up with the monotony until he found an empty container. He knew it was abandoned because the lid was slightly askew. The covers of the containers holding cargo were firmly in place. He brought it to a supervisor, the same one who yelled at him earlier.

Gnash Nuvar was in charge of the shipping and holding on the *Stardust*. He was a Mineralmite, a species of sentient stones and rocks hailing from various sulfurous planets in the galaxy. Gnash was gray-colored and looked like he had a perpetual scowl on his face.

"C'avt! What in the name of the Twelve Core Planets are ya doing with an empty crate?"

"Found it among the deliveries, sir," Hague said, holding the box.

116

"Well then beam it up to sector 7! I think it's 7-G for empty boxes."

"Thanks, sir," Hague said. "It would be helpful if someone taught me instead of the basic instructions on the screens," he muttered under his breath.

****

Karson mingled with the workers while they waited for further directions. There were members of the *Stardust* and several members of the Galactic Federation that were a part of the Terraforming project. The Federation soldiers were using wheeled vehicles in their aid with the herding.

"You'd think the Feds would have better equipment than us," a spacer commented.

"Well, that's part of the Terraforming project," Cecelia the female Krillean said. "Shape the planet to make it habitable for life, then give people the bare minimum to get started."

Karson was about to ask what she meant as he remembered Dawson saying a similar comment when the first mate showed up. He was riding a hovercraft larger than Karson's Ferret, aptly named Boar, shouting, "Let's go!" As he thrust his fist into the air, Karson heard the various cries and shouts of spacers, Feds, and cattle as they began to herd the cows out of the *Stardust*. Karson jumped on his Ferret and began to join the drive. His orders where simple; keep the cattle in line, don't let them stray too far, don't be too far away either. He was giving a stun phaser in case of difficult cattle. However, he was ordered to not shoot anyone, even if attacked.

Karson rode along the drive. Due to the technology of the Feds stationed on New Kansas, the trip went slower than initially planned. While the hovercraft could quickly

117

overtake the cattle, and they would not want to go that fast, they could have been traveling a little quicker than the land-locked vehicles. He was happy and sad when they reached their destination. He parked his craft on the edge of the road and made sure that no animals got anywhere near him. Only one or two beasts attempted to, but him firing his phaser into the ground caused enough fright to put them back in line.

After the cattle were secured, they waited while the first mate and the leading official discussed payment and other legalities. Once those were guaranteed, the company returned to the *Stardust*.

****

The final crate was placed into the transporter when Hague smiled. That was the last one in his section. He glanced around as he wiped his forehead, everyone else seemed to be done with their cargo or very close to it. He headed back to the supervisor when Boris walked in.

"If you are finished here, I need help in the kitchen. Karson is not back yet, and I could use all the help I can get."

Hague nodded as he followed his recovering crewmember. *How strange, back on Nergal, we usually would've stuck to one job and would never have asked anyone else for help. Only in the direst of circumstances did we ask for help. But here, we all seem to work together, even if Boris is a bit rough.*

He was in the middle of loading up the dry dishes when Karson came in.

"How'd it go?" Hague asked.

"Not too bad, but I didn't do anything special."

"As long as you did your job, I'm sure you did fine."

Karson just was not sure.

Chapter 21

Late Night Secrets

It was late at night when Karson and Hague made it to their bunk. Both had not been this tired since their first day on the *Stardust*. After both had washed and gotten into bed, Karson decided to come clean.

"I need to tell you something," Karson said.

"Can't it wait till tomorrow morning?" Hague whined. "I'm so tired my suction cups hurt."

"No, it's about what happened in the locked room."

"I thought you said you just saw a box? Did you actually see something?" Hague sat up, a mix of wonder and slight anger in his bulbous eyes.

"Yeah, I saw something," Karson admitted.

"Why didn't you tell me?"

"I'm telling you now, C'avt. After I got out of the room, I got scared. I was so close to getting nabbed that I didn't want to talk about it in case anyone was listening. But now, that we are here on New Kansas, we can talk about it."

"What's to talk about?" Hague asked, "that depends on what you found."

"Plans for a ship. A big ship."

Karson went on to explain the details of the *Pegasus*. When he finished, he looked at Hague. "That is the mystery on the ship. Those plans."

"Have you told Dawson yet?" Hague asked.

"No, I wanted to tell you first."

"Well, I guess there's not much of a conspiracy then," Hague said dejectedly.

"Well, there might be," Karson offered.

Hague blinked questioningly at his friend.

"Dawson is a cyborg, right? He also claims to have been on several deep-space voyages. He also has some bitter remarks about the Galactic Federation."

"Who doesn't, Pleiades?" Hague laughed. "I don't understand what you are getting at."

"Those plans seem like a big deal! They could change the fate of the galaxy. Imagine if someone who didn't like the Federation found it?"

"He could sell it to anyone," Hague answered, realization in his eyes.

"Or even make it. That's why I didn't want to tell you both. I'm not sure I can trust Dawson."

"He seems harmless enough," Hague replied.

"But we don't know. Also, we have no idea if he won't spout off to anyone else out there."

"Well, regardless, we should be safe if you do feel like Dawson would do something. We can't figure out anything else now."

"You are right," Karson said.

"You still should have told me. I could have helped you with this burden," Hague said long after they had settled down for the night.

"I'm sorry old friend," Karson said. "I'll remember for next time."

"See that you do."

Chapter 22

The Pleiades Motto

They spent the next few days on New Kansas. Taking a break to resupply themselves before venturing to their next mission. They were heading to Cortsea, an outer core planet, for another delivery. According to Dawson, they would be heading off to look for the treasure of Captain Nova Scarm. During their time on New Kansas, Karson sends a message to his mother. He told her that the first part of the voyage was over, and he was embarking on the second part. He still did not tell her about the rumor of treasure or even of the plans for the *Pegasus*. On the morning of the departure from New Kansas, Hague asked a question.

"Do you think after this we really are going to look for that treasure?"

"I'm not sure I am more curious about what we are delivering in Cortsea," Karson responded as he got comfy on his bunk for the take-off.

"It does seem strange for us to go to this backstar planet only to try to go the outer core. It seems a bit backward."

"Well, we will find out one way or another, right?" Karson asked his old friend.

****

"Set a course for two, six, nine, mark two," Captain Abernethy told the woman at the helm. "Warp factor three."

Looking out the viewport in their room, Karson watched the blur of the stars as the engines kicked in, and then settled into place once they achieved warp three. He felt strange helplessness. His feelings were a mixture of wonder and sorrow. While he was excited about the next step in their adventure, he also was worried that it would be the last step after all.

****

The next evening, Karson was about to set out the food for the evening meal as Hague prepared the drinks when Boris approached him.

"The Captain has requested you to dine with him tonight, Karson."

"What an honor, Karson!" Hague said with joy.

Karson's stomach filled with electric nerves. He felt like he was about to dine with a king. This was it! The chance he was waiting for! He could eat and impress the captain, and soon he would be out of this galley. And when he realized that he didn't have the proper clothes or how to dine with ship captains, he grew queasy.

"What am I supposed to do?"

"Eat with him stupid," the old cook said. "Go get cleaned up and find Bill Shanks, and I'll see what I can do to help."

"Whose Bill Shanks?"

"He is the captain's steward. He is sick tonight, so he should be in his room."

"Well, how does that help Karson?" Hague asked the old cook.

"He can tell him how to act all civil and what not. The rank of captain is a high honor, and he does tend to find himself, a...classic man."

"Well, I'm sure you'll be fine, Karson," Hague said, trying to calm his friend.

Karson was in a daze. He then became nervous, he had not done anything fantastic on New Kansas, but what if he had done something terrible? He had better find this Bill Shanks and learn how to be a civilized man quick!

By now, Karson was in a total panic. He ran out of the room before realizing he had no idea where the Captain's steward, Bill Shanks, quarters were. Then he remembered the computer panels in the corridors.

Approaching the nearest one, he faced the panel. "Where are Bill Shanks' quarters?"

"Please follow the lit panels to your destination." As before, a line of panels lit up, showing the way.

"Thank you, computer."

"You are welcome, Karson."

When he reached Bill's rooms, he pressed the equivalent of a doorbell. It took several tries before the steward shouted, "Come in!"

The door swished open, and Karson bolted inside and headed for the bedroom. Fortunately, as Abernethy's steward, Bill had his own private quarters.

"You have to help me be a civilized man. Worthy enough to dine with a captain."

"That's why you are bothering me? Etiquette lessons? I'm sick. Go away."

"Please, Bill, I don't want to mess it up," Karson begged. "I'm just a dock boy from Tecmula. I don't know anything about captains or ships or politics."

Bill shook his head no. "Listen, kid, even if I wanted to, and believe me, I don't, I wouldn't have enough time. Etiquette takes years of training to accomplish. Though I do suggest getting some better clothes. That might help a lot. Oh, and don't mix up your spoons."

"Spoons? Plural? As in more than one? Like for soup or…"

But the door was shut, and Bill Shanks was inside his room, leaving Karson all alone.

****

After Karson washed up, he headed back to the galley. He was dressed in a simple but clean uniform. It was all he had. As he entered, he heard Boris call out.

"Wait. You can't go dressed like that."

"These are the only clothes I have," Karson said.

"We brought nothing but the clothes on our backs and some old uniforms," Hague added.

"Not true. I picked up some stuff for you both at the New Kansas colony." The cook took both of the cabin boys to the supply room and handed each of them a bag. "Think of it as a personal thank you from me to you boys for covering the kitchen when I was sick."

Karson took the bag. Hague had a puzzled expression on his face.

"Go ahead. Open it up." Boris smiled for the first time.

They did so. Inside, they found two sets of clothing.

"The first one is for everyday attire. The second is for more formal occasions."

"Like when I eat with the Captain?" Karson winked.

"The timing was pure coincidence," Boris said. "I have no idea which the Captain wants to eat with."

"No, Boris," Hague interrupted, "it's luck."

Karson smiled, "Born under a lucky star."

Karson quickly changed into the outfit. It was a sharp-looking suit fitting any young spacer, especially one with desires to enter the academy or be a pilot. He asked the computer for directions to the Captain's quarters. When he arrived, he knocked.

"Enter," the first mate called out. Karson entered the room, realizing that it was nothing like the rest of the ship. His earlier glimpses through the open doorway hadn't allowed him to really see the interior. The room was clean, orderly, and fit for a king.

The room had two large windows. Looking through them, he saw the most beautiful view he'd ever seen: a blue, red, and brown colored nebula. Once more, he made up his mind that someday he would become the captain of his own ship.

The first mate cleared his throat, bringing Karson back to the present. He moved to a round mahogany table and sat at the only open position. He breathed heavily as he almost slipped out of the chair. The material was a lot sleeker than what he was used to. He braced himself on the chair and gracefully re-took his seat. He smiled but was bright red with embarrassment. The navigation officer, Reg Tavish, smiled at Karson and tried to calm the boy.

"First time eating with a captain?" Tavish asked.

"Yes, sir," Karson replied as nervously brushed his shirt, trying to avoid wrinkling it.

"Well, don't worry, everyone here is pretty friendly. I've seen you talk with Commander Wagoner from time to time, right?"

"Yes sir, just the other day the commander was teaching me about…" But Karson never got to finish that sentence because there came another from the other side of the table.

"All rise for Captain Jon Abernathey," First Mate Tucson Scalemander said.

Everyone stood up as the Captain entered his quarters. Karson gulped audibly and tried to quiet the sound of his heartbeat.

****

Back on Nergal, Gloria read the message her son had sent her. It was a quick message due to the distance between the planets. Karson had paid for a quick and short message instead of a longer message that would take longer to send. Messaging between worlds was pretty standard in this day and age. Still, between underdeveloped planets to outer core planets, messages tended to be on the slower side. Not only was speed a factor, but cost. The longer the message, the more it was out of pocket.

Gloria stood up and looked out the door. She was doing well, Jasper and Nuba had frequently been visiting, which helped her loneliness. But she still missed her son. She was not thrilled with the fact that there was another portion of the voyage, but there was nothing she could do about it.

Her wrist communicator began to go off.

"Hello?"

"Gloria! It's Jasper, how are you today?"

"Oh, hey there, Jasper. I am doing well. The landlord finally got someone over here to fix the stove. Now three burners work. Oh, and Karson send me a message! Not too detailed, but they made it to New Kansas on time."

"Oh good," Jasper called back through the communicator. "I hadn't heard anything bad from the station, so I was hoping he was fine."

"The *Atlas* can find information about ships?" Gloria asked.

"Not exact information, but I can always access ship logs to see if they make it to their destinations on time or stuff like that."

"Well, that is comforting," Gloria said.

"Did the message say where he is heading to?"

"Cortsea. Not very happy with that location."

"Awh Gloria," Jasper assured her. "Cortsea is a rough planet, but the *Stardust* can take care of herself. It's an Outer Core planet too like Nergal."

"Nergal is several parsecs closer to the Core than Cortsea is," Gloria said.

"I'll keep an extra eye out then if you'd like?"

"Thank you, Jasper, I appreciate it."

Gloria walked back to her chair and sat. She was worried about her son, but deep down, her mother's intuition told her that he was all right.

Chapter 23

Diner with the Captain

The Captain entered the chambers as everyone stood at attention. This was more of a formality than based on Abernathey's personal tastes. Karson panicked and attempted to do a salute, which failed somewhat humorously. The officers smiled and exchanged glances. Their reaction puzzled Karson. He knew that everyone was watching him, and any mistake he made could cost him, but Captain Abernathy smiled and took his seat.

The captain sat at the front of the round table with Scalemander and Wagoner on either side. Karson was sitting between Lieutenant Tavish, the helmsman, and Lieutenant Shawnee, his guide when they first appeared on the *Stardust*. Lieutenant Tavish, the navigation officer, and the transportation chief Eggleton was also there. Several of the members Karson had met before during his excursions on the bridge. He also took into account that other than the captain, first mate, and Tavish, the rest of the officers were human. Tavish was a species known as a Felidae, a cat-like species hailing from the Central Core planet of Marble. Captain Abernathey was regal as ever. Karson had never officially met the captain, he had only seen him on-screen updates, and when he was hiding in the secured room. The white feathers on his head seemed to strike out against even the cleanliness of the room.

Since the steward was sick, everyone served the meal themselves. Karson served himself some soup and some bread. While the lieutenants took some of the salad as well and some of the other fancier food that Boris or Hague must have cooked up tonight.

As the meal progressed, Karson sat and listened. At the same time, the Captain explained reports, figured, and statistics over this second portion of the voyage. His lieutenants offered their opinions and explanations as they discussed the matters at hand.

Karson thoroughly enjoyed the conversation. After the main course, Hague walked up to form the galley with dessert in a large anti-grav tray.

"Oh good, the desert is here, let us adjourn from the business for the rest of the evening," the captain ordered. The members of the crew got up from their seats, placed their dishes on the other end of the tray, and took some desert from the other end.

"How's it going?" Hague asked.

"Pretty good, the officers have been nice. Mostly just boring minutes about the ship. I'm honestly not sure why he summoned me here."

"I knew you'd do okay. Just keep it up."

Loading the tray with their dishes, the crew sat back at the table as they at the desert. As they finished, Hague made a final sweep of the table, clearing the last dishes. He winked at Karson as he left. For the next hour, the lieutenants and the captain talked pleasantries. They spoke about trivial details, but it seemed to change the dynamic in the room. While they were a team and operating under direct orders from the Galactic Federation, they were also friends. They spoke of their home planets, families, galactic sports, and other nonwork-related topics. Karson could have sworn he was at a dinner party instead of the severe work meeting he had just sat through.

"Well," the first mate said to Karson. "I suppose you are wondering why you were asked to join us this evening?"

"The thought did cross my mind, sir," Karson replied.

This time, the Captain spoke. "Tuscon here has told me about the tremendous help you and your friend have been accomplishing in the kitchens. Hector here also tells me about your studying during the off-time with him and other members on the bridge. These pieces of news are pleasing to me. "

"Thank you, sir," Karson.

"You signed on with us on Nergal, correct?"

"Yes, sir."

"Are you from Nergal originally?"

"No, sir, my family is from Teculma. My late father had a job opportunity on a Central Core planet, and well, during our move, he died. My mother and I found our way to Nergal where we have been ever since.

"I am truly sorry to hear about your loss. What is your father's name? I have many connections on the Central Core."

"Wallace Pleiades."

"Wallace Pleiades? I knew of your father," Abernathy said. "I believe I worked with the captain who was going to hire him. It has been many years, but you don't forget a name like that."

Karson smiled, "Pleiades? Yes, it is hard to forget. Our family motto claims that we were born under a lucky star. So far, my adventures on this ship have proven that correct.

"I would agree with that," Abernathey smiled.

"What would you like to do after we complete this voyage?" Commander Wagoner asked.

"Well, I have thought about signing on to the Galactic Academy. Part of the reason I signed on for this trip was the sign-up bonus. I am not sure I will make it for the next term, but saving never hurts."

"Wise words," Tuscon Scalemander spoke. "Would you train to be a pilot?"

"That would be the plan, sir," Karson replied. "Eventually, I would like to be a captain. After I earned my wings, of course."

The first mate laughed in agreement.

"What about Hague?" Chief Eggleton asked, "Does he have plans for the academy too?"

Karson was not sure. Hague had never spoken about it before. Though he knew if he was going to get Hague out of being a cabin boy too, he would have to vouch for his friend.

"I know he enjoys the technological and mechanical aspects of the ship," Karson answered cooly.

"He has been a good help to me, too," Wagoner interjected. "He was the one who discovered that probe before we landed on New Kansas."

Captain Abernathy nodded, a clawed hand on his beak, an indication that he was thinking.

The company talked late into the night, Karson feeling more at home with every passing moment. It was 2200 when everyone was dismissed for the night. Typically meetings did not last this long, but it was sort of a celebration. The mission to deliver the supplies to New Kansas had gone well. The only thing left was to head to Cortsea. Though for what purpose, Karson did not know.

Captain Abernathy called Karson back once everyone else had left for the night, "Do you like being in space?"

"Very much," Karson replied. "I have always loved to watch the ships at the spaceport. I've dreamed of being in space for as long as I can remember."

"Well, I have heard nothing but good reports of you from Paulie and my lieutenants here. Especially First Mate Scalemander, he was very impressed by your actions on New Kansas."

"Really?" Karson was in shock. "I didn't think I did anything worth noticing, sir."

John Abernathy smiled, "You did what you were ordered, and executed it perfectly. Many young cadets your age fail to do that. Tucson is a bit of an old soul and was very surprised by how you followed orders. The Galactic Academy could definitely use recruits like you. Though at the moment, I could use someone like you."

Karson tried to hide his face, turning flush. He had hoped that tonight would be a good night. But he didn't expect such honors from the Captain.

"Why don't you and Hague meet me on the bridge tomorrow? I'd like to meet your friend, and I have a feeling I can be of some help."

****

Chapter 24

The Truth Uncovered

Karson barely got through the door of his room when Hague attacked him with questions.

"I thought you'd never come home! What happened? Is everything alright?"

"Better than ever!" Karson beamed as he changed into his night attire. "As a matter of fact, we are to meet with Captain Abernathy tomorrow. I think we are no longer cabin boys, my friend."

"Great, Griplar! You are kidding me." Hague had a plastered look of shock on his face. "Well, what will happen to Boris?"

"He was the cook on the *Stardust* before us, he can take care of it now. We have gone through too much to back down now."

Hague climbed up to his bed, "I agree but still can't help worrying. Do you think the Captain will also enlighten us about Dawson's mystery?"

"I honestly hadn't thought of that," Karson admitted. "Maybe he will let us in on the secret?"

"If it is a treasure, it seems very interesting."

"And if not, at least I could have a good chance of joining up with the Galactic Federation."

Hague laughed, "You keep that dream, Pleiades. I would be fine working on ships or transporters planet-bound."

****

The next morning Karson and Hague stood next to Captain Abernathy's chair. They were dressed in the clothes they had gotten from Boris to make a good impression. Hague found it strange that they were on the brig early in the morning instead of in the galley. Though he was not about to complain. With Boris back from sick leave, the kitchen could function adequately without the two of them. Hague preferred to move cargo at this point instead of figuring out the menu each day for their side of the ship.

They were still waiting when First Mate Scalemander approached them.

"Pleiades, report back to the Captain's quarters. Captain Abernathy had an unexpected meeting and told me to send you there. As for you, C'avt, Commander Wagoner is in the cargo hold and requests you meet him there."

Both boys confirmed their directions and reported to their stations.

Karson stood outside of Captain Abernathy's quarters. He could hear movement inside and hushed voices, indicating that he was still in a meeting. This lasted another fifteen minutes until Chief Wiggins of security walked out of the door. He did not notice Karson, but seeing his opportunity, Karson entered the quarters.

"Reporting for duty, sir," Karson smiled.

"Oh good, you got my message. Sorry about that, Karson, but Chief Wiggins and I needed to meet this morning."

"Everything ok, sir?"

"For now, yes. But we will be entering rogue space in a few days, so just going over security protocol."

"Rogue space?" Karson had never heard that term before.

"I can see our lessons can begin now," Abernathy smiled as he retrieved a remote from his desk. "Have a seat, Karson. While this isn't traditional training, the better prepared you are now, the better your time in the Academy will be."

Karson took a seat as the lights dimmed. He then saw a large light blue map appear on the wall in front of him. It was a map of territories that were under the jurisdiction of the Galactic Federation. The far left of the map indicated the galaxy's primary sun. Many planets such as Nergal could have their own or multiple suns. The primary sun was pretty central to their universe, and several of the core planets revolved around that time.

"As you can see here," Abernathy broke his train of thought with a red dot as is climbed over the map. It circled twelve planets in the middle of the map. "These are the Capitol Planets, with Cesaroma being among them." The dot moved and created a more full circle around several planets beyond the core. "This is referred to as the interplanetary sector. Essentially any planet located in the Inner Core and Central Core before you get to the Outer Core." The dot moved away from its current position and began to form a single line tracing a line of planets at the edges of the map.

"I'm sure you are aware of this, but these are the Outer Core Planets. Nergal is here and over in this direction," the dot moved as the Captain spoke, "is Teculma. Though further away from there is where New Kansas will be put on our Galactic Federation maps with the next update. I will say that while updates can be a nuisance, I can't imagine ancient sailors who relied on old copies of maps."

"Where is Cortsea?" Karson asked.

"Ah, right here," he moved the laser to a planet that appeared to be in between Teculma and Nergal. Though Karson imagined the distance between the planets was farther than the map would let on.

"All of this is to put a frame of reference for you," Abernathy continued. "Now, this area that I am circling around the outer core? This essentially is rogue space. While it is charted, Federation control is weak in these areas. Planetside is pretty secure but still dangerous."

"As in meteor showers or other planetary dangers?"

"I wish it was only those. Unfortunately, it also includes pirates."

Karson gulped audibly. While he had heard stories of pirates attacking spaceships and spacers, he did not think that the Stardust would have a run-in with them.

"One particular pirate, Captain Flint Grimlocke, has had a warrant on his head for a bit too long. He stole a ship from a Capitol Planet and has been reported to have been in this area of rogue space. While there have not been any recent reports, Chief Wiggins and I felt it best to review reports and plan accordingly."

This pirate must have a spine of duranium to have stolen a ship from a Capitol Planet! I wonder if he is after those plans I found? Or perhaps, maybe Dawson was right, and there really is a treasure on board. Karson thought as he absorbed all this information.

"Well, that is enough about one term for the moment," Captain Abernathy snapped his claw fingers, and the lights came up, and the map was removed from sight. He walked over to the door with Karson on his heels. As they made their way to the bridge, the Captain put his hand on Karson's shoulder affectionately. "You have just taken your real first step into a much larger world, my boy."

****

For the next few hours, Abernathy continued with his lessons for the future recruit. He even allowed Karson to give an order to the helmsman. Afterward, the young man went to the science station, and Commander Wagoner showed him and Hague how to map the stars. It was one of the best days of Karson's life. He couldn't stop smiling, especially when he realized that he loved learning everything about spacecraft and travel.

In the afternoon, Karson took lunch with Abernathy. The Captain decided to test his new protege further by asking him a question.

"I suppose the men have told you about our plans after our last delivery?" Captain Abernathy asked.

"You mean the treasure of Nova Scarm?" Karson smiled. "Yes. But I thought that was all spacer tales."

"I did too until I learned the truth."

"Do you think we have a chance of finding it?"

"If I didn't believe it, I wouldn't have refused these last two cargo shipments I was offered. After we deliver our last cargo to Cortsea, we will be able to have a real plan about the treasure," Abernathy replied.

"Do you have a map?" Karson asked hesitantly. Even though he was trying to remain a calm and collected soldier, inside, he was a whirl of excitement. He thought that the plans for the *Pegasus* had been the real treasure that Dawson was talking about. But now, a real treasure hunt seemed to be within his grasp.

138

Abernathy grinned. "Indeed I do, but it is only a part of the map. I bought it from Scarm's granddaughter. She needed the credits but had no way to search for the treasure herself. I gave her a fair price, considering she had little in the way of proof that this was the real thing."

"How could you be sure she didn't cheat you?"

"I was able to verify a few details. Various higher up members of the crew also took a chance to help me discover the truth. The map is real, and so is the treasure. She told me that before he died, Nova Scarm had the map broken into parts. We hold the first part."

"How many parts are there?" Karson's eyes grew wide with excitement. Forgetting his cautious attitude that he and Hague had developed on Nergal, he was allowing the story to take hold.

"The second part of it is in the hands of that pirate Captain Grimlocke."

"Well, that complicates things," Karson said dejectedly.

"For now, yes," Abernathy cautioned. "But, once we get that second part of the map, we'll go after the remaining third. I plan to share it with any remaining crew."

"But how would we even get the map from him?

"That remains to be seen. Though I think my officers and I will come up with something once we land on Cortsea."

"May I ask some more questions?"

"Please do," the Captain replied.

"What did you mean by the remaining crew?"

"Well, after we make the delivery, I will ask who wishes to continue with us to search for the treasure."

"I thought that was what we signed up for?"

"Not necessarily. The majority signed up for the two deliveries with plans to get on another crew when we port. Though any who are brave enough to stay with us shall receive a share. I think it would serve you well, and I'd imagine young Hague would also like that."

"But what if they leave the ship to go off on their own after the treasure?"

"Some might. I'd imagine most would remain with me. After all, no matter how much money one might have, if they love being in space, that's where they'll stay."

"But then why..."

"Why would I share it, to begin with?"

Karson nodded.

"I am a wealthy man, Karson. I have served the Galactic Federation for many years after I left my own planet of Rasiris. I have learned and earned many things during my service. And while I don't mind adding credits to my account, most of the crew have been with me for many years. Tucson and Wagoner, to name a few. They're hard-working and loyal. They deserve a share."

"Makes sense, I guess." Karson reasoned.

"Loyalty comes first, my son, the rest comes after."

Karson pondered on the advice that Abernathy had just given.

"Are there other questions?" The Captain asked.

"Just one, if I am permitted."

The Captain gestured to Karson, indicating it was safe to ask whatever he had on his mind.

"What is our delivery to Cortsea? I knew about the livestock and supplies for New Kansas, but I have not heard anything regarding this delivery."

For the first time since he started training, Captain Abernathey looked extremely serious at Karson.

"We are on a mission of galactic importance," he started. "The first mission to New Kansas was meant to offer a means of distraction. While the supplies were needed desperately, the true mission is delivering plans to Cortsea."

"What plans? Federation plans?"

"Yes. Plans for a ship, one that could change the future of the Galactic Federation. When we make port in Cortsea, myself and my trusted officers will rendezvous with Captain Hunter of the Federation. He will then take the plans safely to Cesaroma. I have kept those plans even more secret than Captain Nova Scarm's treasure map. I'll admit I used the lore of the map to throw anyone else off the trail of the plans. But, if anyone discovered these plans, we could be in a lot more trouble than if they found the map."

"I see, sir," Karson weighed the knowledge he had just been informed of. While trying to hide the fact that he had seen the plans for the *Pegasus*. He did not think those plans were the delivery, but now he further shared the caution his captain had.

"Regardless, I don't want you repeating what you know to anyone. Until we deliver it safely to the Federation, we must be cautious."

Chapter 25

Dinner Discussions

Hague made his way to the galley after a long day of working with Commander Wagoner. The only real break the Rhungo had gotten was when Karson came over, and they began to learn how to read the star maps. While Karson was enjoying it, Hague enjoyed the manual labor break. He was more focused on the transport systems and the other inner workings of the ship, not reading a map. *With all of this experience, maybe I could stay on this ship for a bit,* Hague thought. *Pleiades want to go to the academy, but perhaps life aboard a ship is better? Who knows, the way he talks it seems like he will be a captain one day. But he will need a chief engineer.* He laughed to himself at the dream.

Hague and his parents arrived on Nergal not long after Karson, and his mother did. His father, Leyor worked on the *Atlas* as a shipping clerk. He was responsible for seeing the cargo check-in and out correctly for his section on the space station. While all three of the C'avts worked hard in their jobs, money never seemed to be enough. A common thread of friendship between him and Karson. They had known each other for years, growing up as kids, attending school, and it was even Hague's father who got them jobs planetside on the docks. Hague did not miss his home planet, but he did not like living on Nergal either. When he signed up last minute for the *Stardust*, he thought this would be a waste of time despite the money. Now, he was beginning to feel like he could really make a living for himself out in the black depths of space.

After he got his food, still slightly in his train of thought, he saw Karson sitting at a table by himself. He walked over.

"Sure is weird being on the receiving end of food this time, right?" He teasingly asked his bunkmate.

"Hey, it still tastes like we made it, so I am not complaining," Karson joked back.

The two friends talked and shared what they had done on their first day of training. Hague went on and on about the different types of ships they had in the bay. He told me about how Commander Wagoner began teaching him how to repair the anti-grav lifts and how to troubleshoot technical difficulties with their computers. Karson shared the details of everything except for the plans about the Pegasus. He would fill Hague in about those tonight.

They started to make their way to their rooms when a shout from a nearby table got their attention.

"Hey! Why don't we play some cards tonight?"

Karson and Hague exchanged looks as they informed their crewmate they would be right back with the deck.

When they got to their bunk, Hague went to change as Karson picked up his cards.

"The treasure is real."

Hague walked in from the bathroom, "is it?"

"According to the Captain. He claims he has part of a treasure map. He says once we land in Cortsea, he will be offering anyone a share if they choose to go with him."

"I thought Dawson told you all that?"

"The sharing, yes. That Abernathy only has part of the map, no."

"Interesting," Hague wrenched his hands together. "So that is the plan? Go after the treasure after this last stop?"

"Affirmative," Karson looked around, making sure they really were alone.

"I have a feeling you have more to tell me?" Hague suggested.

"Yes, but it is very secret. Our delivery to Cortsea is those plans I told you about."

"The…" Hague was about to say its name when Karson covered his blue mouth.

"Yes, that. The Captain doesn't even know I told you. So keep your mouth sealed tight, alright?"

"Sealed like an airlock," Hague replied as he dragged his finger over his lips, further emphasizing the point. "Anyway, I'm more curious about the map. Did you find anything else out?"

"Other than a dangerous pirate has the second piece, not much."

"And now we have pirates," Hague said with a smile. "This voyage keeps getting better and better!"

Karson could not tell if his friend was serious or if he was joking.

"Oh come on, Pleiades. Are you scared of pirates? What is this, a spacer story told by your Uncle Jasper?"

"Well, he did tell us the legend of the treasure after all," Karson replied.

"Okay, you got me there. But pirates? Who would be crazy enough to attack this ship? Not only is it a Galactic Federation ship, but it is huge! Plus, our defenses are top-notch. Did you even get a chance to count how many personal fighters we had in the bay last time you were there?"

Karson chuckled, "Well, I was a little busy getting sent to the brig after all."

"Let me give you peace of mind then, Karson. We are plenty of protected. Plus, in a couple of days, we should be closer to Cortsea and close to more patrolled areas of space."

"Still…" Karson started.

Hague blinked his eyes three times rapidly as he spoke, "Well, no one is attacking us tonight. And I don't know about you, but I could use a couple of card games. Shall we?"

Karson smiled as he picked up the deck, "after you, old friend."

With that, the two companions returned to the galley for a lovely night of cards. Although while they were having fun aboard the starship somewhere else in the galaxy, someone else was having a tough time aboard their new vessel.

Chapter 26

Life Gets Worse

Serena awoke in a sweat. According to her clock, it was still early, and she felt her stomach lurch as if they had just been hit with laser fire. She rolled out of her bed and staggered to the communal bathroom in the room. She felt the bile first, and then Serena hurled everything from her stomach into the toilet. Her eyes watered, and she felt the wave inside her belly lurch again. More of the dinner she had eaten came up, followed by frothy bile.

One of the crew looked over from his bunk, grunted, and turned back to whatever dream was still in his head. Serena gagged and hit her forehead on the edge of the toilet as another wave of nausea overtook her. This was awful. She had never been so sick. Not like this. The overwhelming stench of her own vomit was unbearable, and she lay down on the floor next to the putrid-smelling toilet, which she'd forgotten to flush. She heard a low groan, miserable and forlorn, and realized it came from her own dry, cracked lips.

The next thing she knew, Fingers stood over her, and she was back in her bed. She felt like she was on fire. Sweat clung to her matted hair. She was so hot, and then she was shivering with unbearable cold. She gagged, and Fingers stepped back as she leaned over the side with a dry heave. Nothing came up, just pain like a knife in her stomach, and her body was drenched in sweat. When she leaned back in her berth, she realized someone had removed her outer blousy shirt, and she wore only her cotton undershirt. She rolled onto her side, conscious of Fingers standing so close.

"Ya got food poisoning, lad. It's a bugger, ain't it? Couple mates are as sick as you are. Just gotta let it run its' course. Me, I didna eat that fish the cook gave us last night. Don't like fish."

It was Lonnie, the youngest pirate, she saw next. He was an alien known as a Splinthair, a rodent-like species from various planets in the Outer Core. He had a sponge and was dipping it in a somewhat murky bowl of water and wiping her face and neck with a cloth soaked in cold water. "You'll be okay, Drake," Lonnie said in a soothing voice. "I think the worst is over. But, ya need to change your shirt, mate. It's a mess. I found a clean one for ya that should fit."

Serena rolled onto her side again and panicked. She couldn't take her shirt off in front of these men. All these months, she had hidden the fact that she was a girl. Like the pirates of old that sailed the sea, she knew that a woman on board was terrible luck. If they discovered she was a girl, they'd surely blow her out a torpedo tube, or shoot her right in her berth.

Serena groaned. "Nooooo…too sick. Leave me alone." She swatted at Lonnie, trying to remove her shirt.

Suddenly Lonnie jumped back and looked around the room. "Blimey, Drake, you're a bloody girl. A girl!" He said in a hushed voice. "No wonder we've haven't had any luck finding a ship to prey on."

With all the strength she had, Serena grabbed Lonnie by the shirt and pulled him close. The stench made him cringe. "You can't tell anyone, Lonnie. Promise me."

"But, you're a girl, a woman! We can't have a woman on board; it's bloody bad luck."

147

"Please, Lonnie, they'll kill me."

"And if I don't tell Cap'n, we could all die out here – the ship is running out of supplies, and we haven't come across any prey in days. And you're to blame. You're the curse. Who in Hades woulda thought we had a girl on board?" Lonnie dropped the washcloth, and backed away from the berth, his face contorted with fear. "A bloody curse!"

Lonnie turned and ran for the turbolift. *I had better tell Grimlocke, because sure as dried bones, our lack of prey is caused by that girl.* Lonnie poked his head out from the turbolift after it opened onto the bridge, but before he could step out, he was accosted by one of his crewmates.

"Lonnie, get yerself in here. We've spotted a freighter, and the cap'n wants everyone ready to board her. The gods be fickle, but we got ourselves a good one! Captain hailed it, and they're transporting food and other supplies to be sold at their next port."

Lonnie did as he was told, and said not a word about what he'd discovered. He wouldn't snitch on the girl, but keep the information to himself and use it to his advantage when the time was right. *Might be able to get some extra food rations from this one then.*

Several days later, Serena was back to her usual self. She cleaned the captain's quarters while he was on the bridge. She hated cleaning, especially someone else's room. Because of her own ordeal, she felt sorry for the servants that had cleaned her room for her over the years, even if some of them were androids. After all, they were sentient beings, too, and she suddenly realized how unfair it was to make them do the dirty work.

She was discovering she had been a spoiled brat. If any good was going to come out of this situation, it would be that she would no longer expect others to clean up after her.

She left the captain's cabin and went to prepare the large table that he and his men sat at. Six plates for six ugly men, she thought. As she left, the captain's men paraded into the room, bushing her aside. They had no idea she was a girl, if they did, she would be a corpse floating in space, and any disaster on the ship would be her fault as far as they were concerned.

When she returned with the bread, the door was closed. She heard them talking.

Standing dead still and keeping just far enough to the right so as not to trigger the automatic door opener, Serena pressed her ear against the crack near the door.

"Our scanners indicate that a large transport ship the *Stardust* has been sighted in the area."

"That's a Federation ship, is it not?"

"It is, sir, but look at the size of it! I'd bet there would be plenty of things that the *Antares* could use that we could siphon off that ship? The *Cirrus* could be modified as well. Not to mention the medical equipment or technology it has. Maybe we could even take some short-range ships? Personal guard dogs of Captain Grimlocke and his fleet!"

There was a long silence before Serena heard one of the pirates reply.

"Do we have the coordinates yet?"

"Aye, the *Stardust* is a day or two out. Once we're closer, we'll prepare to attack."

Serena waited a few moments to make sure there was no other information. She heard the men start to eat again. Then she moved in front of the door, which opened.

Walking inside, she placed the bread on the table. She masked her fear in front of the men. Fear and hope.

They were going to attack the *Stardust*, one of the most influential and elegant freighters in the quadrant. She feared the battle, and that she would be asked to take part. But hope was almost as strong as her fear. Perhaps she could escape; get to the *Stardust*, and be rescued. That is if the *Stardust* won the battle. Surely if this ship was a part of the Galactic Federation, there would be more crew, maybe even soldiers on board. Hope soared, but then fear took over once more. What were the chances she would survive? They would see her as a pirate, not the kidnapped young girl she really was. The fear and hope danced in her head, twirling, dipping, and grinning.

"We should hear from our spy on the *Stardust* in a day or two," Grimlocke said. He rubbed his hands together. "She'll make a fine addition to our fleet."

The men laughed and nodded. It would be an excellent addition indeed.

Chapter 27

Solo Flight

Karson's lessons on how to be a captain and how to run a ship continued for the next few days. The more he learned, the more he felt that he was on the road to making his dreams come true. Every afternoon, Captain Abernathy worked with him. Teaching him how to read maps, evasive maneuvers against pirates, and all the other things the captain felt the future recruit would need.

"Have you been practicing with the computer simulations?"

"Every chance I get. I've been working with a couple battle scenarios, but I haven't won one yet."

"Why don't you run one for me?" The Captain suggested.

"Okay."

The Captain left his chair and nodded to Karson. "Let's include the bridge crew. It'll be good practice for them, too."

Karson's eyes lit up with excitement, but there was a tinge of fear, too. He didn't want to totally screw up in front of the crew. Looking around, he saw smiles and nods of encouragement.

"Go ahead, son. The chair won't bite you," Abernathy said. "Computer, make the battle simulation about to be run as realistic as possible without hurting anyone or damaging the ship."

"Acknowledged."

Karson hesitantly sat in the Captain's chair. He looked at the instrument panels in both chair arms, and his eyes blinked twice in rapid succession as a feeling of power rushed through him. He sat back, and then with a nod, he said, "Computer, run battle simulation Cardinal two."

A few seconds passed before the computer said, "Cardinal two battle simulation ready."

Karson looked at the Captain.

"Let's see how you handle it."

"Ready," Karson told the computer.

Two pirate ships appeared on the main view screen, coming out of nowhere, one on each side of the ship.

"Enemy ships off the port bow sighted, Captain," the helmsman said.

"Red alert!" Karson ordered.

The words had barely left his lips when both ships open fire.

"Evasive maneuvers." Karson did his best to contain his excitement, fighting to keep his voice regular but firm as phaser fire raked both sides of the ship. The ship responded just like it would if it had actually been hit, and he found himself and the rest of the crew being thrown from side to side in their seats. Those standing grabbed onto anything they could to maintain their balance.

On-screen, the pirate ships followed the *Stardust* as the helmsman did his best to dodge the continued phaser fire.

"Target both ships and fire!" Karson ordered.

The battle continued with all three ships fighting to become the victor. Some of the shots missed, while others raked various portions of the ship, including the nacelles.

"Target their engines and fire torpedoes!" Karson ordered.

One of the torpedoes hit the engines of the pirate ship on the port side, followed by more laser fire. The ship's engines blew up in a spectacular display of fireworks. It dropped back, unable to continue the battle.

"Yes!" The helmsman shouted. "Direct hit, captain, one ship is dropping out of warp."

"Continue evasive maneuvers and concentrate everything you've got on the remaining ship," the acting captain ordered.

Seeing its sister ship fall behind, the remaining enemy vessel executed a set of complicated maneuvers and fired its own torpedoes. It had not done so before in hopes of capturing the *Stardust* and reusing the ship. When the torpedoes hit, several panels on the bridge released a shower of sparks and blanked out, just like they would had they been destroyed.

"Repair teams to the bridge," Karson shouted, hitting the com on his chair.

The computer kept the order confined to the bridge since no actual repairs were needed.

"Phasers are down," the science officer told Karson. "Prepare to be boarded."

At that point, the simulation shut down, and everything returned to normal.

"Not bad for a rookie," Captain Abernathy said. "But, you need more practice." Seeing the sad expression on Karson's face, he added, "Don't be discouraged. It takes a lot of study and practice before you get it right, but don't worry, you'll get better."

Karson listened while Captain Abernathy talked about alternative ways to handle such a situation, adding, "I'm proud of you, Karson. You're learning fast. I have no doubt that someday you will make a fine captain."

****

Chapter 28

The Meteor Shower

They were caught in a meteor storm the next day. It was easy to avoid the big ones, but the smaller one pelted the shields mercilessly, breaking through the ship in a couple places. The turbulence caused several injuries among the crew. On the bridge, one woman Feladae was thrown against her station, breaking her leg. Karson hurried over to her.

"Let me help. I'll take you to the sickbay."

In between moans of pain, the woman thanked him. "I'd never get there myself."

"Name is Karson Pleiades, what's yours?"

"Tonks LaRue," the Feladae responded. "Sorry, this is how we get to meet."

"Well, you didn't do this to yourself, so don't worry," Karson smiled as he helped her sit down. Medical personnel had been sent all over the ship to help with any incidents like this. Still, Karson figured he could help out given the situation. He approached a nurse and explained the situation. Fortunately, the nurse had an anti-grav chair they could use to escort the female Feladae to the sickbay.

Once Karson was able to get Tonks comfortably in the chair, he took her to the turbolift. He programmed it to take them to the sickbay, and while it moved effortlessly along the shoot, the two decided to talk.

"This is my first flight on this big of a cruiser," Karson started.

"Well, I'll admit this isn't my first," Tonks giggled. "Though this is the most embarrassing injury I have ever received on duty."

"Have you been in any battles?"

Tonks looked up at the young man, "Have *I*? Oh yes, several. Nothing worth knowing or even worth being recorded on the Federation archives, but yes. My favorite skirmish was when my father and delivered supplies to the newly terraformed Barbossa, well it was newly terraformed when we got there. Anyway, my father and I were responsible for delivering some pigs to the settlers when we got ambushed by rustlers."

"Rustlers? Like thieves?" Karson clarified.

"Essentially, very happy we didn't deal with that back on New Kansas. But yes, my father and I, and our crew, were surrounded. We were stuck in the pig herding area, phasers shooting everywhere, people shouting! It was a lot of fun."

Karson was beginning to wonder if Tonks hit her head when she broke her leg.

"Thankfully, local reinforcements showed up, and none of the pigs were harmed. Though I did take a phaser bolt to the arm," she rolled over her sleeve to reveal a sizeable pink scar amid her tortoiseshell fur. "Dad had to give me some rib for that."

"Who was your father?"

"Captain Cousteau La'Rue, and he still is," she winked. "He now works for the Academy has a teacher. I heard you might be interested in applying?"

"I am," Karson said when the turbolift reached its destination.

"Well, let me know when you do," Tonks said with a smile. "I'll have my dad be on the lookout for your application."

When they arrived at sickbay, several injured crew members were already waiting. Karson eased his companion onto a biobed before going over to the doctor.

"Think you'll be ok, Tonks?" Karson asked.

"Once the doc does his work, I'll be fine," she purred.

Karson smiled as he left his new friend to talk to the ship's doctor. He tapped on his shoulder.

"My name is Karson Pleiades. Is there anything I can do to help?"

The doctor, who was a human female, turned around, gave him a surprised look. "I'm Doctor Kai. I'd be more than happy for an extra pair of hands. Are you sure it won't bother you? I don't need someone throwing up all over the place."

"Back on Nergal, I once helped my uncle and local farmers deliver a set of twin calves. Does that count for anything?"

"That it will, son. I'll put you to work, then."

Doctor Kai showed him how to use a hand-held device to heal cuts and contusions. For the next two hours, he helped repair wounds and broken limbs after the doctor set them. While they worked, Karson used the opportunity to question the doctor.

"How long have you been on board the *Stardust*?"

"This is my first voyage," the doctor replied.

"Have you ever worked in space before?"

"No."

"Did you have your own practice before that?" Karson asked.

"I did back on the Capitol Planet Olympus, but I grew bored with that life. I'd always wondered what it would be like to live in space. I had no family ties, so I applied for a position with the New World Space Community, and within a month, hired on with the *Stardust*."

"New World Space Community?"

Doctor Kai explained as she took off her gloves. "An organization that recruits people to help terraform planets, establish life, or make life better on the planet they are on."

"Then why didn't you stay on New Kansas?"

"Didn't want to be on a freshly terraformed planet. Figured I could help best in the worlds that are already settled rather than start from scratch.

"Are you glad you made the change?"

The doctor wrinkled an eyebrow. "Most of the time. I'm not comfortable with having the possible threat of a pirate attack over my head, but so far, we've managed to avoid them."

For the remainder of the storm, Karson helped Doctor Kai with the injured and even helped her organize things in the sickbay. He figured as soon as the storm cleared, he and Hague would be sent back to cabin boy duties, so he decided to postpone that as long as possible.

****

The *Stardust* had finally managed its way through the meteor shower. While cosmetically it took several dings, the rest of the ship was sound. Each section of the ship started to clean up and do damage control. This was the first storm for Karson and Hague. The crew were used to these storms and knew the procedure during and after them.

Up on the bridge, Lieutenant Shawnee touched the tiny speaker in her ear.

"Captain, I'm picking up some unusual static on the outgoing channel."

"What kind of static?" The captain asked.

She listened a moment or two longer and then turned toward Abernathy. "I think it's another communication riding piggyback on the message we sent out after the storm. Alerting the Galactic Federation that we were all right."

"Are you sure?" Captain Abernathy asked.

"Yes, sir, I'm *sure* that's what it is," Lieutenant Shawnee responded.

Abernathy rose to his feet and hurried over to her. "Block it. Quickly!"

Shawnee's fingers danced over the touch screen.

"Well?"

"I was able to interrupt it, but I'm afraid some of the transmission got through before I stopped it."

"It had to come from somewhere on the ship. See if you can trace where the signal originated from."

"Yes, sir."

Abernathy's feathered brow wrinkled. Had enough of a signal gotten through to whoever the enemy was? Probably so. *Whatever was or wasn't said, it was perhaps enough to give their location to the person on the other end of the communication.* He returned to his chair, saying, "Keep this confidential until I find out who is responsible for this."

"I've traced the message's send location to the engineering bay, sir."

The Captain turned to Chief Wiggins, "Send a team to engineering. Commander Wagoner, and I will meet you there."

159

Chief Wiggins ran to the turbolift, shouting orders through his communicator. Usually, Abernathey would send Scalemander and stay on the bridge, but since he didn't know who sent the message, or it's purpose. He decided to check this out for himself.

"First Mate Scalemander, you have the con."

"Aye, aye, Captain."

****

When they arrived in engineering, the security team had already entered the room. It blocked the exit so no one could leave.

"What's going on?" Chief Engineer Silas Holbrook asked as he approached the Captain. "Why are my people being contained?"

Hague was one of the contained workers. He had been sent down at the start of the meteor storm as assistance to the team. He had done an excellent job rewiring the computers and realigning the compression coils. He was about to leave when Holbrook got the orders that no one should go.

Abernathy and Wagoner quickly found the station in question, but no one was there.

"Who just used this station?" The Captain asked Hague

"I'm afraid I don't know," Hague answered. "I was busy realigning the compression coils."

Abernathy looked around at the others in the room. "Did any of you see who was sitting here?"

All shook their head except for one man.

"Someone was working there, but I only saw the back of him. I didn't have any reason to pay attention to what he was doing," one crewman offered.

"Do you remember anything about him? Hair color? Build? Anything? Race? Anything at all?" Captain Abernathy asked.

"I'm sorry, sir. I believe he had blond hair and a slender build, but you can't tell much from behind when a person is sitting down."

Feeling the hair stand up on the back of his neck, the Captain quickly glanced at Wagoner. They both kept their faces calm, but both had an idea of the danger ahead of them.

"Can you check the logs?" Wagoner asked Holbrook.

Before Holbrook could answer, Hague was already at a different station trying to do the same.

"I'm sorry, Captain," Hague said. "It looks like they didn't log into the system. They probably used a blank account since they only wanted to send a message. Wouldn't need any clearance for that."

Holbrook looked impressed. The Captain, however, did not.

"Perhaps it is nothing," Wagoner said, a sign to Abernethy to change subjects.

"Carry on," the Captain said curtly and made his exit with Wagoner.

Once they were out of earshot, Wagoner spoke up.

"Do you think someone is after the map?"

"That or the plans, Hector." John Abernathy replied his claws on his beak.

"Grimlocke?"

The Captain slowly nodded his head. He didn't know who or how, but someone had attempted to make contact with the most dangerous pirate in the galaxy. And that someone was currently onboard the *Stardust*.

Chapter 29

Politics

That night Captain Abernathey called a secret meeting to be held at dinner. Karson and Hague had also been invited to join them. They were in their quarters, changing into the second outfit that Boris had got them.

"You said the Captain was in the engineering room? Karson asked his friend.

The blue Rhungo replied, "Yes. He and Commander Wagoner were looking for someone. Didn't really explain who or why."

"Was this during the meteor shower?" Karson questioned as he put on his shirt.

"Yeah, right after we got out of it. I was down there, and I tried logging into the station where their mystery person was at. Didn't work, but Officer Holbrook was impressed."

"Maybe that's why we are invited to dinner tonight?"

"I don't think my helping got us an invitation, Pleiades. I think the captain might be suspicious of us."

"Why would he? We have done nothing but help in the time we have been training."

"Think about it, Karson. We started working under the Captain and Commander Wagoner a bit ago, the Captain informs you about the plans and the treasure. We get stuck in a meteor shower where someone sends a secret message, and it happens to be in a room I am in."

"Hague, why would they suspect you?"

"I am your friend, right? Suppose the Captain thinks you told me?"

Karson blanched. He had not considered that. While he initially told Hague about the *Pegasus* before he was told not to, Hague made good points.

"So I propose," Hague continues, "we keep a decently tight lip tonight. Not too quiet where they will suspect us, but enough to learn from our superiors."

"What do you mean?"

"Whoever sent that message was smart enough to use a blank account. I doubt anyone who hasn't had ten minutes of military training would know to do that."

"So, it could be an officer?"

"Either that or someone a lot smarter than they are letting on."

Karson pondered for a few minutes, trying to figure out who it could be,

"Think it could have been Dawson?"

"I had not thought of him honestly," Hague commented. "My initial suspicion is that crewmember who saw the individual at that station, but couldn't identify them."

Karson nodded in affirmation. "Shall we go before they send an all call for us?"

This time it was Hague who nodded. As the boys made their way to the turbolift, Karson began to mentally go through the list of people he knew on the ship. It was not a very long list since the personnel of the *Stardust* was vast. However, it did not rule anyone out.

****

Karson studied the men around the table. He was sitting next to Hague, who, in turn, sat next to Chief Eggleton. Karson was seated next to Tavish, who sat next to Lieutenant Shawnee, who sat next to First Mate Scalemander. Chief Wiggins sat next to

Eggleton and across from Salamander sat Commander Wagoner. The seating assignments were similar to when Karson first showed up for dinner, the only differences were Commander Holbrook and Hague's appearance.

The dinner proceeded like the last one did. The Captain came in last, and everyone stood up till they were ordered to be seated. However, instead of eating and discussing, they would start the discussions before they ate.

Captain John Abernathey began, "Ladies and Gentlemen. I have summoned you all here due to the events that transpired today. First and foremost, I want to thank everyone for doing extra duties during that meteor shower. Particularly Hague C'avt for assisting Commander Wagoner, Holbrook, and myself. Karson, who was helping Doctor Kai during the storm, and to Tucson Scalemander for covering the bridge when my attention was needed elsewhere."

Congratulations were offered and handshakes, much to the chagrin of Hague and Karson.

"Also a huge thank you to Lieutenant Shawnee. Her attention to detail was invaluable today. Which leads me to our next point of contention."

The oxygen seemed to have been removed from the room when the Captain made that comment.

"An unidentified individual sent an unauthorized communication wave at the end of the storm. Shawnee, would you mind explaining further?"

Shawnee stood at her seat while simultaneously Abernathey took his.

"In accordance with Galactic Federation standards," she began her speech. Karson made a mental note that she seemed exceptionally prepared for this. Whether that was an order from the Captain or she was hiding her own guilt remained to be seen. "After we safely navigated through the storm, we sent out an 'all clear' communique. Essentially informing any Federation personal that we did not need assistance and that we would make our next delivery on schedule. I was reviewing our logs when I noticed that someone piggybacked on our transmission. The details of the message and who it was sent to were not able to be recovered, unfortunately."

For the next hour, the officers and lieutenants debated and discussed the events that transpired. Hague was questioned slightly, but it was more of a formality of his involvement, rather than accusatory questioning. Suspects were mentioned. Ideas were named. But there was no real resolution to anything. Karson could not help but also wonder if no one was intentionally saying the plans or the treasure map. Karson figured that a few if any, crew members were aware of Karson's knowledge of the matters. *They may be trying to keep it a secret*, he thought. *Or perhaps even among the elite, only a select few know of the cargo.*

The meal was served. Everyone enjoyed the brief respite from the questions and the tension. Hague ate in silence, but he was observing everything. *Everyone seems to be relaxed*, he thought. *But this could be due to the lack of questions.* He scanned the table, taking mental notes of the interactions he was witnessing. The Captain, first mate, and Wagoner seemed close. The security, engineering, and navigations chiefs seemed to be keeping to themselves. And then there was Karson, doing his best as well to find out anything involving this presumed spy.

After being served the first course from Bill Shanks, Karson was determined to ask a few questions.

"I have a question," he started as everyone was getting ready to continue the discussions.

"Go on Plieades," First Mate Scalemander encouraged. *I doubt this boy or C'avt had any direct involvement,* he thought. *Though considering their lack of experience, they easily could be unexpecting pawns.*

"Why would someone piggyback one transmission on top of another?"

"The individual who sent it didn't want the rest of the crew to know what he was doing," Shawnee replied.

Captain Abernathy, seeing what Karson was trying to prove, also made a comment. "To add on to what Lieutenant Shawnee was saying. They would also piggyback a message if they did not want the recipient to be known who they were or vice versa."

As the Captain responded, commander Wagoner gave him a puzzled look. Then he realized that the Captain must have told Karson and or Hague about the plans for the *Pegasus*.

"Captain, I would like to address the elephant in the room," Chief Wiggins announced.

Hague felt you could have cut through the tension with a phaser bolt after that announcement. *If he brings up the plans, that could jeopardize everything.* Though Hague reasoned that every one of the officers would have an idea of the plan.

The Captain nodded curtly, also wondering what Chief Wiggins would announce.

"I forgive if I am overstepping my bounds," Chief Wiggins started. "However, if everyone in this room is not aware of what we are carrying with us, it is high time they were made aware."

Karson started to sweat profusely, a sign of his nerves. Tucson and Wagoner quietly reached for their phasers, in fear that the security chief would reveal too much.

"The *Stardust* is carrying part of a map originally believed to have been owned by Captain Nova Scarm. According to our sources, the third portion of the map is missing. However, the feared Captain Flint Grimlocke has the second part."

So what the Captain told me was true, Karson thought.

Chief Wiggins looked around, "I have reason to suspect that the individual who piggybacked that communique is working for Grimlocke."

"That seems like a pretty bold accusation," First Mate Scalemander responded. He was relieved that Wiggins had not announced the *Pegasus* plans in front of the rest of the crew. As far as the Venomae officer was concerned, only himself, Wiggins, the Captain, and Commander Wagoner were cognisant of the plans. This procedure was put in place before the voyage even started. The four officers had worked with each other for years and naturally only trusted each other. While Tucson could trust the rest of the officers in terms of the treasure map, he was not entirely clear of loyalties when it came to the involvement of the Federation.

"Though it is a fair one," Waggoner, picking up the unspoken cue from Scalemader, said. "We are carrying with us part of a key that could unlock a planet's worth of treasure. A few months ago, Grimlocke's team was able to infiltrate Capitol

168

Planet space and sneak off with a mighty vessel. With that ship at their disposal, they pose a greater threat than you might think."

"Weeks ago, a communique came to use also alerting of a missing person. That person was Viscount Cloudracer," Abernathy continued. "For anyone here who may not know, he was an exceptional space captain of the Federation. His ship was supposed to have reached its destination days before the communique. Judging by the last marked location, I would not be surprised if Grimlocke or another pirate intercepted them.

"Captain Couldracer's personal ship, the *Cirrus*, was indeed a private force by itself," he continued. "One of the fastest ships if need be. So I propose we keep everything on high alert until we make port in Cortsea."

"Should I send an all call tomorrow, Captain?" Shawnee offered.

"Negative. I would rather keep this to ourselves. That is the reason I summoned you officers here, so we could all be on the same page."

Karson and Hague exchanged glances.

"We should be in Cortsea territory day after tomorrow," Scalemander said. "So we are not out of the backstars just yet. And while we will be in the territory of the planet, it does not mean we will be safe. If Chief Wiggins is correct, and someone is leaking information to Grimlocke, then we will all need to be on high alert for those two days. Anything unusual or suspicious should be confidently reported to any of us."

The rest of the officers continued to discuss plans for finding out if there was a spy among the ship. They continued to discuss strategies when dessert showed up. Bill Shanks brought in some form of pastry and served it to the officers. He made a sour look at Karson and Hague, a sign of jealousy, but said nothing.

Bill could be a suspect, Karson thought. *He is the steward to the Captain, and if anyone had any close connections, it could be him.*

Chapter 30

New Assignments

Once the dessert was finished, Karson and Hague were about to leave when Captain Abernathey asked them to stay behind. The other officers left, all except Wagoner and Scalemander. Hague was nervous. Out of everyone at the meeting, he felt that he and Karson were the most suspect. Since they were asked to stay behind, his fears were amped. He did not know how he could prove their innocence, but he would try his hardest. Karson had the exact opposite feeling. He felt that since they were asked to stay behind, the Captain and other officers must trust them both. Though there was a fear that the Captain would question him if Hague knew anything about the *Pegasus*. He figured he would deal with that when the time was right.

"Boys," Abernathey began. "I appreciate your maturity and honesty during our meeting tonight. Though I am afraid, I can only reward that with an assignment."

Karson's ears perked up.

"John, let me," Tucson asked with his Venomae cultured accent. "Karson, you have been working with the Captain pretty closely the last few days. Hague you have done the same with Wagoner."

Both boys nodded in agreement.

"As you heard in our meeting, we reach Cortsea territory in two days. Though it may take another day or two to reach port. Once we get to port, we are pretty safe. Though now, and even after we make our last delivery, Grimlocke might be a threat."

Scalemander continued. "So, I am afraid I will have to ask you two to work under me, indirectly, until we can, for sure, confirm or deny this threat."

Hague looked a bit hurt, "Does that mean I can't work with the tech anymore?"

Hector Wagoner laughed, "Not at all, lad. In fact, I will need you to help Commander Holbrook and his team with repairs and even preparing our fighter ships. We may need those ships up and running sooner than we think."

"What would you like us to do then?" Karson asked.

"Espionage." The first mate said flatly. "Wherever you are stationed the next few days, keep an ear out for anything. I know you, Karson, play cards with the crew during meals; use that to your advantage. If we can find any leads to who is behind this, we could be saving lives as well as treasure."

Karson and Hague nodded in agreement, they would have to spy to find who the traitor was.

"Karson, until we get this figured out," Abernathey said, "I will need you to work under and report to Tucson here. Is that alright?"

"Of course, Captain."

"I'm afraid our lessons will be on hold, at least for a bit," he smiled as he spoke.

"Anything to help out, sir," Karson said.

"Me too," Hague added. "I was honestly afraid you would have thought it was us, sir."

The three officers laughed.

"Not at all," Wagoner said as he slapped the Rhungo's back with affection. "Plenty of witnesses saw where you boys were at during this communique."

Captain Abernathey then informed everyone about the plans for the *Pegasus*. Keeping the five of them in the same loop would also create more unity between them.

"Do you think they are after the plans?" Hague questioned.

"There's a chance," Wagoner said. "Those plans not only are worth a guaranteed fortune if ransomed, but they could be used for dark purposes. The ship those plans are designed for might even be worth more than the treasure of Nova Scarm."

"You don't think the treasure is real?" Karson asked boldly.

"I'll believe it when I see it," Wagoner retorted. "However, those pirates are real. As is this threat to our security."

They continued to discuss plans and responsibilities. Tomorrow Hague would report to the shuttle bay to assist with repairs and preparations. While Karson would start working in the galley and report to the first mate after lunch.

"That way, we have ears in two different places," Tuscon reasoned.

While Karson was not thrilled to be back in the kitchen, he knew it was their best option. He could figure out if Boris or Paulie were involved. Also, being close to an ample common space could be beneficial. Karson could listen in to conversations to see if he could find anything. Once everything was settled, the boys made their way back to their quarters.

Once they were gone, Abernathey spoke alone to his commander and first mate.

"This complication could also prove fruitful," John began.

"Go on," Scalemander said.

"We could use this traitor as a means of taking us to the pirate who has the second piece of the map."

"Sounds rather risky, John," Wagoner said.

"But think of it, Hector," Tucson commented. "If we could defeat Grimlocke. We could be doing the galaxy a good service."

"And we would have the next piece of the map," John added. "I am only suggesting this plan in case all else fails."

"I'm not sure I like it," Hector said. "I would rather avoid them at least until the *Pegasus* plans are safe."

"The plans are the utmost priority," Abernathey assured.

"And when we find this traitor," Tuscon snarled. "They will talk. I promise you both that."

Chapter 31

Bluffing

The next morning, after breakfast, Karson found Dawson taking a break in the lounge. The area where he saw was otherwise unoccupied. Karson decided to use this moment to question the cyborg.

"How's it going?" Dawson asked when he saw Karson walk up.

"Well, it was better before the meteor shower," Karson admitted. "They got me back on kitchen duty till things smooth out again."

"Well, that is unfortunate. Though it was fortunate that we made it through that storm. I've heard of bigger vessels having rougher time out here with that."

"Where do they have you stationed today?" Karson asked innocently.

"Communications," Dawson said as he ran his fingers through his thin hair. "Being a cyborg, I have a few technical skills that others don't."

"Such as helping me get to a transporter?"

Dawson chuckled, "exactly my friend. Speaking of transporters, did you happen to stumble on any news of the mystery?"

Karson turned his head and stared at a couple crewmen having a friendly argument at the other end of the lounge. He hadn't told Dawson about finding the plans for the *Pegasus*. This was the perfect opportunity to ask him what he knew.

"No," he lied. "Why do you ask?"

"Just wondering."

For some reason, a chill ran down Karson's spine. Was Dawson the traitor? His former cellmate had questioned him repeatedly about the treasure. Was it because he really didn't know about the plans for the *Pegasus*, or did he want to find out if Karson could confirm his suspicions? If Dawson was a spy, telling his former cellmate might put him in danger. He decided to play it cool.

"Did you hear about that communique issue that happened yesterday?" Karson questioned the cyborg.

"That's why they want me helping communications today," Dawson replied. "Some sort of piggyback message. I'm pretty sure it was an accident, an error caused during the storm."

Karson grew suspicious, "Really? I overheard some engineers say it might have been a secret message."

Dawson rolled his human and cybernetic eye, "It is possible. But I doubt it is as exciting as people are making it out to be."

Says the cyborg who keeps asking me about the ship mystery, Karson thought.

"Let's say it is a spy, what could one do on a ship as large as this one?"

"Well, I suppose there are several things he could try. He could stir up trouble and cause a mutiny. He might even jettison the cargo into space."

"I just don't see them jettisoning the cargo into space. What would be the point?"

"Well, I don't see a point now since the majority of the cargo we delivered to New Kansas. But we have another stop to make, whatever that delivery will be."

"Do you think he could cause the men to mutiny?" Karson asked.

"Anything's possible."

"Are loyalties that fragile in deep space?"

"Depends on the situation. I don't we have been out in space long enough, or have had nearly the amount of misfortune, for a crew to think of mutiny. However, there is the treasure that Captain Albernathey spoke of before we took off. That alone could turn a spacer into a pirate if the greed was strong enough."

"Pirates!" Karson pretended to be shocked. "I would hope we wouldn't have any of those on this ship. I grew up with my uncle telling me stories like that."

"The threat is more real than you might think, lad. If pirates ever capture the ship, the crew won't have much choice. It will be a join or die decision. It might be different if we were on a vessel they had no interest in, such as the average cruiser or ship. However, the *Stardust,* a fine merchant cruiser of the Federation? This alone is both a target and a prize."

"Do you think someone sent that communique for that purpose?"

Dawson shrugged. "Haven't a clue. All our hypotheticals may be completely unfounded. All I know is that a ship like this would be a valuable commodity to the enemy."

They grew silent for a few minutes until Karson spoke again.

"Well enough of that. I better get back to my duties before Paulie starts yelling for me. But today, after lunch, a few of us are sitting around for a game of cards if you'd like to join us?" Karson offered hopefully.

The cyborg chuckled his mechanical laugh, "If the men don't mind my cybernetic eye, then I'd love to join you all."

Karson had a puzzled look on his face, "Can you see through things with that?"

"No," Dawson answered flatly, "but they don't know that." He winked his robotic eye to add emphasis to his point.

****

Karson was busy loading the dry dishes onto a table for the lunch meal. Since Boris was back to primarily serving by himself, they decided to make lunches a self serve option. That way, the food would be ready for the crew, but the kitchen team would only have to worry about cleaning instead of serving. Karson finished loading another table when Hague walked up.

"Hey, I finished a bit early and figured I'd give you a hand," the blue Rhungo said.

"Good, I could use a quick handloading these tables."

The boys went into a routine quickly like they had weeks prior when they were just cabin boys. As they worked together, they filled in each other with the information they had gotten this morning.

"I have a few suspects that I told Wagoner," Hague started. "Not much, but it is a start."

"I spoke with Dawson," Karson said.

"Well? Did that do you any good?"

"I still have my suspicions, but not sure. I invited him to play cards after lunch. I'm sure I can rope in a few others too."

"You have an idea, don't you?" Hague asked the question that he already knew the answer to.

Karson smiled, "Let's pull the old fashioned on them?"

"Thought you'd never ask," Hague chuckled back.

****

The "old fashioned" was the same plan the boys used to pull at the Planetary Rings tavern. Karson would play cards while Hague observed. Usually, this was used to find the tells of his opponents so they could earn a little extra cash. This time though, it was to see if there was a mutineer among them.

Karson sat at a table with five other crew members as he dealt the cards. This was their last game before going back to their shifts. Dawson was among the members of the crew and Karson's new friend Tonks. The other three members were human men who worked with Hague in the shuttle bay earlier that day.

Hague observed each game. While Karson was doing an excellent job keeping them all entertained and talking, there was nothing for either of them to go on.

"Last game folks," Karson started. "Escape pods are wild this game."

Everyone looked at their hands and asked for the appropriate cards to exchange. Once that was settled, the betting began.

Several of the crew picked up coin currency on New Kansas, though it was never confirmed if it came from their own pockets or betting against others. This would serve in place for credits for now. Once they reached port, the winner could exchange the coins for Federation credits. Since real money was on the table, it made the games a bit tense.

"Raise 2," one of the engineers started. "I'm not in a rush to head back to the shuttle bay."

"Raise 3," one of his companions said. "Albert, you never want to work."

The third engineer spoke, "Lay off, Otho. Raise 2."

Dawson spoke next, "Raise 1. Well, Barnet," he spoke to the third engineer. "Seems you boys were busy today."

"Oh yeah," Tonks interjected, "up on the bridge we were repairing systems from that shower yesterday. Raise 1. They think there was some error yesterday."

Hague and Karson discreetly turned their attention to the Feladae.

"Raise 1," Karson said. "I've been in the galley again all day, so nothing exciting here."

Albert, the first engineer, spoke next. "Raise 1. Yeah, yesterday after the shower, us engineers were stuck in our bay until the Captain and Wagoner showed up."

Otho, the second engineer, said, "Yeah, wanting to know about a message? I don't remember. But whenever the officers get a bee in their pants, they always crack down on everyone, right?"

The table laughed wholeheartedly. Hague observed that comment and took note.

"Fold," Barnet said as he excused himself from the table. "Keep your winnings, I'll head over to the bay to cover for you guys if this game runs long."

Or are you excusing yourself because you are up to something? Hague thought.

The game was slower than previous games. Since actual betting was taking place, everyone felt the need to protect their investments. Tonks was the next one out. Followed by Albert. The last three players were Karson, Dawson, and Otho.

"Raise 1. Say, Dawson," Otho began. "You were working with communications today, right?"

"I was. I should get going there too before I get in trouble again." He stared at his cards, wondering if he should fold or keep pushing his luck.

"Something about a ghost message?" Karson asked, seizing his moment.

Dawson continued to stare as his cards as he fingered the few remaining coins on his side of the table. "I think it was that. Raise 2."

"Raise 3," Karson stated. Now the pressure was really on, both on the game and in the unknown interrogation.

"Probably something to do with the shower yesterday. Sometimes these events create glitches in the computer systems. Lots of small issues can get through. Call," Otho said as he laid his cards on the table. "2 Pair of Moons."

Dawson shook his head, "Can't beat that." He pocketed his remaining change.

"Cosmic Flush," Karson replied as he showed his companions his cards.

Otho shouted some obscenity in a language no one bothered to translate.

As they cleaned up and were about to report to their duties, Hague asked a question.

"Say, Otho, are you sure you didn't get a glimpse of who was operating that station yesterday?"

"Nope, just saw someone there for a bit, but I was too busy repairing another station to take details down. Pleiades, next time we play, I won't lose." He smiled, and he left.

****

That evening, the boys met in the captain's quarters with the first mate and the captain. They informed them about the card game and who was involved. Though even with that information, it did not look likely that anyone would have an answer.

"Any leads?" Tucson Scalemander asked.

181

"I'm afraid to say I am suspicious of Dawson," Karson began. "Not because he is a cyborg but because when I first met him, he told me about the treasure. He even alluded to a mystery on the Stardust. He could be secretly talking about the *Pegasus*, but he could also be just talking about the treasure map."

"It is possible," Abernathey said. "He was put in the brig early on the voyage for snooping. He could be the traitor. I'll have Luitenant Shawnee to run a check tomorrow to see where he was supposed to be when we were in that storm."

"What about you, C'avt?" Scalemander asked.

"Dawson is a pretty good suspect. Especially observing him at cards today." Hague began his report, "Though I am actually suspicious about an engineer named Otho."

"I was more suspicious of Barnet," Karson added. "He left right when the topic of yesterday's meteor shower came up."

"Could be a sign of guilt," the first mate said.

"Why, Otho?" The Captain asked.

"I asked him about when you and Commander Wagoner visited us yesterday. If he got a good look at who was operating that station." Hague said.

"He was the one I spoke to yesterday? I did not know his name," Abernathey said.

"I did not know if it was him at all, sir," said Hague.

Karson looked puzzled, "Then why did you ask him, Hague?"

Hague smiled, "To see how he would react. He never once mentioned the Captain or Commander Wagoner visiting us in the bay. Even when we complained about the events of yesterday. So when I asked if he was sure about his claim, I was testing to see if that was even him."

"So now we have a name to put with a face at least," the Captain added.

"Unfortunately, I think that is all the leads we have," said Karson.

The first mate nodded and seemed happy with the information. "We'll check into it further, but I think we need to keep looking."

****

Chapter 32

"All in."

It was late afternoon the next day when Karson was taking his lunch break.

"Hague, you coming to lunch?" He called on his wrist communicator.

Static. Then, "Sorry, Karson, stuck under one of the fighter ships. Literally. I'll visit ya in the galley when I am done. Over." Static.

Disgruntled, Karson made it for an unoccupied table. He was enjoying his quiet when Barnet walked over with three other members of the crew in tow. One was an Arinsepod, a race of aliens that resembled insects. Karson was not familiar with the men other than Barnet, and that was only due to yesterday's game.

"I brought some friends, why don't we play one game of cards? Since I didn't stay too long yesterday," Barnet asked.

"Sure, gents! Let me just go get my deck from my room." Karson got up and turned around when he felt a sharp prod on his lower back. He then felt a sizeable clawed arm wrap around his shoulder, it was the Arinsepod.

"Name's Garx," he said in an almost too friendly tone of voice. "Why don't you lead us to your quarters for them cards?"

Karson started to sweat, was Barnet, the traitor, and these men were his cronies?

"Sure thing, let's go." Karson sauntered as Barnet came up on his other side.

"Keep your cool kid," he warned Karson. "And this will be over before you know it."

The group walked until they were in the corridor where the bunks where. Karson started to lead them to his when Garx swiftly spun him around and pinned him against the wall, phaser to his head.

"Make a move and yer toast, human." Garx snarled.

"Take his communicator and search him," Barnet ordered one of the men. "Gilete, take his card key and go to his room. You know what to bring back."

"Do I at least get to know what this is about?" Karson asked as he was being searched roughly by the three other men in the group.

"Consider it payback doubled," Barnet said.

"Here is his communicator," one of the men said. "Nothing else on him."

"For what?" Karson asked, "Mad cuz, I took your money yesterday?"

"That is part of that, but the boss can tell you when we bring him to you," Barnet replied coldly. Just then, Gilete returned with a large bag of coins and a deck of cards. Barnet accepted them and placed them in his coat pockets. "You will go with us to our next destination. Garx here has a smuggled phaser on you, don't be stupid."

The young man debated on risking it all and calling for help, but the corridors were suspiciously empty. It was as though someone had cleared them out ahead of time. Karson nodded as he was spun around again and marched like a criminal.

****

Halfway there, Dawson, who had just left a turbolift, saw out of the corner of his cybernetic eye Karson with Barnet and his men. The cyborg changed directions and began to follow the group. Something did not seem right. When he saw the men holding

Karson prisoner, he knew his friend was in trouble. He recognized Barnet from the game yesterday and figured this could be about money.

"What's going on here? Why are you treating Karson like that?" He asked as he walked up to the group.

"Nothing. Just keep to yourself." Barnet ordered. "Orders from the Captain."

"Then where is he?" Dawson asked.

"He had to help with a problem on the bridge, which is where we are taking Karson to. Just run along. Things are fine here."

Knowing he couldn't fight them all on his own, Dawson pretended indifference and left to find help.

****

When they made it to their destination, Cargo Bay 2, Barnet ordered Karson to sit and had Grax keep watch of him.

"Get back to your posts," Barnet ordered. "Two of us can handle this one until the boss arrives. Gilete, find that cyborg. I have a sneaking suspicion he is going to find help." Two of the men went back to their posts while the man named Gilete went to locate the cyborg.

They didn't have to wait long until their boss showed up.

It was Otho.

"Good work Grax and Barnet," Otho said. "Once I get my money back, you two can get a nice tip." Barnet smiled for the first time that day.

"This is what this is about? You sore because I beat you in cards?" Karson asked with a tint of hope.

"Part of it, but mostly due to you snooping about, Pleiades," Otho replied.

"Snooping?" Karson tried to act stupid.

"I've had my eye on you for a bit, son." Otho said, "I know you are trying to figure out who sent that communique the other day. I realized that after your blue friend asked me that question yesterday. Don't worry, he will be taken care of in due time."

"And don't think of denying it," Barnet chimed in. "I've seen you talking to the commander and Captain Abernathy quite a bit lately."

Karson was trapped. Otho had sent that communique after all, and Barnet was his accomplice.

Just then, Otho brought over a large crate and put it between him and Karson.

"Keep a phaser on him, Garx," Otho ordered.

"What is happening now?" Karson asked.

"A game, son, your very last."

As Otho spoke, Barnet produced the bag of coins and Karson's deck and placed them on the table.

****

Hague was walking over to the galley when he heard his communicator go off.

"Hague! Pick up, Hague!"

The Rhungo scrambled to answer, whoever was yelling at him, it was not Karson.

"Hague here, over. Who is this?"

Static.

"It's Dawson, we got problems. I think Karson is in danger."

"Karson? Where is he? I haven't been able to get a hold of him."

"Barnet, the guy from cards yesterday, was walking him to see the captain supposedly."

"That doesn't add up," Hague said. "Can you find them?"

"Give me five minutes, and we can go give our new friends a surprise," Dawson said.

Static.

****

The game had progressed until Karson and Otho only had a few coins remaining to bet. Regardless of the outcome, Otho would win this time.

"Raise 1," Otho said.

"So, what happens after this?" Karson asked.

"You raise or call," Otho smiled.

"I meant after the game, I doubt that I'll take this money back with me even if I win."

"You are right about that," Otho said. "Place your bet, and I'll answer the question."

"All in." Karson shoved his remaining coins to the center of the crate.

"Call," Otho revealed his hand. "This time, I have the Cosmic Flush."

"That you do," Karson said in shock.

"Only one hand in the galaxy can beat this," Otho said smugly.

"This one?" Karson beamed as he placed his cards on the crate.

All the light from Otho's eyes was gone.

"Warp Cosmic Flush," Karson said. "My family motto is 'born under a lucky star,' if you didn't know that." Karson leaned back with a smug look on his face. He didn't know what would happen after this, but he knew he put Otho in his place in terms of cards.

Otho drew his own phaser and stuck it in the young man's face, "Not so lucky now, though, huh?" As he spoke, Barnet scooped up their winnings.

"Before you kill me," Karson gloated. "Can you at least be true to your word and answer my question?"

Otho smiled as he warmed up the phaser, "Like you said. The plan is we go 'all in' now."

"We?" Karson asked.

But before his captor could answer him, the lights in the bay turned off, even the emergency lights did not go on. The only light in the bay was from the encryption keypads on the crates and the lights of the warming phasers. Karson stomped down hard on Otho's foot and ducked, trying to make an escape. His captor cried out and immediately grabbed his foot and hopped to keep his weight off it.

Karson slipped past the Grax just as a phaser bolt shot. All Karson heard was the shot and a groan of pain. Weaving in and out of the cargo, he used the commotion to cover the sound of his flight. Heading for one side of the room, Karson worked his way up until he reached the front corner. There he hid behind a stack of containers.

"Find him, Barnet!" Otho yelled. "He's in here somewhere. If he gets out, our boss will have our hides!"

189

The room grew quiet except for the sound of footsteps made by the men searching for Karson. The young man was glad for the silence. Listening hard, trying to pinpoint where they were, he slowed his breathing, believing it would give him away. This time, he knew the danger was real. And this time, he was alone. No Hague to help. No Abernathey to save him. No one. Still uncertain if Dawson was the other spy or not, he had no idea if anyone would be coming to his rescue or not.

Panic nearly made him run from his hiding place for the door. Reason told him it was a foolish move. Instead, he carefully checked the area around him. Seeing it was clear, he tiptoed from his hiding place to another pile of containers and ducked behind them. Sweat ran down the sides of his face in streaks.

"You'll be given a choice, and if you make the right one, you have nothing to fear," Otho continued, trying to throw off his voice as he made his way to the door.

Karson didn't believe a word. If they caught him, he knew they would murder him. Checking again, he slipped from behind his present location and scooted to the next. There he leaned against the wall and once more slowed his breathing. As each move brought him closer to the door, his excitement grew, overshadowing some of the fear. He dared to hope that he would make it. Checking the area around him, he spotted one of the men thirty feet away. Karson ducked back and waited. Seconds later, he looked again. Seeing no one, he headed for the next hiding place, but this time, Barnet spotted him, and a shout went up.

"There he is, shoots!"

As they started to shoot phaser bolts, Hague walked out of the turboshoot. He ducked when he saw phaser fire and quickly yelled into his communicator.

"Dawson! Turn on the lights in Cargo Bay 2! I need backup!"

They flashed on instantaneously as Dawson left the other turbolift, with several men in tow. One security officer started firing on Otho and Barnet, who also returned fire. Karson hit the ground and slowly crawled his way to the turboshift, away from the phaser fire. As he crawled, he saw Grax lying dead on the ground. Karson could not help but pity the villain. Killed by his own boss. Once he made it safely to the other side, he turned to find Hague grinning at him.

"Let's get out of here!"

"Head up to the bridge and warn the Captain!" Dawson shouted as both sides exchanged phaser fire.

The boys nodded and entered the turbolift with the destination programmed for the bridge.

"Well looks like you were right," Karson said as he hugged his friend. "It was Otho."

"Well, Barnet was a part of it, so we are even," Hague grinned.

"How did you guys find me?"

"Dawson found me after he saw you guys. We were able to trace the communicators from Barnet, and when we figured out where you were, we mounted a small rescue."

"The lights too?"

"All Dawson, guess we owe him for being suspicious," Hague admitted.

They left the turbolift and went to the Captain's quarters. There they saw Tonks.

"I need to see Captain Abernathy now!" Karson exclaimed.

"He was summoned to the bridge," Tonks said. "There's trouble up there. Follow me, I'll take you there."

When he reached the bridge, Karson spotted the Captain and ran to him.

"Captain Abernathy, I know who sent that communique! It's…"

The Captain turned around to hear what Karson was saying, when someone yelled, "Pirates!"

Chapter 33

Grimlocke Appears

Looking up in alarm, Abernathy ran for his chair. Karson followed.

"We found him," Karson insisted.

Captain Abernathy looked down at him. "We'll talk about it later. Red alert!"

The bridge darkened slightly as the lighting turned from soft white to red, followed by the blare of a siren.

"It appears we have some company."

"Is it Grimlocke?"

"Not sure yet," Abernathy said bitterly.

"There's another pirate ship!" The helmsman shouted.

"Where?" Captain Abernathy asked.

"Beyond the bow."

The Captain looked up at the viewscreen. Seconds later, he spotted it, a second ship came into view, heading straight for them. "Blast it, Grimlocke. I didn't count on two. Evasive maneuvers. Target both ships and fire phasers!" He shouted.

Karson ran to a small storage compartment on the bridge, grabbed a phaser, and remained near the captain. As a young boy, he and his friend, Hague, had participated in numerous mock phaser fights. Still, he had never wielded a real weapon. He wasn't even sure if he would hit anyone, and he prayed he wouldn't accidentally shoot one of the *Stardust*'s crew members. Still, he had to do what he could to protect his captain.

Boom!

One of the panels near the engineering station blew out as the approaching pirate ships raked them with phaser fire. The deck shook so hard that Karson had difficulty staying on his feet. *The Stardust* returned fire.

"Direct hits, Captain," Commander Waggoner reported. "Shields down to 80%."

"Target their phasers," Abernathey ordered.

Phaser fire shot through space.

"Direct hit on both ships," Waggoner said. "Damage minimal."

"Go after the cruiser and turn that alarm off," Abernathy said. "Her shields won't be strong, and if we can take her out, we can even up the odds."

The noise receded, but the light continued to flash red.

The three ships flew out and around each other, repeatedly firing, their movements seeming to follow a graceful but deadly dance in space. Several explosions rocked the Cirrus.

"Phasers on the smaller ship are down," the science officer shouted.

His words brought a cheer from the bridge crew, but the Stardust was taking a beating.

The first pirate ship hit them with a barrage of photon torpedoes, causing more explosions.

"Hull breach on decks two and five," Waggoner said. "Shields at 45%."

Captain Abernathey punched the intercom on the arm of his chair. "Repair crews to decks two and five."

"Waggoner to engineering. Commander Dietrich, I need more power to the shields!"

"We're doing our best, Captain, but if I throw more power to the shields, I'll have to take it from something else. The ship is taking a beating."

"Take it from all non-essential systems. We've got to hang on long enough to take out that last vessel."

A moment of silence followed before Dietrich finally spoke. "Shields at 60%. I'm sorry, Captain, but that's the best I can give you."

"Let's hope it's enough," Captain Abernathy said.

Fortunately, the *Cirrus*'s only weapons were phasers, so she could be safely ignored for now. If she survived long enough to reach the pirates' base, heavier armament would be added.

"Helmsman, bring her around and fire torpedoes!" The Captain ordered.

This time, the shields on the pirate ship suffered, but they weren't down yet. The two ships continued to exchange fire. Already heavily damaged, the *Stardust's* shields gave out first.

"Communication from the enemy ship," Shawnee called.

"Bring it up on the main screen Lieutenant Shawnee," Abernathy ordered.

The view of space disappeared from the screen, replaced by the head and shoulders of the pirate captain. "Captain Abernathey, we meet again," Captain Grimlocke said.

The captain nodded and looked his enemy in the eye. "That we do, Captain Grimlocke. I don't suppose you've decided to relinquish your part of the map to me?"

"Not quite, I came here to take yer part off yer hands. There are lots of dangerous ships out here by Cortsea. I figured I'd offer a helping hand," Grimlocke said with a smile.

"A gentleman as always, Grimlocke."

"As a gentleman, then, I offer you a choice: give me the map, or regret doing it the hard way."

"The second pirate ship is still with us, Captain," the helmsman quietly told Abernathy. "But she's only got one shuttlecraft on board."

"We're not giving up without a fight," Captain Abernathey said defiantly at Grimlocke.

"Have it your way, Captain, but don't say I didn't warn ya," the pirate said with a wicked grin. The screen flashed away, revealing only space.

Captain Abernathey slowly reached his communicator. He changed the settings so it would be a complete all call to the entire *Stardust*.

"Attention crew of the *Stardust*. This is your captain speaking. We have currently engaged an enemy pirate ship. I repeat: we have engaged an enemy pirate ship. I need all pilots to report to hangar bays immediately. Officers and Lieutenants, we will be doing attack plan code Delta, make sure your teams are following suit. I need all hands on deck: We are at war."

****

Chapter 34

Preparations

As the sirens continued to blare as Abernathy turned to Karson. "You said you found the traitor?"

"It was Otho, sir, he admitted it to me," Karson said.

"Where is he now?"

"In Cargo Bay 2, sir," Hague replied, "he is currently engaged in combat with some members of security with Barnet, his accomplice."

Captain John Abernathey's beak hung wide open, first pirates and now this? "Of course, this would all come to boil now." He turned on his own communicator, "Chief Wiggins, please take a squad to Cargo Bay 2 if you have not already. It seems we found our mystery communicator."

Static. Then Wiggins' voice broke through, "already on it, Captain. I'll be putting them in the brig. Once we deal with the pirates, we can handle these two."

"Affirmative, over," Abernathy said as he turned to address the young men. "Hague, head down to the Shield room, try to offer any assistance there. We need those shields to hold as long as possible. Karson, you report to Hangar Bay 2 to help the pilots get ready."

"I can fly a ship," Karson interjected.

"Not when it comes to pirates. I can not risk a member of my crew or a valuable ship. Please understand," the captain tried to reason.

"Captain! Should I scramble the fighters?" An officer questioned from the bridge.

"Let's go, Karson," Hague said as he dragged his friend to the turbolift.

Time seemed to be whirlwind for the two young men. Both reported to their stations and did their best to assist during the chaos.

Hague was not entirely familiar with shield generators, but he offered input when asked. He took care of the minor details of the jobs so the professional engineers could focus more on the task at hand. They were able to bring the shields back up to 80%, but due to the fire they were taking, it kept fluctuating dangerously. The longer the shields held up, the less damage the *Stardust* would actually take. Being a Federation vessel, it had powerful shields as well as bays of fighter ships in case of such situations. The threat of enemy ships was always a threat out in the deep black abyss of space. However, even a great ship like the *Stardust* had its limits. The crew worked diligently to keep it from that point as long as they could.

****

Karson had a bit of an easier time in the hangar bay, but the chaos was everywhere. He raced about helping pilots get into their gear and into their ships. Once the pilot was loaded in, he would run to the next one. It was here that he found Dawson again.

"Dawson! I'd give ya a hug, but maybe after we beat the pirates," Karson called as he ran to the next and final pilot.

Dawson gave the young man a hand with getting the pilot ready, and once the pilot was in the fighter, he spoke.

"Think nothing of it, had to help ya out. Were you heading now?"

"Into a ship," Karson said boldly as he walked to the last one in the hangar.

"Have you ever flown a Sparrow before?" Dawson asked as he walked behind his friend.

"Not in real life, but in simulations," Karson said.

"You can't fight against pirates! That ship is huge! The cannons on those alone are enough to blast you apart."

"I know," Karson replied flatly as he reached the ship.

"You know the *Antares* also has fighter bays, right? Those ships are better models than our own Sparrows. Those pirates are not playing around either!"

Karson nodded as he put on his helmet.

"Well, I didn't save you just to let you die now," Dawson said as he climbed into the cockpit.

"Dawson, you can't stop me," Karson replied.

"I'm not," the cyborg replied.

Karson looked puzzled. "Then what are you doing in there?"

"Plugging into the system, seeing if I can give you a bit of extra help."

"Plugging in?"

"Like I've told ya before," Dawson chuckled, "sometimes being a cyborg has its perks. These cybernetic implants do a lot more than their primary functions."

Karson joined in the laughter as his friend jumped down. "Well, I better help ya before someone yells at me," Dawson winked.

Once Karson was settled in the ship, he bypassed the voice command and switched on the navigations and programmed it for flight. So far, things were going exactly like the simulation. He smiled with pride. To think that a few months ago, he was trying to fly a ship by using the operating systems for help. He grabbed the wheel and flipped the switch to start the thrusters. His stomach did a little flip as he felt the Sparrow pushed its way out of the hangar bay. He was defying orders, and he knew he was taking more risks than just spending time in the brig. His life was on the line and the chance of never seeing his mother again. If he did not make it back, his mother could have a harder time making money to make ends meet. Then there was Hague, his best friend. *No*, he thought to himself, *I am making it back. No matter what those pirates throw at me, I will make it back to the* Stardust *alive.*

Chapter 35

Dog Fight

Karson's ship flew through the emptiness of space as it raced to catch up with the other pilots. He was about to turn into their frequencies on the intercom, to receive and give orders, when a robotic voice rang through the cockpit.

"Karson! Can you hear me?"

"Dawson?" Karson thought aloud as he felt the ship lurch a bit due to his distraction.

"Awesome, I tuned into your frequency perfectly."

"Wait, you can do that?"

"It's not the best since I don't have control over the ship, but since my eye is cybernetic, I can 'see' everything."

"Like my scanners and whatnot?"

"Precisely, my friend. I'm heading to the shield generator rooms now. Figured I can try to help Hague too."

"Isn't that a dangerous multitask?" Karson grew nervous as he approached the ships.

"Don't worry Karson, I'll be mostly helping you. But making it look like I am helping Hague, see?"

"If you say so," Karson gulped as he switched his targeting computer on and readied the cannons.

"A Sparrow is designed to be small guard support," Dawson lectured, "their cannons may not be as powerful as the pirate ship's defenses. But you might be able to take a ship or two out. And they are very speedy, which may be your saving grace."

"I have the targeting computer on too."

"That will also help."

Karson put on a brave face even though no one could see, He sharpened his focus on his opponents. He saw the cannons from both large ships firing on each other and a flurry of smaller laser fire from the smaller fighter ships. He saw other Sparrow fighter ships alluding and combating the enemy fighter ships. The color of the ships gave the advantage in this space dog fight. While the fighter ships of the Stardust were light brown in complexion. Denoting mute colors to be associated with peaceful intentions, the enemy ships were better suited for actual space combat.

"I can barely see the enemy ships, Dawson," Karson called out.

"Just what I feared," Dawson's voice had grown more staticky, a side effect of all the firing around him, "those are Galactic Federation Class-A Ravens. Named after their dark and reflective color, they were designed to be camouflaged perfectly with the emptiness of space. A new addition to their stealth."

"How did a pirate crew get their hands on those fighters?" Karson questioned as he began to fire his cannons on the enemy ships that drew too close.

"Stole them and their ship, lad," Dawson explained. "I heard that a Galactic Federation ship was stolen from the Capitol Planets by pirates, but I didn't think I would live to see it."

"*This* is that stolen ship?"

"Aye lad, I didn't know we were facing against Captain Flint Grimlocke and his crew. I'll help ya Karson, but if it gets too dangerous, I'll need you to fall back."

Karson pretended to not hear him as he fired back at the enemy ship. He did an evasive maneuver and was able to get under the enemy ship, which he quickly fired on and sent the ship spinning out of control before it exploded.

"Got one!" Karson screamed in triumph over his intercom.

"Keep it up!" Dawson encouraged, "the fewer fighters attacking the ship, the easier our job will be at the shield generators."

****

At the bridge, Captain Abernathy gave an order, "Lieutenant Shawnee, what is our status on the fighters?"

"All our bays are scrambled, and we have taken little loses," Shawnee reported.

Even a small loss is great when it is unnecessary, John thought bitterly to himself. He reached to grab his intercom, "Commander Wagoner, report on the shield generators."

"We are keeping it steady above 60%, Captain," Wagoner's voice was heard over the intercom. "If those fighters can keep the enemy at bay, we might be able to outlast this."

First Mate Scalemander walked up to the captain, "do you think we could outrun or outlast against Grimlocke?"

"Hard to say," Abernathy stroked his beak as he replied. "Grimlocke won't give up his portion of the map unless he is about to lose."

"Should we send a distress signal?"

"We tried, the *Antares* is scrambling our code somehow."

"Galactic Federation regulations prohibit that type of tech on a vessel of that class," Scalemander responded astonished.

"It is Grimlocke," Captain Abernathy replied bitterly, "no doubt his crew did plenty of modifications to it. I wouldn't be surprised if his weapons were altered as well."

"Are you implying…"

"That Grimlocke is toying with us? Yes, Tucson, I am."

A horrified look took over the first mate's face, "what would you like me to do, sir?"

"Let's keep putting on the pressure, but be ready in case we fail."

The first mate nodded.

****

Dawson made it to the shield generator room and made straight for Hague. When the Rhungo saw him, he smiled but then quickly grew confused.

"Dawson? What are you doing here?"

"No time!" The cyborg said as he opened up a panel and pretended to keep busy.

"Hey, this panel needs help, not that one. What game are you playing at now?"

"I'm helping Karson pilot a Sparrow, so I need to look busy to keep helping him."

"Karson's flying? But the Captain will kill him for that!"

"If the enemy doesn't first," the cyborg replied bluntly, "so help me out and cover me."

Hague groaned but agreed. He continued to fix his panel as he heard Dawson give advice and directions to his friend. Hague figured that any help would be necessary to keep his friend alive. After he fixed his panel, he got up to inspect the next one, still listening to the cyborg.

"Good, keep it up... How are they positioned? Okay, try to do that trick you did earlier...You got someone behind you! Keep it going...Spin now! Fantastic! Great shot!"

Hague felt his heart racing, his friend was locked in life or death combat and here he was helping the shields. Truthfully, both friends were working hard to protect the other. Karson fighting off ships so Hague would get the shields going, and Hague working on the shields so Karson would return to the hangar bay.

Just then, a loud crash was heard and felt that shook the entire *Stardust*. Crewmembers braced themselves as more sirens blared, and emergency lights flashed. Hague had slipped and fallen into Dawson, who, in turn, slid and hit the opposite wall with a clanking thud.

"You okay, Dawson?" Hague asked as he helped his cyborg friend up.

"Fine, just a bit banged up. Karson, did you see what hit us?"

Silence.

"Well?" Hague looked worried.

"It was fire from the *Antares* itself. They are starting to fire several cannons at once, trying to break us down in large waves. Like an ancient battering ram."

As if to prove a point, another hit landed on the shields that sent the ship shaking. Dawson and Hague scrambled to climb up as they heard an officer shout over the intercom.

"Shields down to 20% Captain, another fire like that, and we will be blown apart!"

The minutes felt like hours as they waited for a response from Captain Abernathey.

Chapter 36

Final Call

Safety on his ship, Captain Flint Grimlocke, starred arrogantly out at the scene that lay before him. He saw his fighter ships turning the crew of the *Stardust* into debris and its shields flashing in and out like an emergency flare. He was glad that his men had installed that signal scrambler when they had abducted the *Antares*. Now the second part of the map would be his.

"Any word from Abernathey, Sharky?" The pirate captain asked his first mate.

Sharky, a blonde human, replied, "Nothing yet, Captain. But they really can't take another wave of fire like that."

Grimlocke smiled again, "that you are right, my friend, that you are."

****

At the bridge of the *Stardust*, Captain Abernathy and his officers stood and debated.

"Shields are almost gone, any more energy we siphon from the ship could cause a deplete in life support. We are just about out of firepower as well," Wagoner reported.

"Shawnee," the Captain ordered, "tell the fighters to retreat. We can't win this fight."

"Are we about to try to negotiate?" Scalemander asked.

"We can try," Abernathey replied, "if we can save the *Pegasus* plans, then we should be safe. I'll try to entertain Grimlocke as best I can then try to barter our freedom for the map. Then we can send a signal."

"Think Grimlocke will let us get out alive?"

"I can only pray."

****

Karson had just taken out his third fighter when he heard a female voice rang over the intercom.

"All fighters of the Stardust, please return to the main hangar bay. Retreat. I repeat: retreat to the main hangar bay."

Karson did not argue but began to turn around and head back to the hangar bay. He figured he had little time to get back before they would shut the doors to prevent enemy ships from sneaking on. *If they are ordering us all to return to the main bay then we must have lost a lot more pilots than I thought*, Karson reflected bitterly as he raced back.

"Karson, Hague says to meet us at the bridge when you get here," Dawson spoke over the intercom.

"You got it," Karson replied. *Perhaps Abernathy has a better plan. I know he will focus on keeping the plans safe, and then the map. Maybe I could help protect them.*

****

Karson left the turbolift once it reached the bridge. He spied Hague and Dawson with Captain Abernathey and First Mate Scalemander and hurried over to them. As he approached, he could hear the captain giving an order.

"Send a wave to Grimlocke, it's time we play his game."

It was only a few minutes before Grimlocke again appeared on the screen in front of the entire crew.

"Ready to surrender?" Grimlocke mocked.

"We are willing to negotiate," Captain Abernathy corrected.

"You had yer chance for that earlier, Abernathey. Now that part of the map will be mine. I hope you set the table for me because I'll be visiting your ship shortly."

As he finished speaking, the communication faded to static.

There was a long pause on the bridge before another message was heard. This time it was a voice-over Captain Abernathey's intercom.

"Captain, the pirates have boarded the hangar bays! Repeat the…" Chief Wiggin's never got to finish his report as a phaser fire cut him down.

Abernathy activated his com once more; this time, it was an all-call. "Attention all crew. We are being boarded by pirates. Security to the hangar bays."

Officers and lieutenants took control of their own teams and began to shout orders and preparations. Security was being sent to the shuttle bays as well to protect them. In case that some of the crew could escape.

"Get to safety," Captain Abernathy shouted to Karson and Hauge.

"I want to help," the young man argued.

"I can fire a phaser," Hague complained

The Captain shot a pirate leading more off the turbolift and briefly turned to the young men.

"You boys are not soldiers. Up here, they'll kill you. Down below, you both stand a chance. Go to the galley and stay with the cook. You're both young enough that the pirates will probably make you join their crew."

"I don't want to join their crew," Karson protested.

"There's got to be another way," Hague joined.

Just then, another wave of pirates boarded the bridge, shooting everything in their path.

"You boys can sneak off in the shuttles if worse comes to worst. You two have lives to lead. You two need to make it back home."

Hearing those words, Karson and Hague gave in. Then Karson remembered the treasure map and the plans. They had to get them before the pirates did. He grabbed Captain's arm. "Sir, the map and plans."

The Captain reached into a pocket and produced a key. "It's in my locker. Get it before the pirates do."

"Aye, sir."

Chapter 37

A Mirror of Captains

Slipping through the pairs of battling men wasn't easy. Karson ducked phaser fire as Hague shoved a pirate aside. That caused the pirate to shoot the leg of another pirate, allowing an officer and crewman to finish him off. They ducked into the hallway and raced to the captain's quarters. Having no weapons of their own, speed was their only option. As soon as they saw the door, they ran for it and slipped inside. Karson went to Captain Abernathey's locker and found the tablet with the map and another with the plans. He passed the map tablet to Hague.

"I have the *Pegasus* plans, you can take the map."

"You trust me with the map?" Hague looked curious and touched.

"Of course, once we get to safety, we can have both on a chip or something. But for now, let us keep them separate. If the pirates get the map, we lose the treasure..."

"But if they get the plans, we could lose the galaxy," Hague finished.

Karson gave a solemn nod.

After checking to see if the corridor was empty, they headed for the mess. Once they got to the stairs, a photon torpedo blasted into the galley, creating a huge hole. The alarms sounded as a vortex sucked up everything from the kitchen. Hague hit another emergency shut off switch as the doors closed around the kitchen, sealing everything else from being sucked out.

Karson and Hague fell to the ground. They had been bracing themselves from the suction, and it was a miracle that neither of them had been blown into space. He then noticed Hague crying.

"Hague?"

"Borris...I saw him...he...didn't make it." Hague began to sob. Karson wrapped his arms around his friend as he too felt sorry for the cook. But he soon roused up his friend, both knowing that sitting and crying would solve nothing. They had to think of another plan.

"Where could we get a phaser?" Karson asked.

Hague sniffled the last of his tears and replied, "I have no idea. We couldn't take on all those pirates anyway."

"Hey, come on," Karson encouraged as he helped his friend to his feet. "While we are alive, there is hope, right?"

"You might have been born under a lucky star," Hague said, humor at the edges of his comment, "but I am not so sure about the rest of us."

As they left the corridor, they were surrounded by a few pirates, the boys surrendered, figuring if they were together, they would have a better chance for survival. They were marched up to the bridge with a few other captors among them.

When they arrived, Karson saw the meanest, ugliest man he had ever seen standing tall in front of Captain Abernathy. Hague noticed that the only officers that were standing with the Captain were the first mate, Commander Wagoner, and Lieutenant Shawnee.

Just then, two pirates knocked Hague and Karson to their knees and dragged them to a group full of bound members of the crew. Karson recognized Tonks and Dawson among them. Hague nodded to his friend, a sign they should keep it quiet. Since most of the attention was on the two captains, Hague and Karson were able to slowly move closer to Dawson.

"What's going on?" Karson whispered to the cyborg.

"Captain Abernathey is negotiating with Grimlocke."

"Is he really in a position for that?

"Not sure, lad," the cyborg whispered.

"Surrender, and I'll let the last of yer crew live!" The pirate captain roared, breaking up the conversation between the captured.

Captain Abernathy looked around. Only three of his officers were still on their feet. Many were dead, others wounded too severely to fight. He suspected it was the same throughout the ship.

"Do as he says. Put down your weapons and surrender," he told his crew, sending his words through the intercom so all could hear him.

A few continued fighting, but soon it was all over. The pirates had won. The pirate captain gave orders to sweep the rest of the ship for survivors. It was almost half an hour when the remaining members of the Stardust were brought onboard the bridge.

"That's all that chose to surrender captain," Lonnie said with a smile.

"Those who decided not to?"

Lonnie chuckled, "Otho did a decent job recruiting for ya captain. A dozen or so workers have pledged loyalty to you."

"That should help replenish the troops. And the rest?"

"Took a nice deep space sleep."

The pirate captain grew another evil grin. He turned from his first mate to address his new captives.

"My name's Captain Flint Grimlocke, the scourge of the deep space, and I am the only acting captain now." He scanned the bridge, too many female members of the crew for his own suspicious blood, but there were still plenty of male workers that could do the dirty work for his own men. Grimlocke decided to play the power game. He knew that Abernathy had the first part of the map, but any extra goods would also be welcomed aboard his ship.

"My first order," Captain Grimlocke said, "is that we take a look and see what kind of cargo they have onboard." His cocky attitude turned ugly when his first mate returned to the bridge with the bad news.

"There's no cargo, Captain," Sharky reported hesitantly.

"What do you mean there's no cargo? Is that true?" Leaving the captain's chair, he stalked over Lieutenant Shawnee and grabbed her by the arm. "Is that true? There's no cargo?"

She wanted to spit her reply at him, but knowing she was already on shaky ground, she kept her calm. "That's right. We delivered our cargo of food and supplies to a Federation colony."

"And being a colony, no doubt fairly new, they had nothing to ship out. Did they?"

"Nothing."

"Nothing, what?" Grimlocke said, giving her a nasty shake.

Shawn knew he wanted her to call him, sir, but she wouldn't. When her silence continued, he shoved her.

"Let her go, Grimlocke," Abernathey warned. "You have issues with me, leave the crew alone."

"Have it your way." Turning to Sharky, he said, "Load the women into escape pods and set their courses for Cortsea. By the time the shuttles get there, we will have been long gone. Round up the male prisoners and put them to work. I want the crew's quarters and every last room on this ship search for valuables." He then turned to Captain Abernathey, "let us take our little party to the shuttle bays then, shall we?"

****

The pirates put the captured crew to work, hauling anything of value up to one of the shuttle bays for inspection. Captain Grimlocke leaned against one of the *Stardust*'s shuttlecraft and watched as his first mate related their puny treasure to him. Abernathey was standing with two armed pirates guarding him. Scalemander and Wagoner were also under guard but placed further away. No member of the Stardust crew was allowed to talk to each other. Captain Grimlocke ordered no phaser to be spared in case of disobedience.

Grimlocke told him what to keep and what to offer to his crew. Then with two of his men in tow, he went to check out Abernahtey's quarters.

Stripping the room of everything valuable, including the clothing, he dumped in all in the captain's suitcase.

"Take this to my own quarters," he ordered one of his crewmen.

215

"Aye, Captain."

****

Grimlocke returned to the shuttle bay with his men. Karson noticed the almost calm look on Grimlocke's face. It made him uneasy.

"Did you find what you were looking for?" Abernathey taunted Grimlocke.

"Don't get cute with me, John," Grimlocke replied as he aimed his charging phaser at his head. "Where is it?"

Abernathey chuckled and looked down at the ground. He would not reveal the location of the map. He did not think that Grimlocke was aware of the plans for the *Pegasus*, and he planned on keeping him in the dark as long as possible.

Grimlocke gave an order to bring the remainder of the crew, both pirate and captured. It was time he played his final card.

"Gentlemen," he said with an evil charm in his smile. "While I appreciate the bit of entertainment, you have givin' me, but it is time we end our games. Where is the first part of the map?"

"What map?" Dawson asked from the surviving members of the crew. A few small smiles escaped, but the team remained silent.

Grimlocke returned the grin as he placed his phaser on Commander Wagoner's head. "Captain Nova Scarm's treasure map. The map that leads to his final treasure, or what may be left of it." He turned to face Wagoner, who still remained calm, "ringin' any bells?"

Hector Wagoner slowly shook his head, which he knew would be his last action.

Karson flinched as Hague moved his head towards him, neither wanted to see what happened.

A few of Grimlocke's men moved Wagoner's body away as the pirate captain moved his phaser to the first mate's head. "How about we try this again, Tucson? Though, I know Hector's stubbornness is a side effect of your mentoring after all these years."

Tuscon Scalemander smiled as he reflected on his long life out in space. His adventures under Captain Abernathey's command, his first voyage, and even the few moments that brought him joy on this voyage. "Hector is a bit more tight-lipped than me, I am afraid."

Grimlocke smiled, but so did Abernathey, he knew his first mate better than what Grimlocke was thinking.

"So hear me, Grimlocke, you may search for a thousand years on a thousand planets, and you will never, never, find that treasure."

Grimlocke's anger took over, but it was a long time until the smug smile of Tuscon Scalemander was erased from his memory. He then placed his phaser to Captain Abernathy's head.

"Your men are loyal to you, always have been. Though, I don't think we can end our rivalry so soon. So, I think I'll put you in an escape pod. Off with you now," Captain Grimlocke said with a laugh.

Two pirates escorted Captain Abernathy to the escape pods and shoved him inside one. As soon as he blasted off, they returned to the bridge. The remainder of the

Stardust's crew wanted to lash out at them, but overwhelmed and unarmed, they were helpless.

A pleased smile crossed his face. "Bring Otho to me," he ordered the other pirate.

The pirate returned shortly with Otho.

"Who's the cook on this ship?"

"Boris, but he's dead," Otho replied.

Captain Grimlocke growled and placed his hand on his phaser.

"But it's okay," Otho stammered. "Karson and Hague used to do most of the cooking when Boris was sick. We took them aboard back on Nergal. But they were the ones who were on to me about the communique. We should blast them into space."

"They found out about you?" Grimlocke said, his eyes ablaze with hatred.

Otho stammered, realizing his mistake, but the pirate captain simply shot him with his phaser.

Captain Grimlocke turned to his men. "Find them and bring him here."

Back at the bridge, a pirate asked the *Stardust*'s crew about Karson and Hague.

"Are they still alive?"

"Sorry, don't know," one of the captured men said.

The pirate asked a couple more with similar results until Barnet overheard him. He had survived the shootout with security and was released when the pirates took over the ship. He did not know, however, that Captain Grimlocke had taken out Otho moments before.

"You're looking for Karson and Hague?"

"Know who they are?" The pirate asked.

"Why?" Barnet grew increasingly curious.

"Captain wants him."

Barnet smiled and pointed Karson and Hague out and watched as pirates grabbed them both by the arms and pulled them across the shuttle bay.

"Captain Grimlocke won't treat you as nicely as Otho, and I did," Barnet sneered as the boys were ushered past him. "Now, you'll get your just desserts."

Before they could go below, Captain Grimlocke appeared in the shuttle bay, and the pirate took the young men over to him.

"These the ones?" The pirate captain asked.

"Aye, sir."

"I hear you boys used to do the cooking. Is that true?"

Karson remained silent. Hague stared at the ground.

Captain Grimlocke wasn't stupid. With a calculating look, he grabbed Hague and placed his phaser to the young Rhungo's chest. He then looked at Karson.

"Speak, or he dies."

"Okay. I'll talk. Yes, we did the cooking."

"That's more like it." Turning to one of the pirates, Captain Grimlocke said, "Take them to my ship but don't hurt them. If they can cook as well as Otho said, they might replace that old android I have."

The next few hours dragged on as Grimlocke's men loaded the stolen goods and men into the ship. They even made off with a few of the remaining Sparrow ships. Sharky, the first mate, figured any fighter ship would be better than none. He then ordered his men to set charges on the *Stardust* so it would implode once they made it safely out of reach.

Once everything was loaded onto Grimlocke's ship, the vessels pulled away. Both ships headed for some unknown planet, leaving the *Stardust* empty and hanging in space. Karson and Hague bit back tears as they saw their beloved ship implode behind them.

Chapter 38

The Pirate Ship

A large male Krellian shoved Karson and Hague along one of the ship's corridors, heading for the brig. As they passed through the ship, the two friends took a quick look around and discovered that the environment here was very different from that of the *Stardust*.

The crew was a rough band of thieves, killers, and thugs. Although Captain Grimlocke's word was law, the men were quarrelsome and rowdy. It was survival of the fittest, and those unfortunate prisoners captured from other starships became slaves or worse, unless or until they proved themselves as worthy members of the crew. The crew was dressed differently, too. Captain Flint Grimlocke wore an elegant, black, military-style coat with deep burgundy turned-back lapels and cuffs. The clothing of the crew was more colorful, too, no doubt with hidden connections to their lives as pirates or to their own homeworlds.

The pirates separated the two friends. One took Karson to the left side of the brig, and Hague was placed on the far right side. Both friends could not reach or communicate with each other. The pirates threw them down hard on the ground and, after turning off the force field, locked him up.

"Don't worry, someone will come back tomorrow to get yeah. If anyone can remember," Karson's captor spat at him.

Left alone in the dark, Karson paced the floor and began talking to himself. Like the rest of the ship, the cell was filthy and smelled of stale sweat and nastier things left behind by other prisoners.

"This is great. Things were just getting good on the *Stardust*. Now I have to start all over again from the bottom." He kicked the wall of his cell and sank to a metallic shelf that served as a bed. Drawing up his knees, he dropped his head with a sigh of desperation. "I was finally getting to where I wanted to be."

A young man the same age, but smaller than Karson, emerged from behind the guard's station that was never manned. "Did they destroy your ship?"

Karson looked up in surprise and stared at him. Although light streamed in through the door of the security office from the corridor, he couldn't ultimately make out the boy's features.

"Yes. The *Stardust* is no more. They used chargers to destroy it when they took me aboard. How did you get in here? Are you a pirate as well?"

"No, I am a prisoner like you. They stole the cruiser my family and I were on and made me into a cabin boy against my will."

"How did they manage to steal the cruiser?" Karson asked.

"My father gave most of the crew the night off. They were asleep when a cloaked pirate ship caught up to us. They flew two shuttlecraft into our landing bay. None of the crew survived. We never had a chance," the boy said.

As Karson's eyes became used to the darkness, he was able to make out the boy's features a little clearer.

"Was that the second ship that came at us?"

222

"Yes."

"What happened to the rest of your family?"

"They're dead." Tears ran down his cheeks, and he angrily wiped them from his face with his sleeve. "Grimlocke shot them."

Karson blanched. Remembering Scalemander and Wagoner. He then thought about Captain Abernathey, he hoped he would be rescued or that his shuttle would reach Cortsea. He thought about his own mother, how would he have felt if she was taken away from him?

"I'm sorry about your parents. I honestly can't imagine what I would do if that happened to my mother. Why'd they take you prisoner?" Karson asked. Clearly, he couldn't understand what the pirates wanted with the quarrelsome boy.

"My parents pretended I was just another member of the crew. Hoping I could escape, they figured I'd have a better chance if the pirates took me."

"Well, at least we have some hope."

"Why would you say that?"

"If you're not dead, there's always a chance. My friend and I were captured, and I am not sure if any other members of my crew survived. But while I am alive, I refuse to give up hope. We can think of something."

"Do you really think so?" The young man's voice filled with hope.

"Yes, and you should, too. Never give up. Look, once we're back planetside, my friend and I are going to escape. Come with us," Karson said.

"I don't need your help. I can take care of myself."

"Okay, fine. I just figured we'd have a better chance if we stay together." Karson looked away from him.

"Is such a thing possible?"

"Yes, we'll have to be careful, but with determination, I believe we can make it. The pirates won't stay out here forever. They'll have to return to their base planet and unload their loot."

"How would we escape them? It's not like we'd have a phaser with us."

"I don't know, but I'd think of something. What's your name?"

"Drake."

"Drake, you sure are negative."

"I like to think of it as realistic," Drake said.

Karson took a closer look at him and wondered. The young man's features were soft, but with all the dirt on his face, it was hard to tell for sure.

Chapter 39

Unexpected Allies

Karson got up and sat on the metallic shelf next to Drake in the dark cell.

"Why are you in the brig, if you're part of the crew?" Karson asked. "Did you do something wrong?"

Drake shook his head. "The captain thought I was too frail to fight. He didn't want me in the way. Maybe he thought I might try to escape."

"Would you? Would you have tried?" Karson asked, barely able to contain his excitement over a possible friend and fellow conspirator.

"Well, I…," the disheveled boy looked at his cellmate, quickly assessing whether he could be trusted.

"Yes," he said at last with confidence, looking into his eyes, and deciding Karson was a reasonable risk, possibly a great ally. "Yes. I was planning to do just that – try to get off this ship and hide on the *Stardust*. Even though they confiscated our ship, I had no idea the pirates would use it right away. I thought, or hoped, the *Stardust*'s crew would win the battle despite the odds."

Without warning, tears filled the cabin boy's eyes, and he started to cry; quietly at first until his face seemed to crumple. Karson reached over to pat the distraught boy on the back. Then Drake threw himself into his arms. In shock, he hugged the younger boy, feeling sorry for him. The cabin boy was quite skinny and much more fragile than he looked at first. The sobbing boy held onto Karson and shook in his arms, tears running down his dirty face and onto his lips; slightly soft, pink lips…for a boy. Karson studied the small oval face.

"You're a girl," he whispered in the ear next to his chest. Holding the cabin boy at arms' length, he looked closer at the tear-stained face. "You're a girl, aren't you?"

Serena remained stock-still and looked into the brown eyes staring at her. Her mouth opened, but nothing came out.

"The pirates! The pirates, of course. When they attacked your ship, you pretended to be a boy to…to protect yourself." He looked at the quivering girl in front of him. "Amazing that you pulled it off. No one knows?"

The tears and shaking stopped, and Serena looked at him with strong determination.

"No, well, not exactly. I got food poisoning, and when Lonnie tried to change my shirt, he found out."

Karson grew alarmed. "And he hasn't told anyone?"

"He was going to. He blamed me for the ship's running out of supplies and that we haven't come across any prey in days. Said I was a curse."

"Then why didn't he tell his captain?"

"He figured if he had this knowledge, he could use it to his advantage. So far, it has just been covering some dirty jobs that he didn't want to do. Or extra food rations from my own plate."

Karson thought for a moment. "You must be careful. Since he hasn't told anyone yet, he's waiting to use the information later when he can get the most advantage out of it."

Serena nodded. "I thought as much. But how did you figure it out?"

"I don't know exactly. You just seemed kind of soft, and when you…"

"Soft? I'm anything but soft." She held up her skinny arms and flexed her taut biceps. "You call this soft?"

She held out her hands. "Look at these calluses and broken nails. Oh, these nails, so dirty." She curled her hands into fists and hid them behind her back.

Karson started to laugh. His eyes crinkled up as he shook his head and laughed some more.

"What's your real name?"

"Serena."

"Look at you, Serena. You are hidden away on a pirate ship out in the middle of the Atlantic, performing all the duties of a pirate, and fooling an entire crew. And yet, you're ashamed of your broken nails? That is rich!"

"Why, you…you…." Then she looked at the handsome young man and started to laugh. It was humorous if you could stand back and look at it. The relief, the happiness that filled her heart for that moment, was so excellent. She hadn't laughed in, how long? Months? She hadn't smiled since before the day she watched the pirates set her parents adrift in a lifeboat and was forced to get on this horrible ship.

"What are you two monkey boys laughin' at?"

The voice of a pirate cut into their moment of levity. They both looked at the snarly pirate with fear. Had he overheard Karson when he confronted Serena about being a girl?

"Ach, what do I care? Captain's hungry. Lots of celebratin' to do, and he wants a feast. So you," the burly pirate pointed to Karson, "will be workin' with Chef in the kitchen. And you, Drakey boy, will be helpin'," he said, opening the cell door and walking inside.

Inwardly, both sighed with relief as the pirate placed a filthy hand on each of their shoulders. He gave them a squeeze as he pushed them out of the cell toward the galley.

When they arrived in the galley, the cook's back was to them.

"That you, Husk? Or Sharky?" He asked.

"Brought you some new help," Husk replied. "Cap'n says he was a good cook on the ship we just captured." He shoved Karson and Serena toward the cook, who, hearing the sound moved out of the way. "Also threw in Drake too, figured he couldn't do too much damage here. Better make something good if you don't want to be keelhauled."

As soon as Husk left, the cook spoke up.

"Most people call me Chef. I know Drake, but what's your name?"

"Karson."

"Glad to meet you." Chef turned and held out his hand.

He's an android! Karson thought. Though this android was different than the few that Karson had come in contact with back on Nergal. Instead of being designed to resemble more human-like creatures, it resembled more of a robotic skeleton. His gears and mechanisms were rusty brown, probably denoting the age of the robot, his arms and legs were thin and resembled human bones. His mouth was a simple speaker, and his eyes were large screens that had iris' that moved slowly, to mimic human eyes.

Karson shook the robotic hand, trying to stifle his surprise.

"Though I am surprised to see you here, Drake. Guess you got demoted, eh? Must have ticked off the Cap'n."

"No, just thought I was too weak for topside," Serena replied.

"Oh good, so he sent ya my way," Chef grumbled. "Everything is stored exactly where I like it, so don't change anything around."

"Yes...sir," Karson attempted.

"I am no sir, so don't call me that," Chef seemed to snap on the boy. "I am a GX-86 android originally designed for...for…" Chef started to shake a bit before his eyes turned off.

"Is that normal?" Karson asked.

"I am not sure," Serena said. "I actually have never worked with Chef before, just saw him during the meals. Though I have heard complaints about him due to his programming."

Just then, Chef's eyes turned on, and the android began to speak again. "Sorry about that, I am an older model of android, so sometimes my systems just need a quick break. I have been programmed, erased, and reprogrammed for so long that sometimes...I forget what I was originally built for."

"How did you end up on this ship?" Karson asked.

"I was stolen off of some outer core planet way before Grimlocke was captain of this crew." Chef shook his head sadly. "I remember the first captain, a large Zanian named Tublot Kral, he gave me my first reprogram. I have served under several captains aboard various vessels. Like I mentioned, it has been so long and so many memory wipes that I can't recall all the details exactly."

Meeting Chef made Karson's spirits rise, even though he was distressed to hear about his life with the pirates. He figured this android was a much older model than he was letting on. Still, he might have made an unexpected ally after all.

"I'm sure we'll work quite well together," Karson said.

"So, you cooked, too? Are you familiar with any of this technology?" Chef questioned. "Since we took over the *Antares*, I have been having a hard time learning this updated technology."

Karson was a bit overwhelmed too, he thought the kitchen tech on the *Stardust* was impressive. The *Antares* had much more sophisticated tech, he figured better play to their strengths in terms of cooking.

"My friend, who was taken on board with me, could figure this out. I'm as lost as you. So why don't we try to cook something simple?"

Chef nodded, a small gear shifting sound, "They aren't very picky as long as it is good. To be honest, the tech here is lightyears ahead of our previous ship, so they won't be expecting a gourmet meal."

"The pirates confiscated the remaining food stores from my ship," Karson told him. "I used to make chicken stew. My captain liked it. How much chicken do you have?"

"We're out unless there's some in the supplies from your ship," Chef replied.

"We did, but it would take a while to find it. Why don't I make beef stew instead?"

"Excellent idea, I haven't had a chance to see what supplies they stole from your ship. The storeroom is next to the galley."

"We'll be right back," Karson promised as he and Serena headed for the storeroom.

****

Chapter 40

Shields and Chefs

Hague was not having a good time as Karson was. When Husk took Karson and Serena to the kitchen, Barnet had come to pick up the young Rhungo.

"The cyborg wants you," he said flatly as he switched off the shields around the cage.

"Dawson?" Hague asked as he rose to his feet, trying to keep any hope secret.

"The cyborg from the *Stardust*, I don't give two credits what his name is," Barnet said as he escorted Hague out of the brig, phaser in hand.

"Why me?"

Barnet groaned, clearly growing tired of talking with Hague. "Because you are the only person he deems qualified to help him repair our shields. Captain Grimlocke's ship took some decent damage from the *Stardust*. Though clearly, the better side won."

The bitter side you mean, Hague thought. Though this was a good stroke of luck, if he could work with Dawson, perhaps they could hatch a plan to escape this ship. He patted his pocket slowly, still feeling the tablet that held the plans for the treasure. He and Karson had been lucky so far. *It seems like Pleiades' luck is rubbing off on me, but we will see how long my newfound luck will serve me.*

When they reach their shield room, Hague saw Dawson sitting at the control board with three pirates guarding him. Hague recognized two of the guards as being part of Barnet's group back on board the *Stardust*.

"Here he is, one blue Rhungo, fresh from the brig," Barnet said sarcastically, his men chuckled.

"Hague, how good to see you," Dawson attempted a sophisticated accent, "these mutineers can't tell a cooling unit from their own head. Now I will have some fantastic help."

Hague spoke, ignoring their guards, "what seems to be the problem?"

"A generator took a bit of phaser fire on its external exhaust port. Since the exhaust port is shut, the generator won't run. I could use your help troubleshooting this."

The two friends began working on fixing the broken shield generator. While this was a bitter moment, fixing the ship that took them away from the *Stardust*, it was practical. If this ship could not protect itself, other pirates could show up. *If I can see how this ship operates,* Hague thought as he assisted Dawson, *we could sabotage it, should the opportunity present itself.*

***

"Wow, your ship had quite a bit of stuff," Serena said as she and Karson looked through the chaos of the stolen goods for the ingredients they needed.

"Well, we did deliver supplies to a new Federation colony," Karson explained, "though we were also in need of resupplying ourselves."

Once they found everything, the two new friends carted it back to the galley. Karson, Serena, and Chef start peeling vegetables, but they kept getting in each other's way. Chef kept shorting his circuits, which led him to keep rebooting, which was also a problem.

"I'm just in the way here," Serena said. "Why don't I go to the storeroom and organize the stuff they stole from your ship. It's such a mess in there."

"Good idea," Chef replied after another reboot. "Make sure you store the new stuff the same way I have ours arranged."

"Will do," Serena called, heading out the door.

Once she left, Karson figured this would be an excellent time to question the cooking android.

"You said you've been on the ship how long?" Karson asked.

"Uh...longer than I can remember," Chef replied.

"You must have been a part of many battles then," Karson asked innocently.

"Several," Chef said as his mechanical fingers slowly grabbed a carrot to begin peeling. "I can't remember the details, I am afraid."

Karson studied the android as he worked, while he did the job faster than Karson was used to working, the android still seemed stiff in his movements. The screens that were his eyes would often flash on and off, but that did not seem to alarm Chef.

"Sorry," Karson said as he washed the vegetables in the sink. "You said you've had memory wipes and have been reprogrammed countless times. Does that negatively affect an android?"

Chef was startled that Karson would make such an educated guess so easily. Had he figured out his secret? If so, apparently, the lad appeared to be willing to keep it to himself. "Yes." His screen eyes looked around, making sure that only the android and the human boy were the only ones in the kitchen.

"I don't know Drake's loyalty," he began, "though I have a feeling you want off this ship almost as bad as I want."

"You have a desire to leave the ship?" Karson was a bit shocked. He had never heard of an android wanting to do something different than his original programming.

"I...do..." Chef started slowly. Karson was afraid that he would reboot again, a thing that only seemed to happen when Chef was trying to figure things out beyond literal orders. Though to his surprise, the android did not reboot.

"I do not want to be here anymore," Chef struggled to say. "There has to be an error in my programming. A side effect of all I have been through. Although I can't afford to not work hard for the pirates. If they knew how old my make and model were..." His eyes began to flash again.

Karson held his breath.

Chef's eyes stopped flashing as he continued to speak. "I only know I am a GX-86 model of android. I cannot access the files that stored my original programming."

"How old is a GX-86 model of android? I'm from a poorer planet where not everyone has a personal android."

"Old. I am the fourth generation of my android class. Currently, GX androids are on their twelfth update."

Karson whistled in surprise. He knew the android was old, but he didn't think that old.

Chef continued, "if Captain Grimlocke knew that...well...I'd be in the trash compactor before you could shout. If you keep my secret, Karson, I will do all I can in my programming to help you get off this ship."

"Would you want to come with us?" Karson offered.

Chef quickly stood up and shouted, "Error...error...does, not compute." After a few minutes of that, Chef rebooted and answered the question. "You need to be careful with asking me those types of questions. I cannot answer that directly. There must be dozens of secret safe words and codes stored in my memory that override my own primary functions. Let me answer you like this then: You help me, and I will help you. Sound fair?" Karson swore he saw the android wink at him.

Now that they were in accord, things progressed smoothly, and before long, pots of stew were bubbling on the stoves. Karson was amazed at how many things Chef could do, even though he was an ancient specimen of an android.

When the meal was ready, Shark walked into the mess. "Where's the captain's dinner? He wants it now, or heads will roll. Chef you may not know how angry he is, but I do."

"What has got him so upset?" Chef asked as he programmed the cleaning devices.

"Wasn't happy with the loot from the *Stardust*," Sharky answered as he leaned on the wall.

"It's ready," Karson said, bringing a tray of food to Sharky.

Sharky took the meal up to the captain's quarters while the rest of the pirate crew huddled into the mess for grub.

Karson, Serena, and Chef did their best to serve them. Unlike the crew of the *Stardust*, who took their meals buffet-style to make everyone else's lives easier, this crew expected to be served their meals. To make matters even more complicated, various members of the crew were fighting all around him. Karson had to protect the food from spilling or falling off his trays while trying to defend himself. He ducked fists and sidestepped around the combatants. It was survival of the fittest and every man for himself.

During the dinner chaos, Hague and Karson were able to talk for a brief moment.

"Karson! Stuck back in the galley?"

"For now, where did you end up?"

"Fixing the shield generators with Dawson."

"Dawson made it onboard after all. That's good."

A shout from the kitchen brought the two back to attention.

"Stick close to him," Karson ordered, "I made a few allies here. We might be able to get outta this hole yet." Hague nodded as he took two plates and went back to sit with Dawson.

Karson walked back to the galley, it was Serena who had shouted, but he figured it was Chef who needed the help. Once he was back, he saw Chef holding a large tray with food and a bottle of rum.

"Take this to Captain Grimlocke," Chef ordered.

Karson nodded. He did not want to risk sending Serena to the captain. He also figured that if Chef went, there was a chance that one of those security commands he mentioned could go off. He was not about to risk his plans on account of an out of date android.

Karson walked inside the cabin, put the plates, forks, and glasses in their places, and put the food in the center of the table. The only word that Grimlocke said was, "More rum!"

Karson heading back to the galley and asked Chef where the rum was stored. The old android brought him to a pantry that was stocked floor to ceiling with the drink. *It probably was used for emergency provisions before they stole it. Apparently, rum is an emergency provision on a pirate ship out in deep space.*

Returning to the captain's cabin, Karson refilled everyone's glass.

Grimlocke took a long swallowed and belched. "Thanks," he admitted. "Now, head back to the galley."

Karson nodded. He was glad that Grimlocke did not want to talk to him about the *Stardust* or the treasure map. With luck, maybe he could keep himself and Serena safe until they found a way to meet up with Hague and Dawson and plan their escape.

Chapter 41

The Gang's All Here

"Don't you have to get some sleep?" Serena asked Karson as they made their way out of the kitchen. "The bunks are in the opposite direction."

"I'm sleeping in the brig. The pirates stink worse than the grossest member of the *Stardust*'s crew."

"Neither one of us smell that good either," Serena said with a smile.

"Speak for yourself," Karson replied, returning her smile.

"Okay, I don't smell that good," Serena said.

"At least things did not end too badly today," Karson said, changing the subject.

"Could have ended a lot worse, that is for sure. Though I did see Lonnie at dinner." She looked and saw Karson with a worried expression on his face. "Don't worry, I just had to give him extra soup this time. He won't sell me out just yet."

"Can you be sure?"

"If he reveals it, we can always say that he knew I was a girl and never told the captain."

"Is that much of an argument?"

"These spacers still adhere to the old superstition that women bring bad luck to ships. Lonnie having that knowledge will land him in trouble too."

Karson nodded in understanding as they approached the cells.

"Mind if I take the other shelf? I never thought about sleeping down here. It's a good idea."

"Help yourself," Karson replied.

Realizing the cell's odor was missing, she looked around. "You cleaned the place up. What a relief. With no force field, it's almost like a hotel room in here."

"I brought us each a blanket and pillow, too. Makes it rather cozy. Good night."

"Good night."

****

"Wake up," Husk said, giving Karson a not so gentle kick in the side.

The pain brought him awake. "What's wrong?"

" Look, I don't care where you cabin boys sleep just, so I know where to find you both. You need to get down to the galley right now."

"Okay. We're going." Serena said in Drake's voice.

"Time to cook," Chef replied when they arrived. "Unfortunately for you, I can't figure out the systems to get it started. Though, you can start on the coffee, Drake."

As Serena worked on her assigned task, Karson attempted to figure out the machines. It seemed similar to the ones on the *Stardust* but more advanced. It was twenty-minutes before Karson too gave up.

"I can't figure it out," Karson said.

"Know anyone who could?" Chef suggested. "If we don't get the meal rolling soon, it'll be our heads that do the rolling."

"What is going on?" Serena said as she finished loading more dishes into the dish cleaner.

"I can't figure this machine out," Karson explained. "My friend, Hague, could. He worked with our tech on the *Stardust*. But this is more advanced than that."

"Seriously?" Serena asked. "This ship has a more advanced kitchen than your ship?"

"Well, this ship was stolen off the central planets," Chef explained. "It was rumored to be the most high-tech ship in the fleet. Hence why Captain Grimlocke took it. I'll see if Sharky can bring up your friend."

****

"Here is your help," Sharky hollered as they entered the kitchen. "He wouldn't leave without the cyborg, though. But I don't give a rotten Speckledorf tail, who helps ya as long as chow is ready within the next hour. The crew is getting hungry, and so is Cap'n Grimlocke." The pirate first mate left in a huff, no doubt going to ruin another crew member's day.

Karson began the pleasantries of introducing Hague and Dawson to Drake and Chef.

"Leave it to Hague and me," Dawson began as he walked towards the kitchen machinery. "If we can get those shields up and running, we can figure out this tech."

"Dawson, I found an input, want to synch up here?" Hague asked.

The cyborg then produced a thin cord from his clothes. He plugged in one to the machine and the other on his cybernetic side of his head. His cybernetic eye began flashing information as Dawson seemed to read it.

"You're crazy!" Chef exclaimed nervously. "The ship could overrun your mainframe, or worse, you could infect the ship with a virus! Then we would be floating in space with no hope of survival!"

"Hey, I am a cyborg, not an android," Dawson barked. "I can only read the information presented to me. I can't download or upload anything. Also, how dare you accuse me of having a virus you pile of rusted…"

Karson got in between the cyborg and the android, hoping to avoid any fights.

"This is not the time! Dawson, you and Hague figure this out. Once that is settled, teach Chef how to program the systems, he can show us how it all works later. We all need to work together, okay?"

The group all nodded heads and started to perform their duties.

"Look what I found, poison. I'd like to feed it to the crew," Serena said.

"But that would leave no one to run the ship. I don't know about you, Drake, but I can't fly a vessel this big." Karson replied.

"It would just be our luck we'd be found by another pirate," Hague said dejectedly. "Let's not forget the companion ship that is also going along with us."

"The *Cirrus*," Serena explained as Drake.

Hague nodded in agreement as a chorus of yelling started from the mess.

"Where's the food?" One man yelled.

Then the pirates all began to chant.

"If we don't do something soon, we'll be in deep trouble," Chef told Karson.

"Do something, Karson," Serena whispered. "Lonnie might be out there, he might say something if this gets outta hand."

Pulling his deck of cards out of his pocket, Karson ran into the mess. "Anybody brave enough to play me in a game of cards?"

"What's the bet?" A pirate asked.

"Anything you can put in front of you," Karson smiled as he began to shuffle the cards.

The distraction was needed, several members of the pirate crew sat around and played cards.

Karson decided to do a strategy that he and Dawson would do whenever they visited a different or new tavern. He would purposely lose a few hands and even a couple of games to get the trust of the crew. They, of course, would think he was not a good gambler and would be interested in playing another round. Usually, this trick was used to sucker in more bets and make off with better winnings. But for now, this trick was used for survival. The longer he could keep the pirates entertained and betting, the more time he would buy for Hague and Dawson to figure out the machines.

Before long, he had everyone's attention. After the first hand, the men laughed and eagerly participated in the entertainment. Between games, the crew told funny stories until Chef entered the room.

"Breakfast is on!"

Cheers went up, and soon everyone was eating. One of the lieutenants entered the room.

"Eat hearty, lads. Cap'n wants every available android and machine for a complete diagnostic and overhaul of the ship. So everyone else will have to take on the remaining duties."

The men groaned as they ate, but they ate a lot. Partially because they were starving and somewhat to delay the inevitable fate of working. Karson, Drake, and Chef were kept busy by bringing in dirty dishes, loading them into the machines, and sometimes bringing out seconds or thirds of the meal. Dawson and Hague were able to figure out how the food processing machines worked and taught it to the remaining members of the kitchen crew.

During the cleaning, Serena pointed out Lonnie to Karson.

"See? The Splinthair male at the table on the farthest left?"

Karson squinted, "him? That's Lonnie?"

Serena put her fingers to her lips, "shhh, he might hear us. But yes, that is him."

Karson memorized his face as he went to gather more dishes. He would have to keep an eye on him and, at some point, share his information with Dawson and Hague. While he had not told them the truth of "Drake's" identity, he wanted to let his other companions know about the possible trouble. *Things are starting to get a little sticky.* He thought to himself as he brought the dishes back. *Though I do believe we might have enough heads together to form an escape plan.*

When he got back to the kitchen, he was surprised to see Dawon and Chef talking. He was partially surprised because he figured they would've been assigned for that diagnostic overhaul. He also was surprised that the two seemed to be getting along, especially after this morning.

He put down the dirty dishes next to Serena and walked over to them.

"Everything alright, guys?" He asked cautiously.

"Right as rain," Dawson said as he slapped Chef on his robotic back. "Chef and I were just chit-chatting about his programming and issues he has experienced."

"Dawson claims he might be able to help me," Chef explained. "Since he can read computer information with his cybernetic eye, he might be able to figure out what has happened to my programming."

"While that is great, won't the pirates be missing you? Chef, aren't you needed for that diagnostic thing?

Chef slowly shook his head, the gears making straining sounds as he did so. "Not me, too old to figure it out. They put me in the kitchen as the last option."

"What about you, Dawson?"

"The only people who know about me being here is that Sharky fellow. If he comes looking for me, you guys tell him a different lieutenant took me for the diagnostic overhaul. Since we are all so new to the ship, no one really knows us or where we are supposed to be stationed," Dawson explained.

"So, this is the perfect time to figure things out." Karson reasoned aloud.

"Precisely!" Dawson beamed, "though I'll need Hague for help. If I get too deep into this mainframe, I'll need someone from the outside to get me out."

"Is this dangerous for you?" Karson asked Dawson. "You've plugged into a lot of machinery lately. Sorry I am just not sure how that affects a cyborg."

Dawson tapped the robotic side of his head. "Don't worry, Karson. There is still plenty of human left in this skull. With respect to Chef here, it would take a much more advanced piece of equipment to override my own personality." He let out a deep laugh, to which Chef attempted with robotic-sounding "ha ha ha."

Karson smiled, if Dawson could crack Chef's code, the android might be a more significant help to their mission than he initially thought of.

Little did he know that Chef was a much more valuable android than either himself or Captain Grimlocke were aware of.

Chapter 42

Nuts and Bolts

Karson had been able to put them up with a table in the storeroom that was being used with the food from the *Stardust*. Since Serena had cleaned it, there was plenty of room for Chef to lay down on the table while Dawson and Hague stood above him. It was almost like performing surgery, except no one was being operated on.

"So, how exactly are you doing this?" Hague asked.

"Same way I have done before, just plugging in and reading what I find," Dawson explained.

"You should be able to view my files, though I am not sure if you will be able to get into them, Dawson," Chef explained.

"If we can get them unlocked, then you should be able to remember them," said Dawson. "That is the goal, after all. Though would you mind shutting down? I have never plugged into an android before, and since you are like a person and all…"

"Oh, of course, good luck guys," Chef said as his eye screens turned off.

"I don't think that when the ancient engineers thought about designing robots with quasi-personalities, they took into account how odd they might turn out," Hague said.

"Well, this guy has been through a lot," Dawson reasoned, "I do not know much about androids myself, but anyone can tell that Chef here has made more trips out in space than even the oldest spacer."

"Do you really think he is that old? What like hundreds?"

"Probably a couple, look at his structure, most newer models that I have seen on the core are more streamlined."

"The only few I have seen on Nergal looked very humanlike," said Hague.

"Only the wealthy can own that sophisticated type of design. Let me guess, the bosses or visiting dignitaries had them, right?"

"Yeah," said Hague.

"Case in point. Out in the backstars, they can't afford to look like that. Literally."

Hague nodded. He was not aware of so many rules and ideas about androids. He usually had worked on engines or generators, not machines that talked. Also, being out in the Outer Core, and planetside mostly, he did not experience working with androids.

"Since he turned himself off, how will he start back up? Since he is not rebooting, it won't happen automatically."

"Most servant androids have timers set, in case they have to wake up their masters or due to some other purpose. Though often, a voice command from their master is enough. Since Chef here doesn't just serve the captain, I figured he has a timer set."

"Why would an android just shut down other than to fix internal issues?"

"To save battery life, especially on long voyages with no ways of charging. Well, here we go." Dawson plugged in the cord to a port on the side of Chef's head as his own cybernetic eye began to flash.

"Hmmm…"

"What is it, Dawson?"

"I've seen better memory processing units that have been dipped in battery acid, Hague. Chef here truly has seen better days. There is only one answer for this much damage other than time."

"Which is?"

"Too many memory wipes."

"I thought you said you did not know much about androids? Yet you know about memory wipe issues and what designs belong to what social class."

Dawson rolled his human eye as he turned to Hague, "I don't know makes and models, Hague, but I know basic operating systems. Plus, I've been around the galaxy a few times when I was just a human mechanic, remember?"

"Sorry," Hague said. "How many memory wipes do you think Chef has had?"

"I'm not even sure if Chef was his original name. That's how many."

Hague took this time to study Chef. Being unfamiliar with androids, he tried to figure out how he operated, at least on the surface level. He stared and figured out basic principles based on his training under Commander Wagoner. He sighed at his memory. The one thing he noticed was the number of repairs on Chef. Some of them were minor, like joint repairs or wiring replacements. But he looked closely, and under the rust, he noticed that the android had two different types of legs. Upon further inspection, he noticed his right hand resembled a human skeleton hand. At the same time, his left hand only three long digits, and instead of a palm, it was a sphere. *This android clearly has been through a lot. And whatever that has been, it had to have been worth protecting.* Dawson's cybernetic eye kept flashing on and off. The minutes seemed to drag on slowly.

"Any luck?" Hague asked at length.

"This poor android. Not only has Chef had minor wipes, but he has had complete resets too. Normally someone would do memory wipe an android when you don't want the android to remember a password. Or if you sold it and wanted it to think you were its original owner."

"So then what does a reset do?" Hague was afraid to ask.

"You only do that on an android if you want to reprogram him completely. Based on all this photon damage, its happened plenty of times."

"So someone has reprogrammed him too? So he might not even be an android designed for domestic use?" *That would explain all his home-made repairs.*

"And to make matters more complicated," Dawson continued, "it appears as though someone has also encrypted many memories on him. Or at least uploaded files into his memory for storage."

"Why would someone upload files onto an android? It seems rather risky or dangerous."

"Maybe they didn't have a chip or tablet with them," Dawson said.

Hague was about to offer that they upload them to his tablet, but he decided against it. He had not told Dawson that he had the map. He hadn't even told Dawson about the treasure of Nova Scarm to begin with. Although he had grown to trust the cyborg during the few days of working together, he did not want to betray Karson's trust. He would bide his time until it was the right moment to tell.

"Let's start him up again," Dawson said, breaking Hague's thoughts. "Help me find a turn on switch or something."

"I didn't think androids would have something so obvious," Hague commented.

"I figured this old unit might, I remember androids having buttons when I was a younger sailor," Dawson said.

"I didn't think that type of tech was invented in your day," Hague teased.

Dawson chuckled, "Hague, we have been through so much, don't make me kill, you know." They both laughed as Dawson lifted Chef's head. Sure enough, there was a small switch located in the back.

A switch? Now I really haven't seen a model with an actual switch since I was a young boy. How old are you really, Chef? Dawson thought has he propped up the android and flipped the switch.

A small rumble was heard as Chef was brought back on. His screen eyes lit up before he spoke.

"Well? How did it go?"

"Still going," Dawson explained, "I'm still plugged in, figured you could help."

"This is a bit unusual," Chef said, "but I'll see what I can do."

"What is also weird is you only seem to have a backlog of five years of memory. Then you have other memory files, but they are corrupted too. Probably scattered ideas or things that you were allowed to remember," Dawson said. He began to explain everything he told Hague about his memory card.

"Well, that would explain why I can't remember much other than being on this ship and working for the pirates," Chef said. "Some small personal issues that Grimlocke had with a particular captain named Abernathey, but nothing of real importance."

"But I do see encrypted files. Maybe if you remember the keywords, we could access them," Dason said hopefully.

"Worth a try," Chef said, "why don't we try the oldest file? Maybe we can at least figure out one of my first owners."

"I wish they had dates on here," Dawson said. "Then we would for sure know how old you are. Well, there's also a different type of file in your memory, Chef. Someone must have put something there."

"I'm afraid if I try to remember too much, I will begin to reboot," Chef said. "Though I do seem to remember Captain Grimlocke storing a file there. I believe it was after a battle with Captain Abernathey a few years ago."

Fearing that Chef would reboot, Dawson refrained from trying to ask too many deep questions. He was not sure what would happen to his own cybernetic implants. He tried to access the last file that was stored, which was not too hard since there were only five. The only thing that Dawson could read on it was "NAS" and a prompt for a verbal password.

"Does the name Nas ring any bells?" Dawson asked, his hand was on his end of the cord. At worst, he would yank it out of his port if Chef began to shut down.

"Nas? Not really," Chef said, "but it also doesn't seem to trigger anything if I think about it."

"Could it be short for a full name?" Hague offered.

"Maybe it is code for something?" Dawson scratched his chin as he thought. "Nuclear Assistant Systems?"

Chef tried the password, it did not work.

"Navigational Assistant Systems?"

He tried again, another failure.

"What if it is a name and an acronym?" Hague offered. "Like someone's initials?"

"But that could be any name in the universe," Dawson said. "NAS could have infinite name combinations and choices."

Hague thought about it, it did seem a lost cause. He reflected on the names he could remember. There was one name that had those initials. He figured it was a long shot with astronomical odds, but he also thought that a guess couldn't hurt. He walked over and whispered it to the android.

Chef blinked and said, "Nova Andromeda Scarm."

Just then, Dawson screamed as Chef's screen eyes and his own cybernetic eye began to flash with a whirlwind of shapes and colors. Dawson froze and was silent, the colors and shapes scrolling through his eye like an electronic newsfeed on fast forward. The same images and colors were appearing on Chef's screen eyes in the same fashion. Hague almost screamed too, but the words would not come out. *Great Gripplar! Dawson! Chef! Oh no, what's happening? Did I just kill our cyborg and android?*

Chapter 43

The Truth Is Revealed

The reason for the diagnostics and overhaul became evident to everyone. Damage had been caused when the ship flew too close to a large yellow sun that was experiencing a massive solar storm. The computers did not warn the crew of the solar activity, and it wasn't until the ship's sensors were blinded, that they realized the danger. Several sensitive systems overloaded and blew out, and the men were tired and bored. They weren't used to spending so much time making repairs. To make things worse, they were low on the parts needed for the repairs and had to cobble together bits and pieces from some of the non-essential equipment. To add even more issues, the crew had grown complacent by depending on the various machines around the ship to do the work for them. Tempers flared, and fighting frequently broke out. By the end of the afternoon, superstitious space spacers became antsy.

"Look, there's Lonnie," Serena told Karson at the beginning of lunch.

"Why's he looking right as us?" Karson asked.

"I'm not sure," Serena replied.

Karson and Serena exchanged nervous glances.

Lunch went by pretty uneventful. Since Karson and Serena now had the machines up and running, it took less time to prep and clean. However, they kept busy serving tables and cleaning up minor issues. Drake kept far away from Lonnie's table. Karson had no trouble taking some attention on himself. He kept talking to the crew and suggesting games of cards tonight. When he got to Lonnie's table, he suggested the same idea.

"Game of cards tonight, fellas?" Karson asked. "If no one is chicken, I mean."

"Should be fun, Karson," a male pirate said at the table.

Karson was not paying attention and spilled a cup of coffee over Lonnie's pants. The alien jumped up and tried to brush away the liquid.

"Lonnie, I am sorry, I didn't mean it. How about I play a game with only you to make it up?"

"I'll take that bet," Lonnie said, "but how about we play my game?"

"I mean, as long as we all play fair, what's the harm in a little game?" Karson questioned.

"What makes you think I play fair?"

Two of the pirates grabbed Karson's arms and lifted him slightly above the ground. No one was paying attention since lunch that was starting to end. Lonnie still had not revealed Serena's secret, but clearly, he didn't need to when he had his cronies around. Lonnie figured he would push her little whelp friend around a bit, making a statement that he was in charge here.

"Let go of him," Serena yelled. She hadn't found anything she could use as a weapon, so she raised her fists.

The men ignored her as Lonnie drew close to Karson, phaser in hand as he put it to his chest.

"You've been getting close to Drake now, haven't ya?" Lonnie began to taunt Karson. "I think you boys need a little reminding of who in charge around here. Now how should I make you pay for my damaged pants? Could always blow you out one of the torpedo tubes," Lonnie pondered, "a phaser bolt might be too quick for you, brat."

"You won't like that," another pirate threatened. "Without protection, those solar flares will burn you alive. That's if you haven't already died when the vacuum of space sucks the air from your lungs. Don't rightly know which one would kill you first."

Karson tried to remain calm. "Guys come on, just a little accident is all."

"Stop it!" Serena shouted, struggling to keep her voice low pitched. She beat her fists against the back of the nearest man.

He shoved her away. "Off with ya, whelp. Ya hit like a girl."

Lonnie was too focused on Karson to notice Drake's appearance, and upon the word, he snapped his focus on the direction where he heard the word. His eyes locked on with Serena's. He knew his pushing was correct. Now she had accidentally admitted that the two were in cahoots.

His gaze froze her in her tracks.

Karson continued to struggle and beg. He was never so afraid in his life. The men dragged him down the corridor to the nearest turbolift. They were about to pull him inside when there was a shout.

"Stop!" Captain Grimlocke yelled, pulling out his phaser. "If you got something to say, Lonnie, settle it with yer fists ya coward."

The men grumbled but released Karson.

"What seems to be the problem, boys?" Captain Grimlocke asked angrily. He looked at Karson then at Lonnie. "Well? Must be awfully important if it got me involved and wasting my time here."

Serena got to her feet and was about to say something when the ship lurched.

Puzzled, the Captain touched his communicator. "Grimlocke to the bridge."

"Bridge," his first mate, Sharky, answered.

"What's going on? Why'd the ship lurch."

"We're back in business, Cap'n. The repairs are complete, and we're heading for home."

A shout of joy went up.

"Get back to your posts, boys," Captain Grimlocke shouted. "We're back in business."

Cheers filled the air, and the ship jumped to warp speed. Lonnie, too, took up with the cheers and, at that moment, forgot about Serena.

Grimlocke turned to one of his lieutenants. "Tell the rest of the crew to assume their normal duties, and send the ones who should be off duty to bed." Before he left, he grabbed Lonnie by the scruff of his neck and shook him the way a dog does with a rat in its mouth. "Got anything to say now and take up more of my time, rat?"

"No, Cap'n."

Grimlocke snarled in disgust and threw Lonnie on the ground. Lonnie nursed his pride, there would be a time for him to get revenge on the girl and card boy. He would bide his time.

Back in the galley, Karson pulled Serena aside. "Thanks for looking out for my back there."

"You would do the same for me. We are in this together, remember?"

****

Dawson awoke to find himself lying on the floor in the storeroom. He felt his head for the cord that was plugged in. It was not there. He didn't remember too much, he began to stand up slowly when he hard Hague calls out.

"Dawson!" The blue Rhungo walked from the other side of the table to his friend. "Are you ok?"

Dawson braced himself on the table before he spoke, "I don't remember much after you whispered something to Chef."

"Nova Scarm's full name? Yeah, he repeated it, and then both your eyes got all glowy and weird, and then you both passed out. Well, I figured Chef shut down, but still."

"Nova Andromeda Scarm?" Dawson touched the human side of his head, he felt a headache coming on. "His middle name was Andromeda? Wait a minute, how did you know that?"

Hague shrugged, "Karson's Uncle Jasper used to always tell us the stories, and he began it with his full name. It was the only name I knew that fit the acronym."

Dawson smiled, the pain receding in his head, "Well, you were correct, it did."

"I figured it was when the flashing started. But what did it unlock?"

"That memory. That Chef here used to be the android for Captain Nova Scarm."

Hagues mouth hung wide open. "How is that possible? That would mean that this robot is hundreds of years old."

"I don't know how, but it is. I saw those memories. While I can't remember everything, it was the location of the treasure and the pieces of the map. I think that is what that other file is, one of the pieces of the map!" Dawson beamed in excitement.

"I still can't believe this old android is literally that old...I wonder how he has managed to survive."

"Probably was passed on from pirate to pirate. Since his memories were encrypted, no one would know to look there but Scarm himself."

"That is true. So you really think Chef has a piece of the map?"

"I'm pretty sure that is what that file is. I can't remember if I saw it myself or if it was in Chef's memories, though. Question is: how do we get it out?"

"Oh, I have a tablet with me," Hague said, figuring it was time to come clean.

"You've had a tablet this whole time?" Dawson said in outrage. "Do you know how much I could have done with that? It would've taken us no time at all to have fixed the…"

"Dawson, keep it down!" Hague silenced the cyborg, "I had to keep this tablet a secret, okay?"

"Why? What could that tablet possibly possess that made you keep it a secret?"

"Part of the map that leads to Nova Scarm's treasure."

Now it was Dawson's turn to be in complete shock. "So it was on the *Stardust*, wasn't it?"

Hague looked bashful, "sorry, Dawson. We would've told you sooner, but we didn't know who to trust on the ship." *I'll let Karson handle the plans then,* Hague thought to himself.

"Think nothing of it, I am just happy that I was right about it."

Then they used the cord from Dawson to download the file from Chef's memory. Once it was downloaded, Hague examined it.

"Well, what is it?" Dawson asked excitedly.

"I think this is the third piece of the treasure map," Hague said with a smile.

"Third? What part do we have? And who has the other part?"

"I'll explain later, Dawson. Bring Chef to the brig, and I'll get Karson and Drake. We all need to be on the same page for this."

****

In the cell where Karson and Drake were staying, Hague and Dawson filled them in on everything that had happened with Chef. Karson and Serena also had to tell them what happened with Lonnie and had to come clean about Serena's secret. Karson and Hague, with help from Dawson, told them of the legend of Captain Nova Scarm and the treasure.

"Well, now we have two parts of the map," Karson concluded. "If only we could find out where the treasure is located. It appears that it is on the portion of the map that was in Chef's memory. However, there seems to be some security system installed that will only show it when all the pieces are together."

"So, where is that?" Dawson asked.

"Well, Captain Abernathey told Karson and I that Grimlocke had the second piece on his ship," Hague answered.

"Well, what if this is the second piece?" Serena ventured, "I mean, Chef was on the ship technically."

Chef slowly shook his head, "no, no. Captain Grimlocke has no idea that I have the map, he has been searching for the missing pieces as long as I can remember."

"I just wonder how you ended up on another pirate ship after Grimlocke," Karson said.

"Well, we haven't accessed all my memories yet," Chef said, "though I think I must have just been tossed on or stolen or picked up my various pirate crews over the hundreds of years. Who knows? Maybe I was stored somewhere and turned on hundreds of years later. The experience of an android is a weird one."

"Guess you were born under a lucky star," Hague teased Karson.

"So, the next thing we have to do is get the other map piece," said Dawson.

"If we can, we might be able to get back to Cortsea," Karson said.

"What good would that do?" Hague asked.

Karson figured since everyone was now bound together in secrets, it was time he was truthful to the whole newly-formed conspiracy. "Well, Cortsea, I figure would be the closest planet. But also because that was where Captain Abernathey was heading to drop off the last delivery of the *Stardust*."

"Karson, we lost the *Stardust*, and even if we didn't, we are in no position to deliver cargo," Dawson interjected.

"I have it with me, downloaded on a tablet. It was the true secret mystery of the *Stardust*, Dawson. On this tablet are Galactic Federation plans for a new type of starship. One that could change the future of startraveling and spacing as a whole. Though, if the pirates get it, it could be disastrous for anyone out there. The plans for the starcruiser *Pegasus*. Now you see why we need to get to Cortsea? We can try to deliver these plans. Also, we can charter a ship there to take us to the treasure and maybe even find some help for Chef here. Now I think our conspiracy is complete if you will all take part in it. "

Dawson put his partial animatronic hand in the center of the group, "I'm all in. The Conspiracy."

Chef put his three-digit hand in, "Me too, I don't know how many more miles this rusty body can take, but you'll have me till the end."

"You'll help me, I'll help you, count me in," Serena said as she placed her hand on top of Chef's

Hague put his hand in next, "Me too. I've been a part of this conspiracy from the beginning, after all."

Karson put his hand in the circle last as he spoke, "For the treasure?"

They all raised their hands and, in unison, quietly said, "for the treasure!"

Now the conspiracy was complete, and every member would need all the help the others would provide.

Chapter 44

The Conspiracy Search for the Map

Men, who would typically be sitting around the galley singing and drinking, were in their beds snoring. Karson, Serena, Dawson, and Hague sat at the table, furthest from the door to the corridor and talked. Chef was working in the kitchen. It was two days after their conspiracy had officially formed. Hague and Dawson were explaining how they found the shuttle bays. According to Hague, the shuttles themselves seemed easy enough to figure out or control. They even suggested that the shuttles might even have autopilot, which would also be beneficial to their cause.

"Well, I am glad that is settled, but how far *are* we from Cortsea?" Karson asked.

"I'd say only a few days at the most," Hague replied.

"We might be further out than that," Serena said.

"Before we get into that subject, I overheard two of the lieutenants talking about a map," Dawson confided.

"Think they are talking about Scarm's map?" Karson asked.

"Any idea where it's being kept?" Serena asked.

"Maybe the captain's quarters," Hague replied. "Maybe not."

"I overheard Captain Grimlocke telling his first mate that he thought Captain Abernathy might have had it on him when they released the life pod. They've been tracking him ever since, but when the ship's sensors were damaged by the solar flare, they lost him. Grimlocke sent the *Cirrus* out to continue the search, so it's only a matter of time before they get their hands on it again." Dawson said flatly.

"If we got our hands on it," Serena said longingly.

"We can't just take Grimlocke's part," Hague said. "He'd tear his own ship apart looking for it, and as soon as he found it, we'd be goners."

"Not if we copied the file onto another tablet," Karson said thoughtfully.

"Which tablet?" Serena asked.

Karson was hesitant, he did not want the entire map on one tablet, but it was better than losing the plans. "Let's put it on Hague's tablet. We can switch them after lunch. That way, if I am caught, at least the heat will be on me."

"If Grimlocke discovers you with it, or even looking for it, he'll kill you both," Hague warned.

"Then we'll have to be very careful," Serena said.

****

After lunchtime, Karson decided to take Serena with him to do some searching until it was time to start dinner. Karson figured that Grimlocke's quarters were the best bet for the map. They just had to find it on the ship. As they explored the top level, they saw Grimlocke leave his door.

He gave them both the fisheye. "What are you boys up to?"

"Looking for Sharky, sir," Serena said in Drake's voice. "Wanted to follow up with a question he asked me yesterday. Since we don't have communicators or clearance for the hallway ones, we thought he might be up here."

"Alright, his door is over there," Grimlocke said as he began to turn to the opposite turbolift. As he did, his communicator went off.

"Captain Grimlocke," the voice said.

"Here," the captain replied, as he did so, his hand knocked his card key out of his pocket. Karson waited until the captain turned the corridor before he quickly picked it up.

"Fantastic," Karson said as he picked up the card key. "He'll be gone for a while. Let's go check out his quarters."

"What about the man guarding the door?"

"He won't show up for a bit," Karson.

"How do you know?"

"I saw him use it the other day and asked Chef about it. He told me Grimlocke's guard appears five minutes after he leaves. He doesn't want anyone to be able to override the computer to open the door and sneak into his quarters. When your crew is a gang of thieves and murderers, you can't trust any of them."

As quietly as possible, they tiptoed to the door, slipped the key card into the slot, and unlocked it.

Once inside, Karson whispered, "You take that half of the room, and I'll take the other."

"Okay."

They looked everywhere, starting with the chest containing gemstones from several planets. Serena checked the bedding, under the mattress, and beneath the bed itself. Karson examined the shelves containing souvenirs taken from other ships. Then Serena observed the chest that held the captain's clothing and personal articles. At the same time, Karson looked around and under the remaining furniture. Halfway through the search, they froze when they heard footsteps approach.

Karson placed a finger to his lips. Since they had the only key to the room, no one could come in, but if someone heard them or suspected an intruder, they would soon be discovered. He and Becks stood frozen in place until the footsteps moved away.

"Whew!" Karson wiped his brow.

"That was too close. We'd better hurry up and get out of here," Serena whispered.

They continued their search, looking behind pictures for a safe and everywhere they could think to look. No tablet, no map.

"Where would a pirate hide a map?" Serena asked Karson.

He shrugged.

They even checked the undersides of the furniture and drawers. Nothing.

Moving to the captain's chest filled with gems, Karson raised the lid to take a better look. The sight dazzled them both. So much so, they almost didn't see the tablet on top of the treasure.

"Karson," Serena whispered urgently.

Grinning, Karson removed the tablet and tucked it under his shirt. "Let's get out of here."

****

Karson retrieved his third of the map and brought it back to the galley. Handing it to her, he asked, "You any good at breaking passwords?"

Serena grinned. "Actually, I am. There was a game I used to play back home, and I got to be a pretty good hacker. I can't make any guarantees, but I should be able to figure out the passwords for both tablets, as long as you can tell me some personal things about Captain Abernathy."

While Karson helped Chef start dinner, he told her everything he knew about his former Captain. She asked a few questions, and then when she was satisfied, she knew everything her friend did. Serena took everything, found a discrete corner in the supply room, and got to work. Surprisingly, she deciphered both passwords reasonably quickly. When she finished downloading the map and joining the two thirds together, she gave Grimlocke's tablet to Karson.

"I gotta get this back before he misses it," Karson said as he tucked it into the waist of his pants and under his shirt.

Serena took over peeling potatoes and mentally crossed her fingers. *Please don't let him be caught putting it back.*

The guard was still asleep when Karson slipped inside and carefully put the tablet back where he found it. Opening the door, he checked the guard and the hallway. It was empty except for the sleeping pirate. He was almost clear of the corridor when he heard approaching footsteps. Karson turned around and started walking toward the Captain's quarters.

He had just made it to the door, tablet in hand when Grimlocke opened the door. The pirate captain was no fool. He always had a backup in case a card key went missing.

"What are you doing with that?" Captain Grimlocke roared.

"Grimlocke!" Karson went white with fright.

"Lousy, no good thief! Trying to outsmart me and steal my treasure map."

"What?" Karson protested. "No!"

"Shut yer mouth," Grimlocke ordered as he dragged him to the turbolift. He slapped a hallway communicator as he announced, "all off-duty personnel to cargo bay four! Now!"

As the captain forced Karson to the turbolift, he contemplated how he would punish the nosy cabin boy.

"He stole something of ours!" Grimlocke told the crew as they exited the turbolift. The men hissed and booed.

The Conspiracy, save for Chef, were among the men; they had separated a bit. But, they hoped that Karson would not be with the captain when they got here.

"I say we cut off his head!" The captain shouted. "That's what the pirates of old would do." He signaled his lieutenants to grab Karson and hold out his hands.

"No!" Serena screamed.

Two pirates pinned Karson down, one of which was Lonnie. Karson kept thrashing his head about until Sharky firmly pressed his boot to Karson's head. Fear tore through the young man's heart, making him shiver violently. It was all over.

Lonnie passed a repair laser to Grimlocke. While the intent of the laser was to meld various metals together, it could be turned up high enough to be lethal. Though whether it would cut through a neck in a single stroke remained to be seen. Lonnie, however, was very excited to put the laser to the test.

The crew cheered and began to chant.

"Off with his head! Off with his head!"

"No," Karson cried. "Don't. Please! I beg you."

Raising the laser a bit higher, the captain turned it on.

Chapter 45

Ships and Surprises

Karson closed his eyes and gritted his teeth, waiting for the agony that would come when the laser sliced his hands from his arms.

But Grimlocke turned off the tool an inch above his wrist. "I've changed my mind."

Karson's knees gave out. He would have hit the deck without the support of the lieutenants. Hague wobbled, feeling faint, but Dawson placed a supporting arm around his waist.

Karson and Serena smiled until they heard the Grimlocke's next words.

"Cuff him and take him to one of the launch bays!"

The ship bucked, knocking nearly everyone off their feet.

"Captain!" The first mate yelled into the intercom. "Enemy ships have surrounded us. We're under attack!"

Panic overwhelmed some of the pirates as they poured into the corridor.

The captain turned to one of his men. "Ready my personal ship. The rest of you, man, your posts! All pilots to the fighters! Man the cannons!"

The crew scattered like mice, and when the ship shuddered again from laser fire, the one who was supposed to watch the prisoners took off as well.

Hague and Serena pulled Karson against the wall of the corridor to keep him from being trampled.

"We gotta get Chef, then we head for the escape pods," Karson said.

"If the ship doesn't explode around us, they'll blow up the escape pods, thinking we're escaping pirates," Hague yelled. "We'll never make it."

"Yes, we will," Dawson hollered back. "We can hail the attackers and tell them who we are."

"And what if *they* are a rival pirate ship?" Serena asked.

"Let's just hope they aren't," Karson replied.

As they ran for an empty turbolift, the overhead lights flickered and went out. The darkness made it impossible to see.

"We'll have to make our way through the access ways," Dawson told the others.

Serena looked worried. "We'd never make it in time," she said, echoing Hague's earlier prediction. "The turbolifts may not be working by now."

"Yes, they will! They *have* to," Karson insisted. "Gotta stay positive."

****

The captain reached the bridge just before the lights went out. He shouted orders fast and furious. Running for his chair, he grabbed the first officer by the arm and jerked him out of it. "What were you doing up here? Sleeping? How did they sneak up on us?"

"I don't know! I swear, captain, the main ship came out of nowhere. Ask the rest of the bridge crew. No one spotted it until they were upon us and opened fire."

"We need to abandon ship, captain," one crewman yelled.

"We never abandon ship, you coward. I am Captain Flint Grimlocke! We're pirates!" Captain Grimlocke shouted as he sat in his chair. "Open fire. Hit 'em with everything we've got." He punched the intercom in his chair arm. "Engineering, how much power have we lost?"

"We've lost 40%, Captain," the engineer responded. "We're working to restore it, but the ship's taking a beating. Shields are down to 65%. If this keeps up, they won't hold much longer."

"Take power from everything but life support and weapons and feed it to the shields," Grimlocke ordered. He looked up at the view screen to assess the situation.

A massive warship from the Galactic Federation Spaceforce held steady off the stern. As if that wasn't bad enough, smaller, sleek starfighters from the gigantic ship, zoomed in and out, raking his vessel with laser fire. There were too many targets to get them all, and even if they managed that impossible feat, the warship would finish them off.

"They're hitting us with their fighters instead of the main ship's turret guns," the captain told his crew. "Looks like they want prisoners; let's make sure they don't get any."

****

Karson, Serena, Hague, and Dawson headed back to the galley to get Chef. Chef had stayed behind when Grimlocke entered to guard the tablets with the treasure map and the *Pegasus* plans. Fortunately, the kitchen was on the same deck. About halfway there, the lights came back on, but only dimly. At 30%, it was still difficult to see well, but it was enough. With the ship taking such a pounding, things were chaotic everywhere, most of the men not needed to fly the ship were headed for the landing bays. If the soldiers from the Galactic Federation decided to board her, the pirates planned to cut them down as soon as they left their shuttles.

Karson and the others had to struggle against the men pouring out of the cargo bay, where Grimlocke had gathered them.

"I'll go on alone," Karson called out.

"I'll wait here to help you," Serena said, "Chef is frail and could use all the protection he could get."

"Hague and I will head on to the shuttle bays," Dawson declared. "We might have to fight them all off to get one. Depending on the size."

"Take this," Hage said as he passed a communicator to Karson. Their original communicators had been taken when they were taken aboard the *Antares*. "I stole one from a pirate when we were up there. Dawson's already tuned into it. Let us know when you guys are heading our way."

Karson nodded as the conspiracy split up.

****

It seemed to take forever, but Karson finally made it to the galley. He retrieved the tablets, but he could not seem to find Chef. He called out as the ship gave another mighty lurch, and he heard a moan. There was Chef, slowly walking towards him, he was carrying a phaser, but it was not on.

"Got it when we took the *Antares*," he slowly explained. "Kept it secret till now."

He gave it to Karson, who armed it, in case they would run into any obstacles.

"Come on. I'll help you," Karson said. "We have to get to the escape pods before the pirates start abandoning ship."

"Thank you, Karson. Until I met you, I never cared about remembering anything. Now I want to do something worth being remembered."

272

Karson felt touched, but he was quickly brought back to the urgency of their situation when the ship lurched again.

When they re-entered the corridor, it had cleared somewhat, and they sprinted for the nearest turbolift. The men were in a panic. They knew the ship was doomed. Two men had been ordered to retrieve the massive chest of gems from the captain's cabin. They were struggling with their heavy load as they headed for Shuttle Bay 1 and Grimlocke's personal ship, the *Midnight Wolf*.

When Karson, Serena, and Chef finally made it to the escape pods, Hague and Dawson were defending one from fleeing pirates. Karson ran up and grabbed one of the crew as he was about to step inside the pod. He jerked the man back and hit him in the jaw with all his might. "Ow!" He yelled, shaking his hand.

The pirate swung his fist, catching Karson in the head and knocking him backward.

Chef screamed, and Serena joined the fight, resulting in an exchange of blows until she finally knocked the man unconscious.

"Good job!" Karson cheered.

Serena, still disguised as Drake, smile and bowed.

She was about to move towards the pod, but before she could, Lonnie aimed his phaser at him.

"Take another step, and it'll be your last."

Serena stopped and slowly raised her hands. She wasn't armed and didn't know what Lonnie would do.

"Whatcha going to do, card boy?" Lonnie asked with a sneer. "I should've sold this blighter out to the Cap'n long ago. Ever since she came on board, we've had nothing but bad luck."

Karson moved his hand slowly to his phaser, he might only get one shot.

"Come to think of it," Lonnie said, his eyes maddening by the moment, "the same thing applies to you. You both are bad luck, and I'm tired of my luck running out."

Lonnie began to move his charged phaser when a shot rang out. Lonnie looked surprised and fell to the ground.

Karson stood still as his phaser gently radiated heat.

They both ran and hugged each other.

"Thank you, Karson," Serena said.

"You're welcome," Karson stammered. "Better grab his phaser."

"Come on, you two," Hague called as he and Dawson, carrying Chef on his back, raced back to the ship's doors. "No time! We gotta get out of the airlock! They're gonna launch!"

The Conspiracy barely made it to safety when the pods shot out into space, only to be captured by a tractor beam from the Galactic Federation. No doubt, that was the fate of all the pirates who thought they could escape that way.

"What are we going to do now?" Serena asked.

"I have an idea," Karson replied.

"What's your idea?" Hague asked.

"Do you know how to program a shuttle, Dawson?"

"Indeed, I do. I've flown several different craft during my time out in space. Once, when I was stationed on a trip of mercy to the planet Patuc, I was the one who had to purchase supplies for the kitchen, and the only other store was on the other side of the planet."

"Wait!" Serena interrupted. "How can you fly when you're just a cyborg?"

"Simple, darling, the ship does the flying. I just tell it where I want to go," the cyborg smiled.

Chef hit his forehead with the palm of his hand. "Of course. Why didn't I think of that?"

"Because you've got a bad memory…for now," Hague replied.

"So that's your plan?" Serena asked. "If the ship attacking us is another pirate ship, we'll just be captured all over again.

"Not necessarily," Karson said. "First, we jettison the cargo and the ship's waste. There's got to be a serious amount of debris from all the damaged systems that were repaired. Add that to all the other waste, and it should create a fair-sized debris field. One, we might just be able to hide in until our attacker leaves."

"It might work," Chef agreed. "Dawson, you and Hague take care of that while Karson and I head to the galley. There isn't much portable food made up, but I'll grab as much of the bread and water I can find and anything else edible that doesn't need to be cooked. I know we are several days flight away from the closest planet, and we don't want to starve to death or die of thirst before we get there."

"Great idea," Karson said as he and Chef headed back to the galley. "Serena, can you handle the waste ejection?"

"Yes. I've done it before."

"Good, Dawson, and I can easily take care of the cargo bays from engineering. Then we'll meet up near Shuttle Bay 1."

"Make it 2," Serena said. "And I'll come back here first to help you two carry the food supplies."

"Why 2?" Dawson asked.

"Captain Grimlocke has his private ship stored in Bay 1. I did a lot of exploring after I was captured." She stopped speaking and listened. "Things have quieted down. Either the pirates are fleeing like the rats they are, or we're being boarded. With all the escape pods gone, whoever is left won't need all the shuttles."

"Then we'd better hurry," Karson urged.

****

"This is Captain Scott Bennington of the Galactic Federation Spaceforce *Columbia*. Ceasefire and surrender. Otherwise, I'll be forced to destroy your ship."

Captain Grimlocke stared at the man filling most of the view screen in front of him. Everything about Captain Bennington said that he was a strict, no-nonsense captain. From his immaculate uniform to his salt and pepper feathers that were cut in a short military style. Steel-blue eyes looked back at the pirate over a sizeable dark beak, and Grimlocke could tell there was no mercy hidden within their depths. He had been sent to stop a pirate ship and stop a pirate ship he would.

Instead of replying to Bennington's demands, Grimlocke relaxed in his chair and said, "You look familiar, Captain Bennington. Have we met before?"

"Not likely. However, I'm told I look a lot like my half-brother, Captain John Abernathy. We rescued him, you know, and he had quite a tale to tell."

"No doubt," Grimlocke replied.

The smile on his face reminded Bennington of a snake.

"So, what will it be?"Bennington asked. "Frankly, I don't care one way or the other. Either way, your time of terrorizing this sector of space is over."

"No, I don't imagine you do care," Grimlocke replied. He raised his index finger and tapped his lips a few times before going on. "Tell you what. I'll stop shooting at your fighters. Boarding us, though, is another thing. Then it's every man for himself. If you choose to board us, I can't promise your men's safety. No pirate will give up so easily."

"Fair enough, I've already captured those who chose to use your escape pods."

"And you can have them, too. I've got no sympathy for deserters," Grimlocke growled. "But as for the rest of us, we'll go down fighting."

****

By the time the Conspiracy reached Shuttle Bay 2, only four ships had remained. Karson's idea to jettison everything turned out to be a great idea. So much so that the pirates, who had taken the cruisers, also used the debris field to hide in. Grimlocke sabotaged different parts of his own ship, blowing holes in the hull, which added to the collection of junk. Then he and his men abandoned ship before any of the Galactic Federation's forces came aboard.

With everyone on board, Dawson launched their cruiser, the *Intruder*, and found a spot in the debris. Then, he shut the systems down except for life support, so they couldn't be detected. They made it just in time, too. Knowing Captain Bennington would destroy the pirate ship once he caught it, Grimlocke ordered the ship's computer to take off as soon as the last shuttle cleared the bay. With the added distraction, the Galactic Federation ship took off after them, leaving the shuttles to head for the pirate's home base, the planet Oblistidon.

Chapter 46

Space

Three days had passed, and their food and water were practically gone. The computer flew the ship on course for the nearest viable planet, which they thought would be the home base planet of the pirates. Down to their last container of water, Karson took only two swallows to wet his parched throat, giving the rest to Serena, Hague, and Dawson.

Talking kept them awake during the daytime cycle, which was set according to the time used on the pirate's home base. On the fifth day, a ship approached their position.

"A ship is approaching our sector," the computer announced. "Shall I hail them?"

"Ye..." Serena began.

"No!" Karson quickly interrupted. He turned his chair, one of the pilot's seats to face the forward view screen. "On screen."

As the ship came closer, it matched their speed. Hague sitting in the other pilot's seat also turned to look. Serena joined them while Dawson still sat in the back, and Chef remained powered down.

"It's the *Cirrus*!" Serena exclaimed.

"Computer, block visual. I don't want the crew of the other ship to see who we are when they hail us," Hague ordered

"Visual blocked. The *Cirrus* is hailing."

"Since when do pirates stop to lend a hand?" Serena asked.

"They don't," Karson replied. "They're probably checking to see if anyone aboard is valuable enough to be worth their while."

"You're both wrong," Dawson said in a voice tinged with concern. "We're in a shuttle from Grimlocke's ship. They probably think we're some of the crew in need of rescue."

"What should we do?" Serena asked. "If we don't reply, they're going to know something's wrong."

"Does the *Cirrus* have a tractor beam?" Hague asked, alarmed.

Serena swallowed hard. "Yes, it does."

"We've got to think of something to send them away," Karson said. "Computer, allow the hail, but continue blocking visual."

"Shuttlecraft *Intruder*, do you read? This is the *Cirrus*. We're here to rescue you. Come in."

"If we don't say something, they'll think our communications are down and just tractor us in," Dawson warned.

"I have an idea," Karson offered. "Computer, disguise my voice to sound like that of a gruff, older man, add some static, and let verbal contact go in and out. I want it to sound like our communications are damaged."

"Acknowledge. Opening communication."

"*Cirrus*, is that you?" Karson asked. "Our communicator was damaged by space junk when we left the ship. Visual is out, and verbal is shaky."

"You're breaking up *Intruder*. Slow your speed, and we'll tractor you in."

"No. Wait, *Cirrus*. Have you come across the captain's shuttle yet?"

"What's that? We only got part of your message."

"Have you found the captain yet?"

"Not yet. We went after the *Stardust*'s captain to get his copy of the treasure map."

The four friends exchanged worried glances. If the pirates had found Abernathy, they would have the second third of the map. Which meant the Captain was probably dead. They had no idea that Abernathy had been rescued already.

"Did you find him?" Karson asked.

"No, but we did find his abandoned escape pod."

This was good! Abernathy had been rescued!

"However, " the *Cirrus* continued, "we did find a copy of Captain Nova Scarm's map in the onboard computer."

"He must have put a copy there for safekeeping, but forgot about it when he was rescued," Hague whispered to Karson

"That's great!" Karson tried to sound enthusiastic.

"Say again."

"That's great!"

"Drop out of warp, and we'll tractor you into a shuttle bay."

"Negative, *Cirrus*, Captain Grimlocke has sent us on a short side mission. Your priority should be finding him first. We'll join you afterward when we reach planetside."

The *Cirrus* did not respond.

"Do you think they bought it?" Serena asked.

"I don't know."

They watched the screen to see what happened next.

"Is it leaving?" Hague asked.

Dawson's eyes went wide with alarm. "No, it's not. Hang on. I think they're going to try to tractor us in at warp."

A tractor beam shot past their ship, just missing them.

"Time for some evasive maneuvers," Karson said as he switched off the autopilot and took control of the ship.

"They can't do that. Can they?" Serena asked.

"It's a risk," Dawson replied. "We could end up getting blown to bits."

"What will we do? We can't let that happen," Serena cried.

"We won't," Karson said firmly, his mind racing with ideas as to how to get out of this.

Another tractor beam was fired.

"Computer, what's our current speed?" Hague asked.

"Warp two," the computer replied.

"We can't outrun them," Chef warned, his security systems powered him back on after the first tractor beam was fired. "These shuttles are set for a maximum speed of warp two."

Hague ransacked his brain. "Computer, any chance we can go a little faster?"

"Captain Grimlocke had his shuttles' speed enhanced somewhat. I can give you warp three, but I cannot sustain it for too long."

Karson looked at Serena. "If we change course, we may not find a viable planet in time to save us."

Serena looked back and sighed. "If we let them capture us, we may not be able to get away again."

"Maybe…maybe not," Karson concurred.

"If we don't make it," Serena continued, "at least we'll die together."

Karson searched her eyes, and after a moment, nodded. He realized that their relationship was starting to shift into something more unique.

"Computer, drop out of warp, then before the *Cirrus* can attach a tractor beam, change course and jump to warp three for as long as the ship can handle it without breaking apart. Then as soon as it's safe, return to your previous heading," Hague called out, breaking up Karson's thoughts.

"Acknowledged."

Dropping out of warp, the computer waited just long enough for the *Cirrus* to appear nearby. An instant later, the *Intruder* disappeared, going warp three at a new course heading. They were able to maintain that speed for thirty minutes.

"Dropping to warp two," the computer announced when the ship began to shake from metal fatigue.

"What about the *Cirrus*?" Karson asked.

"There are no ships currently showing on my sensors."

Everyone heaved a sigh of relief.

"Yes!" Serena and Dawson shouted. "You did it, Hague. We escaped!"

Karson grinned broadly as he slapped his best friend on the back. He reflected on how much Hague's quick thinking had gotten them out of scrapes during this voyage. Even back on Nergal, Hague's brainpower was worth its weight in Sarceran gems.

Karson then turned his attention back to the computer. "Computer, have we returned to our original course heading yet?"

"Negative."

"Why not?"

"My sensors are picking up a class M planet ahead on our present course."

Hope-filled everyone's eyes.

"Do you know which one it is?" Hague asked.

"Negative. It is not currently listed on my star maps."

"Can you tell if it's inhabited?" Dawson tried to ask.

"Negative. The ship is still too far out for my sensors to read that type of information."

"If it's class M, even if it's primitive, we should be able to find food and water," Serena told the others.

"I agree," Karson said. "Computer, how long before we're in range?"

"We will arrive at the target planet in two hours, fourteen minutes, and six seconds."

Karson looked at Serena, Hague, Dawson, and Chef. "It's funny how something bad can sometimes turn into a good thing."

"At least we have a chance of survival now," Serena agreed. "If we can stock up on food and water, we should be able to make it to civilization and from there…"

"We go after the treasure!" Karson, Hague, and Dawson said in unison.

Serena and Chef rolled their eyes.

****

Precisely two hours, fourteen minutes, and six seconds later, the ship dropped out of warp.

"Entering orbit of an inhabited planet," the computer announced. "The civilization below appears to be primitive; however, the planet appears to contain suitable food and water."

"What do you mean by primitive?" Hague asked.

The computer ran additional scans and correlated the results. "Thirty-two percent of the landmass is populated, spread over the planet's only landmass, which covers sixty percent of the total area. The rest is covered by a saltwater ocean with small islands located in various areas. Freshwater and plant life is similar, but not the same as Earth's, making it safe for consumption."

"So primitive in terms of actual coverage of civilizations," Hague concluded. "Not necessarily in terms of technology."

Karson and the others grinned in relief. "Excellent. Set us down near a settlement, but far enough out to avoid detection."

The computer guided them to a suitable place and landed. Opening the shuttle door, everyone peeked out. It was dark, and the exterior lights on the shuttle showed that they were in a small clearing surrounded by trees.

"As hungry and thirsty as everyone is, I think we should wait till daylight before venturing out," Dawson said.

"I agree," Serena said, looking at Hague and receiving a nod. "It's been so long since I've eaten anything, I don't feel hungry any longer."

"Computer secure the door and wake us when it's light outside," Hague ordered.

"We may as well get some sleep, so we're fresh in the morning," Serena suggested.

They headed into the sleeping compartment and crawled into their cots. As they fell asleep, no one knew that tomorrow would bring additional complications to overcome.

Chapter 47

Planetside

They all awoke the next morning, hungry, thirsty, and filled with hope.

"Any idea about where we are?" Karson asked Dawson.

"It's difficult to say. Since I have no idea how close or far we were to any other planets when we were onboard the *Antares*. Also, after spending five days out in deep space, I have no way of figuring out where we ventured to. We may be on an uncharted planet."

"The computer could not even identify this planet," Hague chimed in, "if this planet isn't on the star charts yet, no one may know it's here."

"If we find out the planet's name, let's be sure the computer puts it on the chart for this region," Karson said. "I hope the translator can figure out the language."

"It may take a few minutes, but it will," Serena assured him. "Then, we can have it added to the planet's database in case anyone else comes here."

"Aren't we supposed to avoid planets with pre-warp civilization?" Hague asked. "Remember back when we had to land on that planet when we needed to resupply? The planet where that green monster came onboard?"

Karson nodded.

"We had to take all those precautions. We can't afford to mess up with a pre-warp civilization."

"Maybe we should keep its existence a secret," Karson said, thoughtfully.

"Don't worry. If this planet is governed by the Galactic Oversight Bureau, then we should be fine. We might have ended up on a recently terraformed planet with limited technology. Either way, we should be fine," Dawson assured him.

"Then we'd better be extremely careful they don't find our ship. Let's explore our surroundings," Hague said.

"We need food and water for you organic life forms," Chef said, "I will try to use the computer and see if it can map our surroundings. There should be a town or village not too far from here."

Serena took Chef's arm. "I'll help you out," she said, smiling.

"That's right kind of you, Drake, I mean, Serena."

****

Chef ended up getting additional help from Hague as Karson and Dawson planned their next plan of attack.

"We need to find food, then a settlement of some sort," Karson said.

"Aye, once we find some form of civilization, we can figure out where to go from there," Dawson said.

That we can, Karson thought to himself. Now that they had all three pieces of the map, they could, in theory, find the location of the treasure. *But when should we do it? Not now, our survival is more important. But do we go treasure hunting, or try to find Cortsea and deliver the plans?* He weighed these decisions carefully.

Just then, Hague opened the shuttle door and announced, "Got it figured out! We have a new heading!"

"What direction should we take?" Dawson asked as Hague, Chef, and Serena exited the shuttle.

"I checked the computer," Hague said, "and the closest settlement is due north about a mile away."

"North," Karson confirmed. He grabbed a translator from the shuttle, everyone else's had been damaged during their time aboard the *Antares*.

"We must be cautious, though," Chef said. "We have no idea who or what could be out there until we reached that settlement."

Karson thought about it, but Serena spoke first.

"You think the pirates might now about this planet, but are purposely keeping its existence quiet?" Serena asked.

"It's possible. Some of the other shuttles may have ended up here, just like we did," Dawson speculated.

****

As they walked through the trees and foliage, Chef stumbled over tree roots and an occasional rock or two. Seeing this, Hague looked around until he spotted a sturdy tree branch lying on the ground. He retrieved it and, using his pocket knife, removed the smaller branches until he ended up with a reasonably smooth walking stick.

"Here, Chef, use this. It should help," he said, placing the walking stick in the android's hands.

"Thank you, Hague. I don't remember the last time I was planetside. My old parts are in desperate need of repairs as well."

Walking for the next hour, the conspiracy discovered a stream and drank their fill, soothing their parched throats. Further along, a berry bush with plump red fruit provided enough sustenance to take the bite off their hunger, but it wouldn't last long. They left the now empty bush behind and forged ahead until the sound of voices stopped them in their tracks.

Karson put a finger to his lips and motioned the others over to a nearby tree. The trunk and broad expanse of roots above ground was the perfect place to stay out of sight. "Wait here," he whispered. "I'll check it out."

Karson moved toward the sound, careful not to step on any twigs that could snap and give away his presence. His translator picked up enough words to start assimilating the new language. Moving closer, he saw the road and studied the people walking or riding along with it. Based on what he could see, they appeared human. Although their hair colors included a few browns and reds, most were shades of yellow, teal, and green. Eye color was more of a problem, consisting of violet and dark grey. Satisfied, he returned to the others.

"There's a road over there. The people seem okay, seems to be mostly a human population. However, their hair and eye colors are very different than what I have seen on a human. I don't think they're pirates. At least, I didn't recognize anyone."

"Thank heavens," Serena said. "The settlement shouldn't be much further."

When they stepped onto the road, no one paid any attention to them, even though their clothing was better made and utterly different from everyone else's. It was the one time they were grateful for their wretched condition.

"I hope the translator starts working soon," Dawson said as they walked along. "The group ahead of us is excited about something, but I don't know what."

As if on cue, the translator began working.

"They're talking about the birth of a baby boy," Serena said, as she held the translator to her ear with a smile. "Apparently, his parents have wanted a child for years, but until now, it hadn't happened."

Walking was easier for Chef on the packed dirt road. As they followed the others, they talked about what to do next.

"So far, everything seems to have worked out," Dawson mentioned.

"Maybe the Pleiades motto is right. Maybe I am born under a lucky star," Karson said.

"Well, as long as that luck rubs off on us, I don't mint it," Serena added. She was about to say more when three human-like forms, with light blue skin and dark blue stripes wearing masks over the lower part of their faces, came upon them and pointed guns at them.

"Hand over your money," their leader said, his scaled human-like hand gripping a phaser.

"We don't have any," Karson replied, reaching for his own phaser slowly.

Another bandit stepped closer and shoved his phaser in Chef's face.

"He said, hand over your money."

Karson sighed and pulled out his pockets, showing the bandits they were empty. Dawson, Hague, and Serena did the same. Chef merely held his arms up in surrender.

"We don't have anything of value on us," Dawson insisted.

This angered the thieves. After taking a good look at the condition of their hair, skin, and clothing, two believed her. The third bandit, the apparent leader, did not. It had been his idea to rob them. If they had nothing to steal, he would feel like a fool.

"Submit to a search," the leader of the bandits insisted.

At his words, Karson turned and ran. Although he knew these men would have no idea what his tablet was or what it held, he couldn't take a chance of it being damaged. He might be able to give up looking for treasure. Still, the plans for the *Pegasus* were too valuable to allow anything to happen to them.

"Karson!" Hague screamed.

"Stop, or I'll shoot the female!"

"Stop, please,"! Karson heard Chef's voice call out.

"If you don't, they're going to shoot me," Serena's soft voice was heard, trying to stifle tears of fear.

Karson skidded to a halt. What choice did he have? What the tablet held was invaluable, but Serena's life was more important. Turning, he walked back and held up his hands. One of the bandits searched him. Naturally, he found the tablet, and he had no idea what it was. He turned it over and over and showed it to his two friends.

"What is this thing?" He asked Karson. "The thing on the file?"

Karson was stumped. They could tell it was plans for a ship, but what could he say?

"Those sketches you mean?" Karson said, loudly as trying to get vocal help from his friends.

"I don't know for sure," Dawson lied, "but I think it's a plan for some kind of toy."

"A toy?" One of the bandits said.

"Bah, what do we need with some stinking toy?" Another groaned.

"Bah, worthless," the leader of the bandits said as he threw the tablet to the ground, making Karson wince.

The disgruntled bandits left, arguing over how stupid it had been to try and rob a crew. Especially one consisting of three youths, a broken-down robot, and an old cyborg, all of which were obviously nothing more than beggars. The leader, the one who had instigated the robbery, turned and looked at Karson with hate-filled eyes. As far as he was concerned, Karson and his friends had made a fool of him, and he would get even, one way or another.

"Come on," Karson told the others. "We need to put as much distance as possible between our inept robbers and us." He scooped up the tablet, dusted it off, and made sure it hadn't been damaged.

"What's the hurry?" Serena asked. "Other than the fact that I'm starving, the thieves are gone."

"Maybe so, but judging by the look that guy just gave me, I think we embarrassed him in front of his friends. If he gets them riled up as much as he is, they'll come after us."

"Karson has a point," Dawson added, "regardless, we don't want to be too close to people that just tried to rob us."

"The sooner we find food or drink, the happier I will be," Hague groaned.

****

Before the bandit attack, most of the people on the road had been on horseback or in wagons. Being able to travel faster, they had left the five friends behind and vulnerable. Karson did not feel the need to push anyone to go more quickly than a walking pace. With Chef being so old, he did not want to risk damaging him. He also reasoned that with five people together, they would stand a better chance. Despite their previous attempts at robbery. A short while later, the sound of four legged-hooved animals came toward them from the opposite direction. No one said a word as they scurried off the road and ducked behind some bushes. They didn't have long to wait. A troop of local law enforcement rode past, returning from patrol. They stopped briefly as the group hid in the bushed by the road.

"Shouldn't we talk to them? What if they are with the Galactic Federation?"

"What if they are not?" Dawson warned.

Everyone remained quiet.

When the troop was finally past, the Conspiracy returned to the road. An hour later, they came to a sign outside what appeared to be a thriving city.

Chapter 48

Newcomer's Town

Along the dirt road that led to the town was a large sign that read, "Newcomer's Town."

"How appropriate," Hague said. "You can't be any more of a newcomer than we are. By the look of things, it's a wealthy and civilized place. The only problem is if the pirates have found this planet, it's also a perfect spot for raids."

"Look ahead. See the ocean?" Dawson said with a grin. "We've landed in a port town. Smell the clean, saltwater air?"

"I smell fish, too," Karson said. "Let's hope Grimlocke and his men aren't here."

"A word of caution," Hague added. "We must tread carefully and not reveal our otherworldly nature. We don't want to contaminate this planet's natural development."

As they entered the town, Karson, Hague, and Serena were impressed with the differences they saw there, compared to the cities and planets of their birth. A wall surrounded the town, and its streets were narrower and paved with some type of brick. Bold primary colors were used everywhere: on homes and shops, banners, clothing, and even the flowers in boxes under the windows, making the city a delight to look at.

The people wore lightweight clothing, including white pants and skirts, topped with more colorful shirts and blouses. The smell of fish was strong. Small-time merchants fried fish on open grills along the main thoroughfare. The delicious odors made their stomachs rumble.

"There seems to be a lot of humanoids here," Hague mentioned. "Those that look like the ones we saw before and similar to you two."

"Maybe this is a terraformed colony? Like New Kansas, only a bit more advanced," Dawson said.

"You call this advanced?" Serena asked, "I'm shocked that these people have electricity. This hardly what I call advanced."

"This is what it is like on the Outer Core," Chef commented, "the few memories I have about going to port planetside is that they look worse than this. Constantly being on the verge of civilization, without current or up to date resources."

"You'd land on planets that were under the control of the Galactic Federation?" Karson asked.

"Of course, Karson, they stole the *Antares* from the central core planets, remember?" Serena asked rhetorically.

"Well that was different," Karson tried to explain, "that was a bold risk. I am asking if they would regularly land on Federation controlled planets despite their risk."

"Out here on the edges of Federation control," Chef answered, "he who has the most money or the biggest phaser makes the rules."

"Aye Chef is true," Dawson commented, "even here in the backstars, money and appearance seem to rule."

Being dirty and looking unkempt, the local citizenry ignored them. Whoever looked at them wrinkled their noses and frowned. As far as they were concerned, these three must be beggars, and they wanted nothing to do with them.

Without money for food and new clothing, Karson, Serena, Hague, and Dawson had no way to relieve their hunger. They went down to the harbor, where Karson and Hague took on a few sailors in a game of cards. They kept several visitors entertained and quickly started earning some coins.

Although at the dock, Serena, Dawson, and Chef watched a beautiful dual-sunset.

"I have never seen two suns set before," Serena said, "all the planets I have been on only had the central sun."

"Aye lass, it's a big 'verse out there," Dawson commented. He then began to whistle a tune. A country tune that seemed to dance and carry on the wind.

Serena took it all in, for the first time in a few days, there was peace. Granted, they were stranded on some unknown planet, but she was alive at least. The young lady reflected on the loss of her parents, she let one tear escape. She missed them dearly, but she would not let their sacrifice be in vain.

"Drink up me hearties, yo ho," Dawson sang low and slowly.

"What are you singing there, Dawson?" Serena asked.

Dawson chuckled, "an old spacer's song, lass. I think it was a derivative of an ancient sailor song back on Terra Firma."

"Red at night, spacer's delight," Chef added. Saying the only spacer phrase, he remembered being old-timey.

"It means the weather tomorrow will be perfect for a cruise or a voyage," Serena responded. "I did learn a few things while being with the pirates." They all laughed.

Karson and Hague walked up to them, carrying things and objects in their arms. They earned enough coins to purchase a small amount of fish, which they shared.

They ventured to the beach, the sand would be warm and soft enough for the organic beings to sleep on. Chef commented he would need to find a charging station tomorrow, but they were not worried just yet. Serena and Karson began to work on building a fire while Hague worked on cleaning the fish. Dawson decided to spend some time with Chef, trying to unlock more memories. This time, Dawson only found one file, and unplugged before Chef began to verbally guess.

"As a child, my father used to tell me about the spacer's superstitions. I used to go with him on all his diplomatic ventures," Serena told Karson as she gathered dried driftwood.

"That had to have been exciting," Karson commented as he dug a hole which would be where they lit their fire.

"It was on occasion, but it got boring quickly. There weren't many other children my age, so I had to get by on books. Reading was all I had."

"Well, that explains why you are so smart then," Karson grinned.

Serena blushed, "what about you? How was growing up on Nergal?"

"Pretty tough. Work has been most of our lives. We barely graduated high school since we both had to get jobs at young ages."

"Oh my," Serena said as she tossed the driftwood into the hole. "Why did you have to?"

"Well, we were about fifteen. I had to help because my Uncle Jasper needed help supporting my mom. She works hard enough, but I know he helps out from time to time. I used to help out a lot more before I started working. Hague's dad had an accident at his work around that time, so Hague started to work to cover him. He never stopped since it helped the family so much."

Serena blushed again, this time it was about her life of privilege.

****

The fish cooked slowly on the skewer that Hague as rigged up, it was their first one. The three young adults sat on the beach and watched the second sun as it set. This sunset was darker than the others, but it was still beautiful.

"Thanks for taking care of that fish, Hague," Serena said.

"Thanks for finding the water when I was playing cards," Karson added.

This time it was Hague's turn to blush, his blue complexion darkening around his cheeks, "always here to help."

Karson looked out to the sea. "We'll have to sleep out here tonight and look for a map or some way off this planet tomorrow."

"I'd rather stay here for a few days, resting and sleeping under the stars with the sweet smell of saltwater," Hague said.

"So would I," Karson added, "but the longer we stay out here, the more attention we will attract. Tomorrow morning, we should look for a records center or archive library."

"If they have any on this backstar world," Serena groaned.

Dawson then walked up, Chef trying to keep up speed.

"Well good news," Dawson said, "Chef here was able to process his memories and unlock some more. He knows more about the map and the treasure!"

"Apparently, Karson's intuition was correct. When all three pieces of the maps are connected, the location of the treasure on the planet will be revealed."

"That's great!" Karson exclaimed.

"But it doesn't tell us the name of the planet the treasure is located on?" Hague asked as he removed the first fish from the fire and placed the second on the skewer.

Chef shook his head, "No, but I know the name of the planet."

Everyone remained silent, waiting on bated breath.

"The planet Exe," Chef said.

"So 'Exe' marks the spot, huh?" Dawson chuckled.

"Where is that?" Serena asked, "I have never heard of such a planet."

"Neither have I," Hague said."

"That's because it is a secret planet," Chef said, "at the time, Captain Scarm was the first spacer to find the planet."

"So tomorrow we really need to find an archive library," Karson said, "if we can find that planet on a star map..."

"Then we could find the treasure," Hague finished.

"But how do we know if this planet is even on a starmap?" Serena questioned.

"The only way to find out is to look," Dawson added.

The conspiracy ate their cooked fish dinner in good spirits. They talked about their plans for tomorrow and about their adventures over the past few days. Then one by one, they nodded to sleep, surrounded by the slowly burning out fire.

Chapter 49

Archives and Shuttles

The next morning, Karson woke up bright and early. The first sun was rising, so the sky was very gray and murky. Creating an eerie feeling over the beach. Karson stood up and stretched and scratched his arms. *We are lucky that the local authorities did not ask us to leave. Or worse, detain us. I am hoping that this planet is under Federation control, it will be much easier to deliver the* Pegasus *plans. But if not, at least I am hoping it is closer to this Exe planet.*

Karson began to stoke the fire, there were a few embers left. He began to search for debris and other flammable substances. As he stoked the newly-forming fire, Dawson awoke and moved over to sit next to him.

"How'd you sleep, Dawson?"

"Not too bad, whatcha thinking about?" The cyborg asked the young man.

"I wish this planet was more advanced so I could send out a transmission to my mother," Karson said. "Just to let her know that I am alright, ya know? I haven't sent a message since we landed on New Kansas."

"I understand, I wish there was someone out there that I could send a wave to."

"You don't have any friends or family?" Karson asked. "Where are you from?"

"Well, I'm sure there are relatives somewhere on Sarceran, that is my home planet, but I have never met them before. I was a young man of fifteen when I first became a true spacer. I had worked the spacedocks along with my father back on Sarceran. We were not of the wealthy class of that planet. We were taking a short trip one day after my father had saved up for years for it. However, since we were among the wealthy, we were attacked by pirates. I was able to escape on an escape pod back to Sarceran. My parents did not. After the pirates killed my parents, I withdrew all our remaining funds and took on the next charter out, and I became a spacer."

"I'm so sorry, Dawson," Karson said, remembering how, when they first met, he had told him about how he became a cyborg. The poor man's life indeed had been hard.

"However, I've always looked on the bright side, and that has served me well so far," the cyborg smiled.

Everyone else slowly began to wake up, after an hour, the Conspiracy was awake and ready for the next step of the plan

"I think we should venture into town. Even a low tech planet like this should have a records building or a library. Maybe then we can put together the map and figure out how to get to planet Exe." Karson addressed his group.

"I think it would be best if we split up," Dawson cautioned. "We do stand out a bit as a group on this planet. This isn't a busy port planet like Nergal ya know."

"A robot. a cyborg, two humans, and a Rhungo hardly seem like we are blending in," Hague put in, "especially here."

"Plus we have the shuttle to think of," Chef said, "it just occurred to me that she could have a distress signal. Whether that is good or bad, I haven't figured out yet."

Karson snapped his fingers, "that's it then. Serena, you and I go into town while we look for a library. Hague, you and Dawson head to the shuttle. See what you can figure out. We still have the communicator to keep in touch."

"If you don't mind, I think I'll remain here," Chef said. "I'm not fast, and I know I can find a place to plug in or shut down."

"Are you sure?" Serena asked. "Won't that be dangerous?"

"No one will want an old rust bucket like me. Why don't we meet up in the town in six hours? I remember Dawson, and I saw a tavern close by. I think it was called Orion's Belt?"

"Then it is settled," Karson said, "we meet back up here in six hours."

****

"Let's try this way," Serena said, pointing to the left. "The buildings are bigger and look more important."

"What makes a building look important?" Karson questioned.

"Hard to explain, they just do. They remind me of the buildings my father and I went to during his diplomatic meetings."

Coming from a planet hundreds of years ahead developmentally, what he saw didn't overwhelm Karson. Yet there were noticeable differences. Because of the heat and humidity, awnings made of canvas shaded most of the windows, helping to keep the rooms fresher in the afternoon sun.

Like any port town, spacers came and went with their ships. Street merchants were everywhere, selling finger food, lightweight fabrics, handmade jewelry and crafts, seashells, and numerous other things. Street musicians played merry tunes in hopes of earning a few small coins from passersby. The city also had its fair share of pickpockets and beggars.

Serena stopped to admire a shell bracelet. She would like to purchase it, but without the local currency in her pocket, it was impossible. She sighed and smiled.

"It's beautiful."

"Thank you, Miss."

While waiting for Serena, a little boy tried to pick Karson's pocket. Feeling the feather-light touch, he grabbed the child's hand.

The boy's violet eyes seemed to grow as large as saucers. "I didn't mean anythin', Mister, honest."

"It's okay," Karson said in a soothing voice. "There's nothing there to take. I'm penniless, just like you. If I were you, I'd work a bit more on that touch. You've almost got it."

He released the boy, who scooted away like a rabbit down a hole. When they finally found the library, a clerk took them to a room filled with boxes and piles of books on the shelves and floor. They looked through everything, brushing aside dust and a few six-legged orange bugs that covered nearly every surface. Time passed too quickly. In another hour, they would have to return to the pub and start supper.

"There's nothing here," Karson said at last. "Let's head back to that tavern. I'm too tired to keep reading."

Serena and Karson put away the books and boxes and made their way out. Still, when they reached the library's entrance, they spotted the three bandits from yesterday heading toward the library. Now, however, there were five. All dressed the same except for the leader, who wore a red bandana around his head.

Karson grabbed Serena's hand and pulled her away from the door. "This way."

They hid behind the front desk.

"What in the name of Griplar do you think you're doing?" The librarian whispered angrily, her orange eyes shooting bolts of imaginary fire.

Serena raised a finger to her lips and point at the pirates entering the door. Understanding, the librarian remained silent as the bandit leader and his men approached her desk. She didn't know why they were afraid of these strange individuals, but she wasn't about to allow them to become victims of such brutes.

"Got any records of planets?" The leader asked in a loud voice.

"Keep your voice down, sir. This is a library," the librarian said. "If you'll follow me, I'll take you to the room where the planet database records are kept."

As soon as they were out of sight, Serena and Karson scooted out from behind the desk and ran outside.

"That was close, too close," Karson said as he ran.

"Do you think they're looking for the treasure, too?" Serena asked.

"It is possible," Karson said. "We don't know if Grimlocke or Captain Abernathey had the only copies of the pieces."

They quickly exited the library and headed for the pub, Orion's Belt.

****

"What a delicious odor," Dawson commented as they were served.

"A hearty stew," Karson replied. "We did not have enough coin for a feast, but a warm bowl of stew never hurt."

"Good idea," Serena said.

"I am plenty content for a good homemade stew," Hague said, eating his share.

That evening, the pub was full of customers. This was the perfect place to meet in public but also have a private discussion at the same time. They were all beginning to carry a lot more important information with them with every step towards the treasure.

Dawson and Hague explained how the shuttle could fly short distances, but not to the ends of the galaxy. Dawson commented on how he and Hague could fix up the shuttle, but getting into town would be more trouble than it was worth. If they had the parts, which cost credits, they could do the repairs without a problem. Karson and Serena told everyone about their run-in with the bandits at the library.

"It was a close call, but I think we are on the right track. Why don't we head back to the shuttle tonight? We could camp out on that beach, and that can be our headquarters? Chef, you can be head of the basecamp. Tomorrow, Hague, you and I will come back here or find another tavern to play cards. We will need to start making some more coin if we are going to get this shuttle working. Dawson, you and Serena can head back to the library and keep finding out information. I'll move the map pieces to one tablet and leave the plans on the other."

The conspiracy agreed, finished their meals, and began to make their way back to the shuttle.

They did not talk about the entire walk. Karson keeping his hand on his phaser and Serena doing likewise. Everyone moved a little faster than yesterday when they walked into town. Only when they had reached the *Intruder* and checked that no one was around, did they speak.

"When we find the treasure, what will you do with your share?" Karson asked the conspiracy.

"I like that confidence, Karson," Dawson said with a smile.

"Help my folks, maybe set them up nice on Nergal," Hague said.

"I have no need for currency," Chef added, "but I would use my share to help fix the rest of my memories. Maybe donate the rest to other outdated androids like me."

"I'm going to build or buy a ship," Dawson said. "Then I could travel the stars like I love to do and have no one tell me what to do otherwise."

"I think I'd like to travel a bit around the galaxy, but closer to the outer core where there is still some civilization," Serena said dreamily. "Maybe I'll meet someone rich and get married, who knows." She looked at Karson to judge his reaction and found him frowning. Karson withdrew from his disturbing thoughts and nodded.

"Of course, you'll buy a ship and your mother a house back on Nergal, right?" Serena asked, reaching out and taking his hand. "Or would you take her back to your old home planet? If you buy a ship, you could take me wherever I wanted to go."

Her words brought hope to Karson's eyes. "I could. Couldn't I?"

****

Chapter 50

The Ceiling Mural

The conspiracy spent days looking for the location of planet Exe. Dawson and Serena spent hours studying in the library while Hague and Karson kept playing cards at various locations. Karson had asked some of the citizens about Nova Scarm. While everyone knew the tale, no one knew anything about Planet Exe. They, too, were clueless. The bandits were still in town as well, so they had to be extra cautious. The last thing they needed was more competition or more complications. Serena and Dawson had the daunting task of looking for the planet at the library. The records were extensive, even for a world as newly terraformed as this was. It turned out that they were on a Federation planet, but any military visit from the core had been few and far between.

"Figured, the Federation is so quick to terraform new planets that they don't seem to take care of the planets that they already terraformed," Dawson commented quietly in the library.

"But we are under Federation control, do you think Karson could…"

"I wouldn't risk it if the last visit from the core planets was a few months ago. If this area of space is not frequently patrolled, then we also have the risk of pirates. Or even worse, corrupt officials who could venture to make some quick credits if they sold it to the right buyer."

They were on the planet, New California, a small world with eternal summer. They were a few weeks journey away from Cortsea, how they managed to venture that far off, no one knew. They were also one of the few colonized planets in the area. There were thousands of uncharted worlds in this quadrant. A map to help them locate the right one was all that stood between them and untold wealth.

Karson practiced flying with the shuttle nearly every night. With the computer's help, he was becoming a fairly good pilot. By now, they had covered nearly two-thirds of the landmass for cities large enough to have a library but had not yet located the planet they needed.

****

It was on the fourth day on New California when Dawson and Serena went back to the library in Newcomers Town. The day prior, Hague and accompanied Serena and Dawson went with Karson. They had switched partners because Dawson was afraid that it would be suspicious if the exact same two people kept playing cards or researching in the library. Both sat down in the chairs in the large domed lobby. Tired, Dawson precariously propped his chair against the wall, leaned his head back, and closed his eyes. A few moments later, he opened them and stared helplessly at the ceiling. When it hit him, he nearly fell out of his chair.

"Serena, look up."

When she did, she realized that the dome was a painted mural of a planet. A black world with a white label reading, "Exe." Their hopes grew by leaps and bounds. They now had an idea of what the planet looked like. The only thing remaining was to locate the right one.

"Once we're back at the *Intruder*, we can scan this into the computer," Serena said.

"Once it's completed, the computer can search its databases to see if there's a match," Dawson exclaimed.

"Hopefully, it isn't that far from here."

****

That afternoon, Hague tried to see if the *Intruder*'s navigational computer could find the location of the planet. Karson pulled out his tablet and brought up the maps, which had merged into one since they were together.

"Computer, checking the planets with known landmasses in your database, are there any areas similar to the mural that would align with the directions on the map?" Hage asked as the program ran its scan and search of the area.

Several moments passed before the computer replied. "Negative."

"It figures," Serena said. Her voice was filled with disappointment. "How are we ever going to find the treasure if we can't find the planet?"

"Accessing the shuttle *Invader*'s onboard computer...."

Hage exchanged looks with Serena and Karson. She wasn't asking the computer, but since it was running a search, it was worth a try.

"Accessing ancient lore on maps and lost treasures. According to an obscure archive, the identity of planet Exe is a little known planet in deep space."

"Planet Exe could be anywhere then!" Dawson said hopelessly.

"That assumption is incorrect. There are clues listed that refer to a possible location. While in orbit, I scanned this planet and its two satellite moons into my databanks. By correlating all known star systems, eliminating those that do not fit the parameters, and extrapolating the remaining data, I have determined that the planet in

310

question is within reach. However, this particular shuttle will not make it. A faster and more powerful ship designed for long interstellar journeys is needed."

Karson commented. "Apparently, the pirates knew about this planet's existence but have kept it a secret for at least decades. Now that we have the location of the planet and the map, we should be able to find the treasure."

Serena studied the expressions of her fellow Conspiracy members. "I hate to bring this up, but what if we arrive too late?"

"I have been wondering the same," Hague said. "I know Captain Abernathey had a supposed part of the map, and so did Grimlocke, but how do you know they weren't the first ones to get those pieces?"

"I know the last part had to have been safe with Chef," Dawson said. "But the other two parts, it is possible. Plus, we have not accessed all of Chef's memories yet, someone else could have taken the treasure already, and he not be aware."

They all looked to Chef, who was shut down and being recharged by the shuttle.

"My thoughts exactly. If the map is just a copy, we'll be placing ourselves in danger for nothing," Serena added

Karson looked into her eyes. "We have to try. It's the only way I'll ever get my own ship. Besides, we all have worked hard for a share. We've all sacrificed so much, we can't give up now. Don't you at least was some of the prize? The great treasure of Nova Scarm?"

"Sure, but I don't need it the way the three of you do. My family is rich. Once I return to Ceseroma and my family's estate, I'll be fine." She thought a moment then said, "We should download the plans for the *Pegasus* onto a chip or something. I'm sure the shuttle here has an extra one. If we are going to go after this map, we might as well keep the plans safe."

Hague ejected a chip from the *Intruder* and inserted it into the tablet with the Pegasus plans. He downloaded them, then proceed to copy the map and back it up on the other tablet. "That way, we have another backup in case we lose this one."

"I propose a fallout plan," Dawson declared, "if this trip is for naught, we should head back to Nergal. That is where the *Stardust* began this adventure, after all.

"That is our home too," Karson said, "we should be able to contact any Federation ships from there as well. I like the idea."

"Me too," Hague said.

"Then, it is settled. If we don't find the treasure, we have to somehow find a way to get us all back to Nergal. Agreed?" Serena asked.

"Agreed," they all spoke in unison.

That night, they ate the fruit they found on the beach. Karson and Hague had some money, but they saved it for tomorrow. They would try their luck to win more currency. They would have to buy or buy a charter to planet Exe somehow. As they ate, Karson filled in everyone on what he had learned that day at Orion's Belt.

Karson had discovered more information about the bandits, due to playing cards with them. They were local pirates and thieves of the area, referring to themselves as the Bandits. However, since they patrolled here often, they usually only attacked travelers. The local law enforcement had done their best to deal with them, but few reported crimes in this part of space.

"They are mostly Nerwil's from this planet's moon," Karson continued, "their leader's name is Zaxe, and he wears that red bandana on his head. He is not thrilled with the Galactic Federation for terraforming this planet, which is why he usually attacks ships and visitors. Trying to keep them away."

"Now we have to really make sure we don't bump into them as well," Serena said.

"I've also been told that they are searching for the treasure, too," Karson added.

"We will just have to beat them there then," Dawson said with a smile.

Karson inquired into how much it would cost to supply the shuttle with enough nonperishable food and water for the trip. Quickly, Hague and Dawson calculated the cost and expenses of both having a ship and the ability to supply it. It would cost them a bit of local coin, and it was not even a sure thing that they would find one out on this backstar planet.

****

Chapter 51

All According to Plan

The next day found Dawson and Karson at the Orion's Belt pub. Karson was trying to keep his winnings, Dawson was looking for information. A few ships had landed last night, just ships stopping to resupply before continuing on their voyages, so there were plenty of new people to talk to. Karson stepped away from the table to take a break. He had not won a lot of money, but he also had not lost a lot either.

"How goes gambling?" Dawson asked as he leaned up against the bar.

"Taking a short break, waiting for a new table," Karson said as he ordered a drink.

"I think I might have a buyer for our shuttle," Dawson said.

"What?" Karson looked incredulous.

"See that gentleman looking guy over there? The one with the mustache? I mentioned our shuttle to him, and he said he was interested in buying it."

"That could work," Karson had not really given much thought to selling the *Intruder*.

"He said he would be here for three more days. We have until then to decide. I've also talked to several pilots. All are willing to take us as charters if we leave in the next few days. Though they all said, they were passing Nergal and heading into the core planets."

Karson thought about that. While that would make sense on a logical scale, returning the *Pegasus* plans and being safe on a core planet. It would be easier to get home too, but he did not want to give up just yet. They still had three days, they would have to find the treasure.

"I should have gone with Hague and Serena looking for a cruiser. Why am I here? I am the pilot, after all."

"Because you are needed to earn coin to buy the cruiser," Dawson corrected him. "And you are not the pilot, yet."

"Well, how many credits do you think we will get for the shuttle?"

"A couple thousand? I can't imagine that gentleman over there paying full price for it."

"Why not?"

"I told him how we got it here from the *Antares*."

"Fair enough."

"But still, a couple thousand credits can put us on a good line to get a ship. How far away is the planet again?"

"The shuttle's computer said it would take two weeks to get there. Which we know we could not make. But if we get a standard class S cruiser ship, we could make it there in three days."

"We might have to acquire some more credits then," Dawson said as the doors to the pub opened up, and several new faces entered.

Karson took the hint and sat down at a table just as a hand was being dealt.

****

The hours waned as Karson sat and played cards. So far, he had been able to make decent money at the games. He was about to call it quits when the Bandits entered the

315

pub. Everyone grew quiet at first, but after a few moments, the natural lull of the tavern returned. Dawson counted over twenty of them, much more than the three they had run into when they first came into town. He watched in horror as three of them, including their leader, sat at Karson's table.

Karson tried to remain cool. He was thankful that he was not in charge of dealing with this game. However, as he tried to get up, he got looks from the Bandits.

"What's your hurry?" The leader asked in a gruff tone. "Why don't we play a friendly game of 'Orbit the moon'? It is my favorite, after all."

No one argued.

"Your masks please," the dealer asked Zaxe.

With a gruff nod, the Bandits took off their black masks. In doing that, they revealed their jagged, almost animal-like, jaws. Several took off their gloves, revealing more of their light blue skin and their dark blue stripes.

"Satellites are wild," the dealer declared.

The players took turns exchanging cards with the dealer. Once that was done, the betting began. Karson started with one coin, which was raised with each patron until it came to Zaxe, who raised it by five.

Karson could tell he could either make a lot of money or lose it all.

****

Hague and Serena made their way into the pub a few hours after the Bandits did. They met up with Dawson, who was playing hologram billiards with the machine.

"Dawson, where's Karson?" Hague asked as they approached.

"Still playing cards," Dawson said as he made his shot. "How did the hunting go?"

"Well, we found a few decent crafts," Serena said. "They just all cost a bit, even the cheapest one."

The computer lights flashed as the machine made it's shot.

"Well, I found a buyer for the shuttle," Dawson said, "Karson seemed key on the idea that we sell it for credits."

"I can't believe we found someone all the way out here who'd be interested in buying a space station shuttle all the way out here," Serena said. "Especially ours considering the condition it is in."

"We are out here deep in space, lass," Dawson warned. "Sometimes out here, people only come out looking for weird, or dark oddities."

Serena gulped.

A huge roar shot up from the card tables. More shouting and cheering was heard before the sound of broken glass.

"You two get back to the shuttle," Dawson said, "I'll get Karson out of this, and we will meet you back there."

"Hey, I've been in plenty of pub fights with Karson before," Hague protested.

"Not now, Hague," Dawson bellowed, "if they catch you two with us, then it could be trouble. Split up and meet back at the Intruder. Go! Now!"

****

Karson scooped up as many coins as possible. When he revealed the winning hand to Zaxe, the Bandit leader flipped the table in outrage. Now he has shouting and ordering his men to gather the coins as dozen other pub patrons dove for the chance of a quick buck. Karson was used to this type of retrieval. He scrambled on the ground, gathering what coins he could get until he saw Dawson. The cyborg was also scooping up coins, he waved to Karson and gestured to the door.

Karson slowly crawled through the scrambling crowd. He tried not to draw any attention to himself, he did not want to mess with Zaxe or any of the other Bandits.

"Get my coins back ya wormtails!" Zaxe was heard shouting over the crowd.

Karson sweated as he made his way to the door, he looked up to see Dawson just leaving. As he began to stand up, he felt a pair of eyes on his back. He slowly turned to see Zaxe putting on his mask, covering the lower half of his face. He screamed above the roar of the maddened pub patrons.

"We will meet again, boy, I'll be sure of it. Only next time I'll take my money back, and your life."

****

That night, around a bowl of leftover stew, Karson delegated the actions they would take tomorrow.

"We are on borrowed time," he began, "I do not think the Bandits will find us here tonight. However, tomorrow I think I will be a fair game, especially if I am in town. Tomorrow, Dawson will have to get in touch with the buyer. Chef, you'll help him back here with the shuttle preparations. You'll have to wipe the last few days of travel from its memory banks if you are comfortable with it."

"Should be no problem, won't be enough to cause any long term damage, unlike my own files," Chef gave a thumbs up with his human-like hand.

"Good, hopefully, it will be enough credits to buy us a ship. Once we get the credits, oh be sure you get cash only, Dawson, Hague, and Serena will then take the cash and buy one of the ships. I will head to the library. I figured the Bandits may not be looking there for anything, and I can try to study this map a bit more for when we land on Exe."

"Then we can find the treasure, hopefully," Hague added.

****

The next day, everyone went to perform their part of the plan. Dawson was able to find the gentleman buyer at Orion's Belt and sold him the shuttle for 4,000 credits. Chef made sure the *Intruder*'s memory of the past few days, including searches and maps, was erased. Dawson met up with Hague and Serena to give them the credits for the cruiser. When combined with the coins from Karson and Hague's card-playing, they had just over 5,000 credits. Dawson told Chef to head to the library to meet up with Karson.

When he did, the android found Karson at a table with the tablet in his hand and a notebook by him.

"Karson," Chef whispered.

"Chef," Karson whispered back, "what is happening?"

"We are waiting for Dawson to communicate with us after they buy a cruiser. He said the plan until otherwise noted, is to pick us up on the other side of town. Once they acquire a cruiser, that is."

"Fantastic, I've been studying the map here. Hopefully, it helps when we get to Exe."

"Do you think we will be able to find the treasure?" Chef asked.

"I hope so, Chef," Karson replied.

Unbeknownst to either member of the conspiracy, a spy from the Bandits had been listening carefully to their conversation. *Planet Exe? Treasure? They could be talking about Scarm's treasure! Better report this to Zaxe, maybe we will be able to find the cache after all.*

****

"Karson? Come in Karson."

A voice called in Karson's ear, but it sounded staticky and almost far away.

"Karson, come on, man. Where are you?"

He then woke up. He had fallen asleep at the table in the library, his tablet was also in sleep mode. He looked around for Chef as he clicked his earpiece.

"Hey, I'm here, Hague is that you?"

"Thank Griplar, look, we got a nice cruiser. It's a class S, Otter, so it's a bit sleeker in design, not designed for long flights, but it'll get us to Exe in no time."

"Save me the lecture, professor," Karson laughed, "I just need to find Chef, and we will meet you guys on the other side of town."

"Sounds good, over."

Static.

Karson put the tablet and his notebook in his pocket as he began to search for Chef. He looked all over the entire floor that he was on. Nothing. He ventured down the old stairs only to find nothing. *That is odd. Just where has that old android got to?*

He stepped outside of the library. Something did not feel right.

"Make one move, and the old robot gets it," a deep voice sounded.

Karson turned around to see Zaxe standing with ten of his men behind him. One of them, he was bigger than the rest, and he had a scar over his left eye.

"Karson...I am sorry," Chef said.

"It's not your fault Chef, don't you worry," Karson tried to remain calm, but he felt the panic welling up inside of him. He only had one phaser, they had up to ten. He clicked his radio, hoping Hague or Dawson would hear.

****

Up in the Otter, Dawson picked up the wave.

"Huh? Karson? Karson, is that you? Wait...who's that talking?"

"Send the signal to the Otter," Hague said as he piloted the ship. He had learned a bit from Commander Wagoner, and his assistance with flying the shuttle certainly paid off.

The signal that came in was staticky, and it seemed to be coming from far away.

"Boy...we just wanted...imagine my...Nova Scarm..."

"That voice sounds familiar," Dawson scratched his chin. "Trace it, Karson might need more help than we know."

****

Karson slowly moved his hand towards his phaser. If he could get a round off, he would be able to get Chef free. He would have to fire and duck and dodge milliseconds apart, or else he could be mowed down by phaser fire.

Zaxe snapped his fingers as the big bandit knocked Chef down to his makeshift knees. The big bandit chuckled as he did so. Small bits of power amused him, and he enjoyed the small misfortune he was causing. Zaxe felt a more substantial surge of power. He knew this kid had something special on him, he just did not find it.

"Boy, a few days ago, we just wanted to rob some new travelers who picked the wrong route," Zaxe began. "But imagine my surprise when I find out that they not only owe me money now, but they also have connections to Nova Scarm's treasure. My my, didn't we get lucky."

"I've been pretty lucky on this journey, too," Karson replied, cooly feeling for his phaser.

"Well, I think your luck's just about out," Zaxe taunted, "give me the map, and I'll release your android here."

Karson looked to Chef, the old android shook his head as he whispered, "no."

Karson reacted before he could process. He snatched his phaser and shot at Zaxe and rolled toward the library, he yelled into his intercom.

"Hague, I need you at the library *now*! Chef and I got company!"

Karson hugged the side of the building, the staircase offering cover. He could hear people shouting in the library. He looked and saw Chef's robotic body on the ground, with a large hole through his chest.

"No...no..." Karson said.

He crouched as he ran towards him, he grabbed the body and dragged it back as phaser fire started again. He shot back blindly, but hearing a groaning sound affirmed that he at least hit something.

"He didn't have to die," Zaxe called out. "Though I'm not really sure that robots do die. After all, they are just hunks of metal."

Anger burned in Karson. He wanted to lash out on them. To take his phaser and end them all. But, he held back, knowing that would get him nowhere.

"Karson..." a faint voice was heard.

"Chef?" Karson was shocked.

"I only have a little bit of time left, that phaser bolt really did a number on my core drive. Since my mechanical anatomy is so old, there is no hope for repairs."

Karson tried to hold back the tears.

"Thank you, Karson. You and Serena and Dawson and Hague. All of you have given me things to remember. Things I have not...remembered in a long time."

"Your welcome, Chef," Karson said as tears slowly ran down his face.

Chef gave a thumbs-up as his screen eyes shut down for the final time.

Phaser fire brought Karson back to reality and out of his sadness. He looked up and saw a medium-sized ship fly down and orbit around the library.

Dawson stood out of one of the open doors and began firing out of a turret gun that was stationed on the ship.

"Lower the rope, Serena!" Dawson yelled.

Serena hit the button that dropped a rope from the ship to Karson. He grabbed it and yelled up as he continued to shoot at the Bandits, "go now!"

"Hague take us out of here," Dawson called.

Hage piloted the Otter out of New California's atmosphere, they were gone in a flash.

The big bandit walked up to Zaxe, "Cap'n, what are we gonna do?"

Zaxe smiled, "we follow them. Smithly, contact the rest of the crew, tell them to board their ships. Cluny? Where are you? We need to get a trace on that ship, its an Otter class, so it should not have any high tech cloaking devices. Let's get a move on boys! It's high time the Bandits went in search of the treasure of Captain Nova Scarm."

Chapter 52

Lucky Star and Barren Planet

The ship lazily droned on as it made its way to Exe. However, as it started its journey, there was some sad news.

"We lost Chef," Karson said, hanging his head. They had all gathered to stand in the small square space that separated the cockpit from the small hallway that lead to the bunks. The only other room was a bathroom. This ship was customarily designed for two passengers, but it would fit the now four members of the conspiracy decently.

Hague hung his head as Dawson cried silently. Serena leaned and hugged Karson. They had all loved the android. Losing him made Serena miss her old android Sarah even more so.

"I am so tired of losing people," Karson said.

"There's still some hope," Hague said.

"Even after all this? We lost the *Stardust*, Captain Abernathey, Commander Wagoner, Tucson Scalemander, Serena lost her parents, and now Chef! How can there be any hope left when we have lost so much?"

Hage walked over and stared his best friend dead in the eye.

"Now you listen to me, Pleiades," Hague began. "I haven't stood by your side or followed you through all sorts of dangers to just let you give up now. Haven't you always told us to never give up hope? What about that lucky star or motto that you always go on about, huh?"

Karson looked around at the faces of his friends.

"Remember the transporter mess?" Dawson said shyly, "that was pretty stressful, right? But we made it through."

"We have got to finish this Karson," Serena said, "didn't you tell us that if we don't, we would have let all those people down?"

Karson smiled, a mixture of embarrassment and happiness.

"Well, I guess you guys are right. Let's start things off right, what should we name our new ship?"

"The Hope?" Serena offered.

"Too cheesy," Dawson replied.

"What about the *Lucky Star*?" Hague suggested. "After all, we have had our fair share of luck on this trip."

"I like it," Karson said, "The *Lucky Star*."

****

"Are the other ships ready to launch?" Zaxe asked his first mate.

"Aye, sir, the *Venom* and the *Night Serenade* are ready to follow you."

"Good, tell them to wait here until I give the order, don't want to arouse suspicion by having too many takeoffs."

When everything was finally ready, Zaxe gave the order to lift off.

"Well done, mates," Zaxe said when they were clear of the planet's upper atmosphere, receiving shouts of joy and laughter.

"Cluny got a tracer on that ship with the human on it, Cap'n," Brutus, the big Bandit, and first mate, said.

"Excellent," Zaxe replied. "Warm the cannons, let's give those fools something to sweat over."

Brutus gave a wicked laugh of glee.

As they headed for their target, the helmsman spotted something. "Ship ahead. Can't tell its size yet, Cap'n, but it doesn't think it's much bigger than a shuttlecraft."

"On screen," Zaxe ordered. At first, he didn't see a thing other than the ever-increasing size of the moon. "Are you sure, Cluny? I can't see a thing. Set view screen to magnification ten."

"They are there Cap'n I know it," Cluny defended

 The ship finally appeared but was still too small to identify.

"Increase magnification another ten," Grimlocke ordered.

This brought the ship into view enough to show that it was indeed a shuttlecraft.

"Computer, can you identify that shuttle ahead of us?" Zaxe asked.

"It is a class S Otter ship, recently purchased legally on New California. According to the Galactic Transportation Registry, it is called the *Lucky Star*. There are two human life forms, as well as a cyborg and a Rhungo onboard," the computer replied.

"I guess you were right, Brutus," Zaxe growled.

"They must be after the treasure, too," Brutus said.

"That they are, and so are we. Fire over them, just to give them a little scare," Zaxe ordered.

Phaser fire shot out from Zaxe's ship, the *Chameleon*, at the tiny target.

"It missed," Brutus said. "It's too far out of range."

"That is the point, I just want them to remember that we are here. We will pull off in a bit, having them think they overtook us."

Brutus nodded "Then we meet up with the other ships and follow them to the treasure," he said.

"Precisely. This ship should easily overtake them, in case all else fails."

****

Onboard the *Lucky Star*, the computer addressed the crew.

"Warning, we are being pursued by an aggressive Class M Raider codenamed *Chameleon*. They are equipped with level 8 cloaking tech and adaptability sensors. They have fired phasers at our position, but are still too far away to cause any damage."

"What are we going to do?" Serena asked, alarmed.

"On screen," Karson ordered. What he saw made him turn pale.

"What?" Serena asked, tugging on his arm.

"The Bandits have followed us," Hage told her. "It looks like they have spotted us.

"Oh no!" Dawson exclaimed.

"We can outrun them. We have nowhere else to hide," Karson said flatly.

"The *Lucky Star* is five minutes, seven seconds for the warp drive to be ready for activation. Once that is achieved, I will scan for a coordinate to land that can hide the ship temporarily," the ship said.

"Make it so," Karson replied. "And if they begin firing on us again, do some evasive maneuvers."

"Acknowledged."

Even though the *Chameleon* was more powerful, Zaxe was sure to keep the fire away from directly hitting the ship. He knew it would take days to get to the planet. So he figured they could get a little head start, but first, they had to be scared to get the motivation. Zaxe's ship did seem to be gaining ground, but there wasn't enough time to make much difference.

As the *Lucky Star* entered the outskirts of an asteroid belt, they were suddenly rocked by a glancing blow from one of the *Chameleon's* phaser.

"Evasive maneuvers!" Hague shouted.

The cruiser did as ordered, weaving to and fro through the asteroid field. The *Lucky Star* flew what seemed to be a crazy, suicidal course. However, once it was clear that the *Chameleon* on the other side of the belt, the ship returned to its normal speed.

"Blast it, I did not take into account an asteroid belt," Zaxe shouted when they lost sight of their prey.

"Cap'n, I've plotted a course around the belt," Cluny replied. "It'll take longer, but it still intersects with the course our quarry is taking."

"Follow it," Zaxe ordered. "Brutus, contact Squelch and Marmuda on the other ships, tell them to meet us here. We will keep following our prey at a safe distance. Lulling them into a false sense of security."

****

The conspiracy waited in their shuttle for the three days of the voyage. Their supplies had been kept better than when they escaped the *Antares*. However, they were delighted when they entered the orbit of Exe. Upon landing, Hague shut down everything but life support to prevent the *Chameleon* from picking up any sign of their presence.

Sitting in the shadow of the giant crater, everything was pitch black, until the system's sun began to light the area beyond. Even so, the view out the window was bleak and barren. As far as the eye could see, nothing but mountains, grey dirt, the broken remains of shattered meteors, and craters of various sizes were visible.

"Do you think it's safe yet?" Serena asked.

Hague checked the scanners. "The *Chameleon* has assumed orbit around the moon."

"So every time they pass over us, there's a chance they could find us?" Karson asked.

"Actually, the trajectory of their orbit should not be a huge problem. We landed the shuttle near the moon's south pole, while their ship appears to be in orbit around the equator."

Serena and Dawson sighed in relief.

"We made it!" Karson laughed.

Hague and Dawson shook hands and slapped each other on the back as Serena and Karson hugged each other. As the young man and woman hugged, their eyes locked in a look that could mean only one thing. Both blushed and stepped back. Now was not the moment to deepen their relationship. There would be plenty of time for that later.

Still sitting in the pilot's chair, Karson cleared his throat and addressed Hage, who was still in the co-pilot's seat. "What are the conditions outside? Also, do we have a location for the treasure?"

"According to the scanner, this small planet has an atmosphere that is 100 times thinner than Galafect Federation regulations dictate suitable for terraformed planets," Hague reported.

Dawson slapped his hand to the cybernetic side of his face, "I didn't think of the planet not being terraformed. That might complicate things."

"There is enough atmosphere to allow ease of walking, but the air is not breathable. We will need to wear spacesuits to protect us from the sun's radiation. We will also need oxygen tanks to breathe, " Hague said.

"Do we have that equipment on board the ship?" Karson asked.

"Yes."

The whispered sound of a door sliding open brought their attention to an area in the back of the ship where a compartment opened. Inside were four space suits and all the equipment they would need to venture outside.

"Thank goodness for that," Serena said. "It would have been worse if we had come all this way and not been able to leave the ship."

"Well, this ship was designed for two passengers ideally, but I am glad there are spares," Dawson said. "I'm just surprised that this ship so far from the core has all the suits onboard. It is not uncommon that a ship being sold around that area may not have all the basic features."

"I guess we gave this ship the right name," Karson said.

"I can also give us the location of the treasure," Hague continued. "It can be found on what is now the dark side of the moon in a cave deep within the mountains. There even is a small area large enough for us to land the ship."

"Could the *Chameleon* fit?" Karson asked.

"Hmm, hard to say," Hague said. "It could, but if not, they would send a shuttle or pod from their ship."

Dawson then leaned over Hague's shoulder and plugged into the system.

"Doing a quick scan?" Hague asked.

"Something has been bugging me," Dawson commented.

A few minutes passed in silence until Dawson spoke again.

"Just as I feared, there seem to be two other ships in allegiance with the *Chameleon*," the cyborg sighed.

"Zaxe must have a small fleet of ships under his control then," Karson concluded.

"Huge cruisers like the *Antares*?" Serena asked

"No," Dawson said, "they appear to be ships about our size or a bit bigger. But nothing as big as that ship, or the *Stardust*."

"However, they could still beat us to the treasure," Karson reasoned.

"Well, the *Chameleon* is still in orbit, and according to the scanners, the other two ships are still a fair distance out. Zaxe could be waiting for back-up," Dawson said.

"Plus, we have the map," Serena said with a smile, "Zaxe may not know the location of the treasure, even if he knows it is on this moon."

"He would not be able to make it off ship for another nine hours anyway," Hague said.

"Why not?" Karson asked, puzzled.

"According to our thermal readings, the dark side of the moon currently has a temperature of minus 100 degrees Fahrenheit," Hague answered. "No way Zaxe and the Bandits will risk leaving the security of the ship.

"Our protective suits will not be enough to prevent us from freezing to death either," Dawson added.

"Then how are we going to…" Serena began.

"Once the moon has rotated enough to allow the sun to warm the section where the treasure is located," Hague continued. "The ship says that the temperature could increase to as much as 70 degrees Fahrenheit."

"That's a relief," Serena said.

"Well, we can't get the advantage, but at least neither do the Bandits. Let's eat something and try to catch a few hours of sleep," Karson suggested. "Operating system, please wake us when it's time to leave."

"Acknowledged."

After eating some more of their ever-dwindling rations, the Conspiracy laid down on their cots in the sleeping section. No one thought they would sleep a wink, but with all the excitement and danger they had been through, they were fast asleep in moments.

Chapter 53

The Journey to the Treasure

It seemed like they had closed their eyes for only moments when a loud chime sounded, and the computer's voice called them awake.

Startled, Karson jumped up. "What? What's happening?"

"That's the alarm you set, Karson. That means it is time for the next part of our journey," Dawson replied.

Serena sat up and yawned. "Already?"

"Well, it looks like we have been asleep for five hours," Hague said as he checked the universal clock by his cot.

"Let's eat a light breakfast, then we can prepare our suits while the ship flies to our destination," Karson directed. "Hague, any idea how long it'll take the ship to get there?"

"The system navigations report that it will take ninety minutes."

The thought of taking that final step toward finding the treasure erased the remaining fog from their brains. They ate some dried meat and some of the fruit from their provisions, then thoroughly checked the spacesuits they would wear when they left the shuttle. As Karson cleaned up, he put his phaser back in its holster. He looked over to see Serena doing the same.

"Did you hit any of the Bandits back on New California?" He asked her.

"I don't know if I shot anyone, but I know I was trying," Serena said.

"I never thought you'd actually use it," Karson admitted.

"If it's us against the Bandits or pirates, or it means life or death, I won't hesitate."

"Good."

"We are getting closer," Dawson announced.

The two friends returned to the front of the ship. Hague had taken over the pilot's seat as Dawson assisted him in the co-pilot's seat.

"It looks like we'll have to fly through a mountain pass about halfway through that range," Hague said as he pointed to the scanner.

No one said a word as the ship zoomed through the darkness across the barren landscape toward the mountains, which were farther away than they seemed. Once they reached the range, which rose higher than anything anyone had experienced prior, the sun reached its peak and lit the way. The next part of the journey put both of them on edge as the computer flew the shuttle in and around jagged turns, jutting rocks, and high peaks. Serena had to look away.

"You looking a little green around the edges," Karson said. "Are you getting motion sickness?"

Serena nodded. "The first aid kit should have something for it," she said, jumping up and running for the tiny onboard bathroom. Grabbing the kit, she quickly opened it up, grabbed the spray injector with the right medicine, and dosed herself. The relief was instantaneous. Returning to her seat, she looked much better.

One more sharp curve, and ahead they saw a cave opening with a clearing in front just large enough for the shuttle to land.

"This is the cave," Hague said as it landed.

"I downloaded additional information into the map tablet that will help us all navigate the cave," Dawson said as he unplugged the tablet from the *Lucky Star*'s computer.

"It looks like we beat Zaxe and his men," Karson said as he and Serena helped each other pull on their spacesuits.

"That we know of. Hague or Dawson, was there any sign of any of the Bandits or their ships?" Serena asked.

"Nothing came up when we landed," Hague replied.

"What a relief," Serena said.

"Now all we need to do is find the treasure, load it into the *Lucky Star* and escape without the Bandits seeing us," Hague said.

"That's all?" Karson asked. "Piece of cake."

Serena smiled. She knew Karson was putting on a brave front for their sake, and she didn't want to let him down either.

Finishing the final check on their suits, the members of the Conspiracy grabbed a stack of sacks, a coil of sturdy rope, and two powerful lights that we stored aboard their ship. Dawson shouldered the turret gun he had used on the Bandits back on New California. Then they opened the shuttle door. As soon as they were clear, the computer closed and sealed the door.

Karson tapped his communicator. "Computer, don't open the shuttle door for anyone but us members of the conspiracy."

"Acknowledged."

Standing at the entrance, they saw that only a few feet of the cave was lit by the sun. Karson and Hague attached the lights to their helmets and turned them on. Dawson turned on his cybernetic eye, and it became a small flashlight in the dark cave. Serena stayed close to the group, her hand on her phaser, just in case. The darkness beyond was now as bright as day.

"We need to be careful," Karson said, pointing to the stones, rocks, and boulders that littered the cave's floor.

Stalactites jutted down in places, formed by minerals brought down by liquid methane dripping from the ceiling. Some celestial bodies had lakes of methane, ethane, and propane instead of water.

"We'd better not fire a phaser in here," Hague warned after scanning the area with the tablet. Everyone else nodded in agreement.

They carefully moved across the floor, avoiding the obstacle course as well as any puddles of liquid. The path was anything but straight. It twisted and turned, with one side tunnel that branched off and doubled back upon itself. Their progress was slow, but sure, until they came to an area where the path narrowed to only twenty inches wide. Both sides had steep drop-offs, and when they shined their lights down them, the drop-offs appeared to be bottomless pits.

Serena gave Karson a panicked look. "I don't think I can cross that."

Karson moved closer and took her hands. "I know it's scary. I'm scared, too. But we've come so far. We can do it together." When she didn't say anything more, he asked, "Do we really want to give up now?"

"No. Yes…Karson, you and the others go ahead. I can't do it."

"We can do this together," he said as he held her hand.

Tears rolled down Serena's cheeks as she shook her head. "No. I'm sorry. I can't. I can't."

"Hague," Dawson coughed, trying to get the young Rhungo to look up from his tablet. "Why don't we look for another route to the treasure?"

Hague looked up confused, then looked at Karson and Serena.

"What? Oh um, yes, Dawson. Let us go check over here for an alternate way."

Dawson and Hague headed in the opposite direction, trying to give the two some privacy.

Karson led Serena over to a boulder and sat down with her.

"Look at me," he ordered.

Serena shook her head and swiped at the tears on her cheeks. "It's no good. I'm just a coward. I can't do it."

Karson smiled, "I do not think you are a coward."

"You don't know me as well as you think you do."

"Wrong again. How can you possibly think you're a coward? You dressed up and pretended to be male just to survive on a pirate ship. A pirate ship that was captained by the man who killed your parents. Then you helped us escape to New California, in which you helped us discover the planet where the treasure was! Not to mention you helped Dawson shoot off the Bandits when I was stuck at the library."

Serena blinked back more tears.

"Listen. I know they've passed. I lost my father a long time ago too. But, don't you think they are keeping an eye on you to make sure you *do* make it?"

"I guess. But Karson, I'm terrified of heights. If I try to cross, I'll freak out and end up falling to my death and maybe taking you and the others me."

"I have an idea."

Serena fixed him with a look filled with hope.

"The scariest part of crossing a narrow bridge like that is looking down."

"I know, but what if I can't help it?"

"Do you trust me?"

"Yes, with my life," Serena replied.

"Good, because the feeling is mutual. I'll tie a blindfold over your eyes, and walk right behind you. Since you'll be blindfolded, you won't see anything. This way, I can guide your steps, and we'll make it across just fine."

"But, I'll know!"

"First, I will help you calm down. Then we'll make our move," Karson said.

She thought about his words for a moment, then her brow furrowed. "That may be okay to cross over, but how will we get the treasure across?"

"Hague, Dawson, and I could carry it to the other side."

As if on cue, Dawson shouted as he walked to the other two, "we did find an alternate route. Though it will take a long time to get to, I am afraid."

"I had a feeling that there is another way out, otherwise, how would they have gotten the treasure here in the first place," Hague reasoned.

"Couldn't we try that way first?" Serena asked.

Hague shook his head. "We only have so much oxygen. It will be easier to find a second path after we've found the treasure."

Serena took a deep breath. "Okay, I'll do it."

"That's my girl," Karson said, giving her a hug. "Now I'm going to put the blindfold over your helmet, and then we'll take some deep breaths, slowly breathing in through the nose and then slowly blowing it out through the mouth. Ready?"

"Yes."

Karson took one of the sacks they carried and put it over Serena's helmet. "You okay in there?"

"I can't breathe," she replied in a shaky voice.

"Yes, you can. Nothing has changed. Your oxygen tank is still providing you with air."

Serena took a breath and then nodded. "Okay. I'm okay."

"Now do as I say. Deep breath through the nose, then blows it out through your mouth."

They practiced the exercise together. After half a dozen breaths, Serena's muscles relaxed.

"I'm…, I'm ready."

"Good."

Dawson took the lead Hague followed, still scanning the map on the tablet.

Karson led Serena to the narrow walkway. "Now, look down and slide your right foot forward." As she did, he kept his right leg right next to hers. "Now, do the same with the left."

It was slow going at first, but as they moved along without mishap, Serena gained enough courage to move a bit faster. Twenty-five steps later, Karson removed the sack from her helmet.

"You did it. We're safe."

Serena looked back and saw that they were across the passage. She looked and saw Dawson taking a seat on the rocks and Hague a little further off, his light glowing in the dark. She laughed and threw her arms around Karson. "We're safe. Thanks to you. If we didn't have these helmets on, I would kiss you."

Karson grinned, "Once we're back aboard our ship, I'll hold you to that."

"Good. Okay, what's next?"

Hague walked back to the group. "There should be a bunch of twists and turns ahead, with other tunnels branching off."

They continued on, changing directions when necessary until they came to the first prominent marker on the map.

"The rock with the face should be around here somewhere," Karson said, pointing to the highlighted spot on the tablet.

The clearing they were in had numerous rocks and boulders strewn across the cave floor like toys scattered on a child's playroom floor. They looked everywhere, but no clue was in sight.

"We must have missed it somehow. I guess we'd better backtrack," Dawson said.

Karson didn't move. "Wait a minute. It has to be here. Maybe we're not looking low enough."

They examined the boulders and rocks once more.

"Here it is!" Karson said excitedly.

Serna joined him. "Yup, that's a face, all right. Kinda creepy if you ask me."

"Anyway, we're on the right track. Let's keep going," Hague urged. "We still have no idea how far the Bandits are behind us, or close to us."

"Okay," Karson said, looking at the map. "From here, we go..." he paused and pointed his finger to the left passage. "That way. We need to find a small circle of stones with this strange mark on them." He enlarged the drawing on his tablet and showed it to the others.

"Got it," Dawson said. "Let's go."

They walked until they found an irregular circle of stones with the correct markings.

"This is it," Karson said.

They both grinned until they realized that the only way to go now was down a sheer rock face.

"How are we supposed to get down there?" Serena asked.

Karson unhooked an extended length of rope from his belt and spying a large boulder next to the edge of the cliff he tied it tightly around it, making sure it would not slip loose. Then he dropped the other end over the cliff.

"Wait," Serena said. "What about us?"

"Here," he said, handing her the tablet. "Hang onto this and wait here. This looks like a dangerous climb."

"We could try to find the other path?" Dawson ventured.

Hague shook his head, "no time. We have a few more hours left of oxygen, I set a timer for when we need to head back to the ship. Pleiades can handle this, I've seen him tackle more dangerous things along this journey."

Grabbing the rope with both hands, Karson again gave it a pull to test its strength. It held. Backing up to the edge, he looked down, took a deep breath, and started down. The rock face was slippery with different sections sticking out farther than the rest, making the climb difficult. Partway down, his foot slipped, and he lost his grip on the rope.

"Karson!" Serena screamed. Her heartfelt ready to burst.

Karson slipped five feet before he was able to grab the rope again. Both sighed with relief. Working around the jutted sections, he continued downward. His weight pulled the rope above him taut, and although he avoided the juts, the rope did not. Sharp edges rubbed against it, and it began to fray.

"Karson!" Hague called a warning, but it was too late.

The rope snapped, dropping Karson the rest of the way to the ground.

****

Chapter 54

The Standoff

Several miles away, three ships broke the atmosphere of the moon and set their coordinates for the landing site of the *Lucky Star*. The trace they had on the ship was still strong and locked. However, Zaxe was always down to explore his options.

"Cluny, run a scan around the targeted perimeter. Search for another way around."

"I'm sorry, Cap'n," Cluny said. "There's no way around, according to our scanners."

"Then we have no choice but to take the ship to the original entrance."

Cluny checked the navigation systems to ensure that the Chameleon was still en route to the location of the cave.

"But boss," Brutus said, "how can we land with the *Lucky Star* blocking the way?"

"Simple, Brutus, we trap them in the cave."

Brutus nodded and smiled.

Zaxe brought up the communication screen to his seat. The image of Squelch and Marmuda appeared on the screen. Squelch was the acting captain of the *Venom*, and while he looked like any other Nerwil, he had a black eye patch over his left eye. Marmuda was the acting captain of the *Night Serenade*, and his distinguishing feature was the green bandana he wore over his mouth.

"Aye, Cap'n, Marmuda here," Marmuda began.

"Squelch reporting," Squelch said.

"Boys, listen up, I have new plans for you two."

"What do you have in mind, Cap'n?" Squelch asked.

"Marmuda," Zaxe began, "I want you to take the *Night Serenade* and do a full scan of this moon-sized planet. See if there is any life here, or any other goods worth taking, but just record, do not land. After that, orbit the moon and keep all waves out for any other ships. In case Grimlocke or any other pirate is also after the treasure."

"I'll start now, boss," Marmuda said as he turned off his communication wave. A few minutes later, the *Night Serenade* broke off from the other two ships and began to scan the area as instructed.

"Now, as for you, Squelch," the leader of the Bandits laughed "once we get to our location, I want you to not land the *Venom*. Instead, keep it hovering over the cave with the cannons at the ready. Just in case our prey does not want to relinquish the treasure."

"Aye, sir, you can count on me."

****

Karson picked himself up.

"Are you okay?" Dawson called down.

"Yes, just shook up a bit." He was outside the mountain again in the sunlight. "That fall led to an open area. There's a lot of sunlight here. There's another cave down here. I'm going to check it out."

The cave wasn't deep, and the sun's beams lit more than half of it. He looked around for something that would indicate where to search. There was nothing. Going back outside, he yelled up to the rest of the group.

"I think I found it! Dawson, help Hague down here. I need help."

"Look out," Hague called as he tied their last rope around another rock, "I'm coming down."

Karson stepped aside. Hague slipped a bit at the end of his descent, but he managed to pull himself up.

"Finally," Hague said. "This is it."

The two old friends shook hands as they ventured into the next cave.

"Can you believe we made it all the way here?" Hague asked as he scanned the cave.

"If you told me we would end up hunting for treasure, transporting plans of Intergalactic Security, and have a run-in into with two different pirate groups when we first signed on to the *Stardust*," Karson responded as he pulled a collapsible metal rod from his spacesuit. "I would have said you were crazy. How much oxygen do we have left?"

Hague checked the suit readings, "we started with 18 hours worth of oxygen. So far, we have taken up about four hours' worth. However, we can't stay too long here. We still have to make the trip back to the *Lucky Star*, and it took us four hours to get here." He moved slowly to the center of the cave, at which his tablet began to flash.

"Dig here," he said as he too got his collapsible rod from his own suit.

Karson stuck the rod down when it struck something hard and stopped. The friends did not react right away for fear of getting their hopes up. They dug around the obstruction using their hands, the dirt and rocks they moved out of the way slowly revealed a large perfect square. After a few more feet of digging, they found a set of handles on either side of the square.

"We found it!" Karson yelled.

Hague grabbed the handle on his side, Karson did the same as they both struggled to pull it from the ground. They stood struggling and grunting as their muscles strained until it finally popped out of the ground. They rested a moment. Then struggling, but not as much as before, they carried it to where Dawson and Serena were waiting.

Hague shouted when they got there. "It's huge! And heavy!"

"Just how treasure should be!" Dawson squealed with delight.

Serena gasped and clapped her hands. "How are we going to get it out of there?"

"We will have to tie the rope around it, and then all of us will have to pull it up."

"Sounds like a plan," Dawson said.

****

It took all their efforts, but the Conspiracy was able to drag the treasure up to their level. They all took turns as they carried the large gray chest back to the *Lucky Star*. When they reached the bridge, Serena just closed her eyes and held on to Karson as they crossed. Dawson took most of the weight from Hague as they carried the treasure.

"It's okay," Karson told Serena, "we are almost to the end of the bridge. Then all we have to do is load the treasure to the shuttle and head for Nergal."

"It will be nice to be stationary for a bit," Serena admitted.

As soon as they crossed the bridge, they all sat down. Taking a breather before venturing back to the *Lucky Star*.

"We are making good time," Hague reported, "though I would trade a percent of this for an anti-grav lift now."

"Never thought we would be missing one of those, huh?" Karson asked.

"Now there's a bit of a problem," Dawson said, looking at the front of the battleship gray chest.

"What is it now?" Serena whined.

"Passcode needed to unlock the treasure," Dawson said.

"I figured we could hack it on the ship," Hague commented.

"How long is the passcode?" Karson asked.

"Seems to be only four digits. Or letters." The cyborg replied.

Hage took a look at the chest. The passcode pad was old. It actually had physical buttons made out of plastic instead of screens. Although some earlier models of passcode pads still had physical buttons, they were now made of duranium instead of plastic and iron. However, since it was old, the Rhungo was able to quickly deduce the buttons needed to unlock the chest.

"Well, I can see there are twelve buttons that have the most wear and tear," Hague reported, "1, G, 8, K, 7, B, 2, Q, E, 6, W, and X."

"Well, that is a lot of options," Dawson said, "but at least we can figure it all out aboard the ship."

"Wait," Karson said, "the passcode is just four options?"

Hague and Dawson nodded in unison.

"Try," Karson said, "GX86."

Hague typed the code, and there was an unsealing sound that escaped from the chest. The lid lifted up ever so slightly. Karson looked around, everyone in unison had put their hands on the cover, and they lifted it all at once. The light from the Sarcarean gems almost blinded them. There was gold and other jewels as well as ancient forms of currency within the chest.

"There's a fortune here," Serena gasped.

"Sarcarean gems," Hague said.

"Look at those credit piles in the corner," Dawson said, "even those old drive forms of currency are worth a fortune. Maybe even more if they are that old!"

"I told you," Karson replied, grinning.

"How did you guess that?" Hague asked with a puzzled look on his face.

"That was Chef's make and model number, or so he told me. When I heard them mentioned by you, Hague, I figured it was worth a try."

"He had to have been a far older model than that, though," Hague reasoned.

"Maybe he thought that was his model, but it really was the passcode?" Serena offered. "Dawson, you said he did suffer a lot of damage from all his memory wipes."

The cyborg nodded, "aye, he did. He was a good friend, still helping us out even now."

"A true member of the conspiracy," Serena added, a tear in her eye.

Everyone hung their head in a moment of silence for their fallen android companion.

"Alright," Karson said at length, "let's get this back to the ship."

****

The group was almost out of breath as they reached the opening of the cave. The tunnel they had been traveling in was opening up, bringing in more light and slightly warmer temperatures.

"We'd better hurry," Karson said. "I'd like to get away from here as quickly as possible."

As they turned, their ship became in full view. However, Zaxe appeared from behind it, with several members of the Bandits behind him.

"Well now, Pleiades, how nice of you to dig up the treasure for me. I'll consider that an act of kindness and payback for the money you stole from me during our little card game."

"No!" Serena screamed in frustration.

They had been so close.

Chapter 55

The Final Battle

Karson knelt down and drew his phaser.

"The treasure is ours. We found it first," he shouted.

"You stole from us first. We don't take kindly to thieves," Brutus laughed. "At least, thieves that don't work for us."

Dawson slung the turret phaser from his shoulder, the high pitch warming up sound was soon heard by all.

"Get to the ship Serena and Hague. Karson and I will cover you. We're leaving." The cyborg looked the Bandit leader dead in the eyes as he spoke.

"I don't think so," Zaxe said as the *Venom* hovered overhead their ships. "Drop your weapons, or we'll gun you down where you stand."

Surrounded by pirates, Karson knew they didn't stand a chance. He lowered his hand that held his phaser.

"Smart thinking, boy," Zaxe said. Turning to his crew, he was about to give orders when his wrist communicator began to go off. Static at first, but then a voice rang out loud and clear and full of panic.

"Captain help! We are being fired upon! It's the Galactic Federation. Repeat it's the..."

Static.

Zaxe shouted, "blast it! The *Night Serenade* may not be destroyed yet." He turned on his communicator again, "Squelch, go back up, Marmuda, the *Chameleon*, and I will be right behind you once we take the treasure."

The *Venom* ship slowly backed up and hovered away before blasting into space.

Zaxe charged his phaser again, "hurry up with the treasure, men."

The crew got to work while Brutus and another member of the Bandits kept their phasers trained on the Conspiracy. Zaxe walked over, smiling as he still charged his own phaser.

He stopped in front of Karson. "You have no one to help you this time, Pleiades."

"I don't need anyone's help this time," Karson said.

Zaxe sneered. "Famous last words."

As the leader of the bandits prepared to finish off the young man, Hage reacted. With little thought to his own safety, he ran forward, kicked the bandit leader in the shin, and grabbed his phaser arm, hanging on for dear life. Karson used the distraction to duck and roll as he began firing on the Bandits.

"Dawson! Serena! Get the treasure!"

The Bandits and the Conspiracy began to exchange phaser fire.

Hague was able to steal Zaxe's phaser, but he had to get out of range before we could take a shot at the Bandit leader. He fell back to the chest, seeing Karson crawling towards him. He covered his friend until they were able to get the chest and drag it over to the ship.

Dawson saw this and moved towards the ship, his turret gun mowing any Bandit member that got too close to the chest. Hague and Karson had finally loaded the treasure when Zaxe's voice cut above the sound of phaser fire.

"Stop and drop your phasers, or I'll blast the girl's head off!"

"No, Karson! Don't do it. He'll kill us all anyway," Serena begged.

What choice did he have? He couldn't stand there and watch this pirate kill her. Karson dropped this phaser.

"It's better this way," Karson said. "You mean too much to me."

"No!" Serena screamed.

"Do what he says, Dawson," Karson ordered.

"Aye, Captain," Dawson replied.

Karson was shocked and touched, he and Dawson had been through so much, but he had never addressed him as captain before.

"Hague?" Karson asked a tear in his eye.

"Aye, aye, Captain," Hague said as he tossed his phaser outside of the ship

Karson blinked away his tears, he had wanted to join up with the Federation in hopes of one day becoming a captain. He smiled. *Guess that space really does make a captain out of you*, Karson thought to himself.

"Now isn't this a touching moment," Zaxe sneered as he pushed Serena to the ground.

Serena kept her head down as she crawled towards Karson and the rest of the group. Tears stained her face, out of fear and happiness. Karson smiled back at her. If it was all to end here, he would at least be among the people that he loved.

353

"Don't think about following us," Zaxe ordered the Conspiracy as he stepped forward. "Face it Pleiades, I won."

He was about to fire when his body stiffened. Karson was puzzled until he realized a blackened hole was gaping out of the pirate's chest. An officer of the Galactic Federation pushed Zaxe to the ground with his foot.

"That'll teach you to interfere with those under the protection of the Galactic Federation."

Jumping to her feet, Serena ran to Karson and fell into his arms. After their embrace, Karson looked around. The place was swarming with men all in Federation uniform.

"I don't understand," Karson said.

"Where did all these people come from?" Dawson asked.

Captain Scott Bennington of the Galactic Federation Spaceforce ship *Columbia* smiled and introduced himself. "Seems you two made more friends than you realized. Once we rescued Captain Abernathy, he filled me in on everything, and we've been looking for you ever since."

Security from the *Columbia* gathered up the surviving pirates and other affiliates of the Bandits and placed them in the cells aboard their ship. The second ship that landed was known as the *Destiny*, which was to escort the *Lucky Star* safety back to New California. The conspiracy made sure the treasure was safely secured on their ship before joining the crew of the *Destiny*. Since it was better supplied for the three-day journey back planetside.

The conspiracy sat at a small table in the kitchen. While the *Destiny* could house a crew of thirty, only a team of five were aboard. As they ate, they discussed what would happen when they reached New California.

"Providing legal pleasantries are quick," Dawson said, "we should be able to fly the *Lucky Star* back to Nergal."

"Think we will make it in one flight?" Serena asked.

"Even if Nergal was close, which I doubt it is," Hague said, "We will probably need to make a stop or two to refuel and resupply."

"After we land there, do we part ways?" Karson asked.

No one spoke. It was true that before it was found, they all had plans with different journeys. Although after finding the treasure and almost losing their lives to the Bandits, they had formed a bond that no one wanted to break just yet. Although Karson and Serena had developed a different type of bond.

As the tension lingered, the captain of the *Destiny* walked in. He was a human with a gray mustache and goatee. While he was older, he still looked like a pinnacle of physical perfection for his age. He also bore a warm and comforting smile, which served him well during his many years working in the Planetary Relief Division.

"Hello everyone," he started as he took a seat with the group. "Nice to finally meet you all in person. I am Captain Laurence Golightly, and I do have some good news for you. However, I also bear some bad news."

"Well, I knew our luck would run out eventually," Serena sighed.

"Is it about the treasure?" Hague was almost too afraid to ask.

"It is," Laurence Golightly said. "I am afraid that Galactic Federation rules dictate…"

"Of course the Federation would get involved," Dawson muttered, not too quietly to himself. "Did none of the hard work for the treasure but demand a percentage since it happens to be under their already too large jurisdiction."

Captain Golightly ignored the cyborg. "…dictate that since the treasure was found in Federation controlled space, the treasure is technically imminent domain property of the Galactic Federation of Unified Planets and Moons."

"That means we don't get a share?" Serena asked.

"Well, not a true share," the captain spoke softly, "though it is also stated in the code that you four have the right to a finder's fee."

"Probably a tiny share then," Dawson said. "But if you'll accept it, Captain Karson, then so will I." The cyborg said, never taking his eyes off of Captain Laurence Golightly.

"We still deserve that share then, however small," Karson told Dawson before turning to face the captain. "After all, we risked our lives to save it and the plans for the *Pegasus*."

"I am glad you bring up the plans, actually," Captain Golightly smiled. "Since you returned the plans, I was able to negotiate a raise in your finder's fee. I was able to negotiate that each of you receives a 20% fee of the gross worth of the last chest of Captain Nova Scarm."

"Each?" Dawson perked up.

Captain Golightly smiled and nodded, "each. I wanted to make sure you all get your just rewards. While it may be a bit smaller than a four-way-split, I think everyone will be happy with their share once the treasure is calculated correctly. So there is the good and bad news of it all."

Everyone cheered, and even Dawson gave a rowdy pat on Captain Golightly's back.

****

Chapter 56

Home At Last

When they returned to New California, the conspiracy was treated like royalty. The small colony rarely got so many fine military personnel to visit their backstar world. The residents enjoyed the visitation of Captain Bennington, Captain Golightly, and the rest of their crews. Not only was it a nice economic boost to the colony with all the spending from the crew, but it was also an opportunity for the new settlement to deliver their complaints to the captains.

The planetary representatives were able to discuss those policies and lobby for representation in the Federation court systems. While this would appear to be a daunting task, Captain Golightly was used to these types of demands and was no stranger to them. During his extensive years serving the Federation, he had dealt with far worse planets than this one.

Serena was able to make contact with her family back on Cesaroma. Captain Bennington insisted she utilize his ship as it was far more powerful than any beacon on New California. She had been able to contact her grandparents on her father's side. She explained everything to them, with help from the rest of the Conspiracy.

"We were so afraid you were dead," her grandmother sobbed and laughed at the same time.

"When you return home to Cesaroma, we can get everything estate-side sorted out," her grandfather said. "We will start the preparations for your parents soon, however."

"I will make it in time for the funeral, I promise," Serena said, "although, there are a few things I have to do first."

Dawson and Hague excused themselves as Serena told more about her plans. By the end of it, her grandparents had heard the long tale of their adventures. They also realized that something more than friendship had developed between their granddaughter and Karson. Serena's grandparents didn't want to let her go, but they realized she was a grown woman now, and a rich one at that. They gave her their blessing but reminded them of the duties she still had back home. She nodded and smiled.

Karson also sent a communication to his mother. She cried when she saw her son and was so happy to hear that he and Hague had survived everything. She also took note of the attractive young girl standing close to her son.

****

The time had come for them to return to Nergal. Captain Bennington insisted they ride with him aboard the *Columbia*, but they declined. So instead, as a reward for helping his brother's mission, he repaired the *Lucky Star* and modified her weapon systems and life support.

After all the adventures they'd had in space thus far, he wanted to be sure the ship could defend itself whenever necessary.

"Unfortunately, I also have to deliver some bad news," Bennington began, "Grimlocke evaded our capture when we seized the *Antares*."

"Were you able to reclaim the *Cirrus?*" Serena asked, hopefully.

"Unfortunately not, Grimlocke set it to self destruct as he made off on his own ship. That's another reason I wanted to assist your ship, just in case. I think you will be safe though, Grimlocke is a smart pirate, and he won't show up anytime soon."

The journey home took them a week, but they had no issues or interruptions. They even stayed an extra day on the planet Balkwin just to rest.

When they arrived on Nergal, Karson's mother and Uncle Jasper were waiting for them at the dock.

"Oh, Karson, my son," Gloria sobbed, kissing him on the cheek and hugging him fiercely.

"I'm sorry, Mother. You've been through a lot, too, but I plan to make it up to you."

"Karson, you did it!" Jasper Tinsmith trapped him in a headlock and gave him a noogie. He repeated the same with Hague.

"Hague, Karson, who have you brought with you? Jasper asked.

"Name's Dawson," the cyborg introduced himself as he shook Jasper's hand.

Gloria dried her tears and turned to Serena. "And this beautiful young woman with you? I remember her from the message you sent."

"This is Serena Cloudracer," Karson replied.

"Then welcome to Nergal. I'm sure you all have lots to tell us."

When they arrived at Gloria's small home, Karson told her everything about the treasure. Gloria was overwhelmed when Karson told her about the gold and jewels. They then decided to feast with friends at one of the most excellent restaurants in town.

"I have some better news," Karson told his mother. "Tomorrow, we'll pack up everything you want to keep. You too, Uncle Jasper. Serena has offered to let us stay with her on her estate on Cesaroma. We can all finally leave this planet behind us."

****

The next day, Karson hooked up with Hague. They sat on the knoll in their favorite spot, watching people go about their business. When two men carted a massive chest off a recently arrived ship and looked around to see if anyone was watching, Karson and Hague looked at each other and laughed.

"Now that you have a ship, you can visit any planet or solar system you want whenever you want," Hague said.

"Why don't you and your family come back to Cesaroma with us? With your share of the treasure, I know you guys can find a place. Then we can seriously think about joining up with the Galactic Academy."

"Really? My parents would jump at the offer. They've wanted to leave this planet for years now, but couldn't afford the trip."

"I could even join the Spaceforce and go after pirates after we graduate from the Academy," Karson said.

"You'd do that?" Hague asked.

"Probably not," Karson admitted. "With all that's happened, I feel like I've already been through a war. Besides, I'm no soldier. I can barely fly a Sparrow."

"Ah, but you are an adventurer," a man's deep voice said.

Karson and Hague looked up and jumped to their feet.

"Admiral Lucas Darkmatter!"

Admiral Lucas Darkmatter was a posing specimen of his Mineralmite race. He stood eight feet tall and had skin that resembled stone. Although he looked intimidating, he smiled. "I see my reputation goes before me. I want to personally thank you for delivering the plans for the *Pegasus* to Captain Bennington. Have you any idea what could have happened if they had fallen into enemy hands?"

"Yes, sir, I think I do. That's why we all worked so hard to keep them safe."

"It's a fine thing you boys. The Federation thanks you."

Karson grinned. "Thank you, sir. Also, the credit should go to the rest of my crew, not just us."

"However, I have something else in mind that might prick your interest," the Admiral said, "for you and your crew."

"All of us?" Hague asked with a small smile on his blue face.

Karson looked at him quizzically. "I can't imagine what that would be, sir."

"I have a job for you. No, not what you're thinking," Admiral Darkmatter said, holding up a hand to silence Karson. "It's a highly classified job. Something was…stolen, shall we say? Do you have a ship and a trustworthy crew?"

Karson looked to Hague, "will you come with me, First Mate C'avt?"

Hague blinked away a large tear forming in his bulbous eyes. "I'll follow you to the ends of the universe and back, Captain Pleiades."

Karson smiled. "What is the mission, Admiral Darkmatter?"